When you Wish Upon a Lantern

GLORIA CHAO

VIKING

For Anthony. Because of you, my wishes found the light.
And for those who believe in the magic of kindness.

VIKING

An imprint of Penguin Random House LLC, New York

First published in the United States of America by Viking,
an imprint of Penguin Random House LLC, 2023

Copyright © 2023 by Gloria Chao

Visit us online at penguinrandomhouse.com.

Library of Congress Cataloging-in-Publication Data is available.

Printed in the United States of America

ISBN 9780593464359

10 9 8 7 6 5 4 3 2 1

BVG

Design by Lily K. Qian

Text set in FS Brabo

Note about Mandarin Words

In this book, Mandarin words are spelled using the pinyin system. In Liya's point of view, the lines above the vowels indicate the pitch contour of the voice:

A straight line (ā), the first tone, is high and level, monotone.

Second tone (á) rises in pitch.

Third tone (ǎ) dips, then rises.

Fourth tone (à) starts high and drops, producing a sharp sound.

The tones of the Mandarin phrases in this book are depicted as pronounced in conversation in the author's family's accent. There may be some discrepancies with other accents and dialects.

A pinyin umlaut (ü) is pronounced as follows: keep your tongue in the same position as when saying an "ee" sound as in "feed," but then say "you."

There is also a glossary at the end of the book for definitions of the Mandarin words and phrases used.

1

Schloop

LIYA

If there was ever to be magic found on this Earth—this sometimes wretched, unremarkable Earth—it's when I'm standing on the shore of Lake Michigan, the cold water dancing with my bare toes, and I'm looking at a lit-up sky. It's not alight with stars or fireworks or a big, bright full moon, but lanterns. Paper lanterns with people's wishes written on the side, carried into the never-ending dark night by a fire inside that matches the fire inside the sender's heart. What could be more magical than a sky aglow with wishes and dreams?

There are many names for this miniature hot-air balloon—sky lantern, tiāndēng (a.k.a. "sky light," translated literally)—but my favorite is the one my family's Chinatown shop, When You Wish Upon a Lantern, has coined for our community: wishing lanterns. Because to us, the wish you write on it is the most important part.

Today is the first day of summer, June 21, and for the tenth year in a row, the Chicago Chinatown community has gathered at Promontory Point, a peninsula that juts out into the lake with big grassy areas, firepits, views of downtown, and large stone ledges leading down to the waves crashing against the shore. We're here to celebrate a tradition started by my family's little shop that could, which is fifty-one years old and responsible for two new holidays and many, many wishes being granted. In less than an hour, we will light up the sky.

Currently, my parents are managing the table we've set up with lanterns for sale, lighters, and markers. As I approach them to help out, I notice an additional person nearby assisting the surrounding customers. And he knows how to manipulate the sometimes-finicky lanterns as well as I do.

Kai Jiang.

Oh no.

His presence stops me cold. The shock of straight, unruly black hair that's often falling into his eyes, the confident yet humble walk, the lean forearm muscles honed from hours of kneading dough in his family's Chinatown bakery, Once Upon a Mooncake . . . all of that would be enough to stop anyone cold when they see him, but for me? I halt because I have quite the *oh no* history with him, which I attempt to put out of my mind as he gives me a brief, deliberate, right-left wave from several feet away. I try not to let the chilliness of his gesture freeze my insides, but it's all I can think about.

Before, we were childhood best friends, constantly playing together in the alley shared by our family's neighboring businesses. Then, more recently, he started becoming *Kai*, as in Kai with the infectious laugh and defined arms and delicious buns (I'm talking about the breads he bakes, okay?). But before I could figure out what all that meant . . .

I threw up on him. A few months ago. We were having a blast sipping boba tea at the café closest to our shops when he made me laugh so hard that I snorted a boba ball up into my nose (yes, I know, I'm cringing too). Schloop, out everything came. On the table, in my lap, on him. So much on him. I died a little that day. Afterward, I was so embarrassed I steered clear of him for a couple of weeks, even telling my parents I was sick so I wouldn't have to go to our store and risk running into him. But I didn't mean for it to last forever. Somehow the avoidance snowballed, and we've barely seen each other since. Perhaps he's keeping a six-foot splash zone between us (*if it's good for viruses, it's good for vomit* kind of thinking). Or perhaps he isn't who I thought he was, given that he let that incident come between us. Or perhaps the awkwardness of it all is just too much, and every time he looks at me, he sees boba coming out of my nose. Whatever it is, I miss my friend.

Before I manage to give Kai a return wave, my father says, "Kai, thank you, but Liya's here. You should go join your friends."

My mother narrows her eyes at my dad. Then she calls after Kai, "Thank you so much for your help!"

I say nothing as I join them at the table.

"I've told you," my father says to me, "to be careful of him. His family . . ."

His family, his family, his family. I tune him out. My father's feud with the Jiangs is bordering on obsession now. *Their trash smells worse than ours. They don't respect our half of the alley. They filled our shared dumpster with spoiled dough, and when it rose, the dumpster exploded.*

I guess it was for the best that I never figured out my feelings for Kai because the Jiangs and Huangs were becoming the Montagues and Capulets, the Hatfields and McCoys of Chinatown. And all because of garbage.

We didn't have any issues with the Jiangs before this year thanks to my paternal grandmother, the peacekeeper. But after Năinai passed away six months ago, every dumpster incident has led to a heated argument. Now the feud is all my father talks to me about, partly because he's avoiding the one thing we really should be talking about. And on today of all days, I'm so annoyed that I do dare to bring up the forbidden topic.

"It's the first Summer Lantern Festival without Năinai." *The festival she created.* "Can we just . . . have a moment of silence for her?"

That softens him. "I miss her too, Lili." His use of Năinai's nickname for me stirs up too many emotions. I busy myself by straightening the items on the already well-organized table.

Ya-ya would be the more common nickname for someone with my Chinese name, Lí Yă (the tradition is to repeat the last character), but Năinai always thought the *lí* part of my name fit me more than the *yă*. Together, *lí yă* means "will be graceful," but *lí* by itself has several definitions, and Năinai always thought its meaning of "dark" fit me better because it made her think of the dark night sky we love—loved—to look at together. "You are the night sky that other people can shine against," she used to tell me, her own dark brown eyes shining. "That's why you're so special. You put others first and make them shine, and there are very few people in the world who do that."

"Liya?" my mother says cautiously, breaking into my thoughts. Concern seeps from her narrowed eyes and tight jaw. "Are you . . ." She can't even finish that simple question.

I wish she would stop treating me like cracked glass, but I also don't want to tell her I'm okay when I'm not sure what I am. Since Năinai was more of a parent to me than my mom or dad, they don't seem to know how to step up now. After

Nǎinai passed, my parents began tiptoeing around me, afraid to make things worse or remind me too much of her, and their tiptoeing has only increased over time. I wish I could tell them what I needed, but I have no clue myself. I guess my wish is for them to just know what I need, the way Nǎinai would have, and to just do it. My worst fear is that they're right: I'm on the verge of breaking. Without Nǎinai, without Kai, and (in the important ways) without my parents, I've never felt as alone as I do now.

I swallow hard, swallowing my emotions down with my saliva. "What do you need help with?" I ask them.

"We're fine here," my father says.

My mother suggests, "Why don't you join the festivities?"

"But not with him," my father adds quickly. And sternly.

If Nǎinai were here, she would defend Kai. "He's a good kid, the best! Have you seen how kind he is to his family?" *Even the ones who don't treat him well* usually went unsaid. "And have you seen how hard he works in the bakery?" *Working his buns off on the buns*, I would always add, and Nǎinai would roar with laughter, her deep, resonant chuckles filling the air with her distinctive *ha-ha*s that I always loved because she literally said *ha-ha* over and over when she laughed, like it was so funny and she was so happy that she had to enunciate each syllable perfectly.

My mother grabs a lantern and pushes it into my hand.

"Why don't you make a wish tonight?" Her voice lowers and she struggles to get the next words out. "For . . . her. She'd want you to."

I do have a wish I want to send into the universe. But I don't want to do it alone. I also don't want to do it with my parents. Năinai and I had many things that were just ours, and our biggest just-us tradition revolved around the wishing lanterns. I haven't figured out how to do this (or anything, really) without her yet, how to fill that hole, or if I even want to. Her last words to me were *Don't be afraid*. But I've been afraid for so long, ever since she fell ill, and I don't remember how to feel anything else.

I take the lantern, and instead of grabbing one of the markers on the table, I take Năinai's calligraphy set out of my backpack. My father smiles at me. I force one back at him.

"I'll still help people with their lanterns," I tell them.

They give me absentminded nods, distracted by approaching customers.

When I turn away from the table, my eyes land on Shue Năinai. Even though none of us are her grandchildren, the community calls her *năinai* because she loves us all like family and is constantly watching other people's kids or handing out fresh homemade scallion pancakes (the thick, circular, flaky kind that requires mad skills). She lost her husband decades ago, and her children are grown and have moved away.

She's currently standing with Daniel, the young chef who

owns the trendy French-Chinese fusion restaurant around the corner from When You Wish Upon a Lantern. When Shue Năinai catches my eye, she waves me closer. I wasn't going to interrupt, but then Daniel also begins waving me over frantically. Once I'm within earshot, I hear Shue Năinai mention a pot, and I immediately know she's telling Daniel about her gift to the community's most recent newlyweds, who moved into the apartment building down the street to attend graduate school at nearby UIC. I can practically recite the story for her: "I saw a top-notch pot for sale and it said 'good pot' on the side in nice lettering. So of course I bought it—it has to be good! It says so on it! But then, you'll never guess this, when I gave it to them, they laughed because they say *pot* has another meaning! Did you know that? They think it's so funny, the double meaning, but all I can think is, English has nothing on Mandarin. We have so many homophones and clever idioms, and we take them seriously. We're the masters of puns! Even our traditions are based on double meanings, like how we eat fish for the New Year because 'fish' is a homophone for 'surplus'!"

I know her stories better than the back of my hand (because let's be honest, I don't think I could pick my hand out of a lineup).

As soon as I join them, Daniel pats me on the back and darts off. He had given me *thank you for saving me* eyes that I have sadly received often when joining a Shue Năinai conversation. People say she tends to go on. I shake it off and hope Shue Năinai didn't see, then I focus on her. She's a good, if long-winded, storyteller, so I don't mind as she, apropos of nothing, launches into the umpteenth iteration of how she met her husband.

One thing is different this time though. As she talks, her tone is less sad, more nostalgic. Her eyes are clear and hopeful, not clouded with tears. She confirms my observations when she finishes the story on a completely different note than in the past. Instead of talking about how much she misses her late husband or her kids, she says, "If I found love once, I might again, right?"

It's so sweet I want to hug her. But I merely give Shue Năinai a smile and a "Yes!" that is emphatic but not as emphatic as I feel on the inside. It's not in my DNA to show what I'm feeling. Or I guess, more accurately, I've conditioned myself to hold back my full reactions to most things. It started in fifth grade when Mrs. Hearn told the class that Stephanie Lee had won a spelling bee and I clapped enthusiastically, only to realize moments later that she had actually said, "Stephanie Lee was stung by a bee." Then, as I sat on my hands and scrunched my eyes closed, Mrs. Hearn proceeded to tell everyone how Stephanie was extremely allergic but luckily had an EpiPen, which her mother jammed into her thigh right before the ambulance arrived to speed her to the hospital. Stephanie was fine in the end, thank god, but when I opened my eyes, the other kids and even Mrs. Hearn were still staring at me. I had never wanted so much for the earth to swallow me up. I felt horrible, and I suspect everyone else thought I was horrible too, especially Stephanie if she heard about what happened (and given the tight-knit community we live in, she definitely heard).

I relive that memory all the time. Almost as much as I relive the boba one. Now I keep my feelings to myself, and everything I do is from the background, hiding behind lanterns or a blank face. The only person I could be myself around was Kai, pre–boba incident. Post, I'm just as awkward as with everyone else, maybe even more so. I'm usually embarrassed about my need to hide in the shadows, but Năinai used to make me feel better. "You are the night sky that other people can shine against." She viewed my fault as a strength. It made me feel invincible. Special. Loved. But now that she's gone, I just feel small.

"I hope you make a wish for yourself tonight," I tell Shue Năinai.

In response, she holds her unlit lantern up in front of my face. I can read most of the words, but I already know that the few Mandarin characters I'm blanking on are critical. And if you don't know a word, you're screwed. No sounding it out. Sometimes you can infer some meaning if the character in question includes a root or another word you know, but that's more difficult for me than my parents since Chinese is my second language. So even though I speak it fluently, if I'm missing one or more essential characters, I usually have to give up.

Shue Nǎinai tells me her wish when she realizes I need her to: "You know Tang Xiānshēng? Boba shop owner?"

Do I ever. Mr. Tang was the one who brought napkins over on Day Zero. He and Kai both had bent forward to mop up my vomit but I couldn't bring myself to let them. I did it myself, which took way longer and was maximally awkward since they didn't know what else to do but stand there and watch. That's my superpower: I'm the monkey-covering-eyes emoji personified.

Shue Nǎinai giggles softly, and it's so unexpected and cute it distracts me from reliving my boba nightmare.

"My wish is for him. To notice me," she says, giggling again. "He's now single!" His divorce was finalized this year, and his ex-wife moved away to be with her new young boyfriend.

Instead of sharing in her giggles like I want to, all I say to Shue Nǎinai is: "May your wishes find the light," which is what When You Wish Upon a Lantern says to every hopeful customer. Then I put a hand on hers. When our customers are open enough to share their wishes and stories, I want them to know that I am holding their hearts with care, the way Năinai taught me to. Making the wishing lanterns the distinguishing feature of our shop had been her idea, and she was one of those people whose outlook on life, whose pure love and joy for others, made her feel like magic. People confided in her before the wishing lanterns, and even more so after. When she fell ill, the entire community showed up at her bedside, and when she passed, a cloud of mourning descended over Chinatown for weeks.

"Guāi háizi, guāi háizi," Shue Năinai says to me. *Good kid* can be condescending in other languages, but it's the golden compliment in Mandarin when it comes from an elder. It was Năinai's favorite way to describe Kai.

Shue Năinai eyes the lantern in my hand, then raises one eyebrow. She repeats the When You Wish Upon a Lantern customer mantra back to me in Mandarin: "Xīwàng nǐ de yuànwàng zhǎodào guāngmíng."

Then she looks around, wondering what boy I will write a wish about, and even though that's not my wish, I blush. Because there *is* a boy I *want* to write a wish about. I've wanted to for a long time. But I won't. Especially not now.

In silence, I help Shue Năinai fluff up her lantern so it's ready to be lit and sent off. Then I scurry away.

Without meaning to, I glance around until I spot Mr. Tang. I approach him and hover awkwardly, waiting to see if he'll invite me over. But when he meets my eye, he simply gives me a nod hello and returns to his lantern, bending over it more than before. I've been around enough lantern festivals to recognize the subtle hints for wanting privacy. Most likely his wish is personal and he doesn't want to share, but I also can't help wondering if, like Kai, he's scared of me now. Or perhaps the sight of me makes him cringe.

I immediately give him a wide berth (I take lantern privacy very seriously), but I can't stop thinking about Shue Năinai's wish. About how Mr. Tang looked so lonely writing on his lantern by himself. He didn't want my company, but that doesn't mean he didn't want *any* company. Perhaps he wanted a specific someone's company?

I need to find out if there's a chance, if there's any hope for Shue Năinai's wish. A plan is already forming in my head: how to approach Mr. Tang, how to create the ultimate meet-cute for them so that if there are feelings on both sides, *bada bing bada boom*, the fire from inside their lanterns will turn into sparks in real life.

That's what I do. I make people's wishes come true.

Well, I used to. With Năinai. That is (was) When You Wish Upon a Lantern's secret sauce, why our wishing lanterns are the best: when a customer entrusts us with their dreams, we do what we can to make them come true, behind the scenes, unseen. The first time came when I was thirteen, after Lam Āgōng bought a lantern so he could wish for a taste of his past. He told us how homesick he was for Macau, and I will never forget the sadness that surrounded his hunched shoulders when he came in, or how his eyes had shone as he told us about his favorite foods to eat, temples to visit, gardens to wander back home.

"We have to help him," I had said to Nǎinai. Instead of telling me there was nothing we could do, Nǎinai's immediate response had been, "Let's figure out how." After brainstorming and Googling, we found a recently opened Macanese restaurant on the North Side of Chicago that made one of the dishes he had mentioned, minchi (minced beef with diced potatoes stir-fried with onions, seasoned with Worcestershire sauce, and served with white rice and a fried egg). Granting that wish was as easy as slipping the restaurant's menu underneath his door. And when Lam Āgōng came into the shop a few days later, bursting to tell us that his lantern wish had come true and his taste of home had invigorated his old withered soul, that was it, I was hooked. I wanted to grant wishes for as long as I could.

For the past few years until she passed, Nǎinai and I were the unseen genies to our Chinatown community. "Partners in wish granting," we loved to call ourselves. A play on "partners in crime," but way, way better.

In the past six months, since her death, I haven't worked

on any wishes. It's been too hard. But as I look back at Shue Nǎinai fussing with her lantern, a hopeful smile on her face, I feel that flutter in my chest.

Hello, again.

This would be a wonderful wish to start back up with. And conveniently, it would also grant the wish I am about to make with the lantern in my hand.

I pause, taking a moment so my favorite sounds and sights can wrap me in nostalgia. I want to feel Nǎinai beside me again. The sky is pink, set aflame by the setting sun. Along the Point, children run and screech on the grass. Dogs lick their owners, strangers, and each other. Joy dances through the park. I look around at the people surrounding me. People I've known my whole life, the ones who I can turn to for the largest and the most trivial of problems. There's Sung Āyí, who kindly shuttled me to and from the hospital while Nǎinai was sick and my parents didn't leave her side. I wave to her and her two teenage daughters. There's Yang Pó Pó, the sweet woman in her eighties who is so proud to be from Taiwan that she wears a necklace with a pendant the shape of the island. She's known for the adorable paper frogs, fish, cranes, and shapes she makes by hand. And there's Zhang Āyí, who used to feed me the grossest homemade red bean Popsicles that I had to choke down in front of her with a smile. (The more I choked down, the more she fed me; quite the bitter catch-22.)

Every single family I can see has at least one wishing lantern. They dot the sea of people like floating seagulls. Islands. A reflection of the stars. There is hopeful wish-writing everywhere I turn.

Năinai made this happen. She is here, all around me.

The sun sets and night slowly creeps in. I hurry forward down the stone ledges, closer to the water for a little privacy. I think of my năinai, run through memory after memory until I can hear her *ha-ha-ha* laugh and, I swear, smell the citrus-scented perfume she wore because "oranges are lucky." With the calligraphy set, I paint my wish on my lantern in broad, bold strokes, just like Năinai taught me when I was eight.

I wish for Năinai's legacy to live on. For me and my parents and the community to hold on to her.

One by one, lanterns are lit. As darkness envelops us, anticipation is in the air. Hope is on everyone's breath.

Then . . . there's magic.

With one collective inhale, everyone grasps their lanterns and sends them into the air. They flicker orange and yellow and red, gradients across the sky. It feels like the entire Point is lit up by floating glowing orbs shining down on us. I can't take my eyes off them. I can't move. I've done this too many times to count, but it never fails to take my breath away. And I hope to never lose this reverence.

I gently hug my lantern, careful not to squash it, then

I light it and send it soaring up, up into the night. It hovers above me with the rest until, gently, smoothly, elegantly, it gets caught in a breeze and dances away, allegro.

As the lanterns are carried over the water, for a moment I want to reach out and call my wish back. Not because I don't want it to come true (I do, with every cell and heart fiber) but because it feels so small in a sea of dreams, ones that seem more important than mine. After a moment's hesitation, I let go mentally, and with a small wave of my hand, I send the wish out there.

Then I whisper an additional wish into the wind. One I'm too scared to write on a lantern.

I hope one day my other wishes also come true, not just the ones I send into the night sky. Maybe especially the ones I'm too scared to write down.

I don't want to feel alone anymore.

I watch my lantern slowly shrink to a small circle, then a dot of light, then a faint star. And then I focus. Tomorrow, I will put my meet-cute plan for Shue Năinai and Mr. Tang into motion. The only thing more magical than seeing a sky full of wishes is helping them come true.

2

Moth

KAI

I actually didn't mean to park that close to her shop's table. But everyone is so used to me helping out that as soon as I bought my lantern, I was swarmed. I'm currently helping little Bao write his wish for more Pocky sticks onto the side of his lantern.

"Good call, buddy," I say with a high five. As Bao tells me his favorite flavors, I nod continuously while dutifully writing them onto the creased rice paper.

Liya's shoulder-length hair and cat-eye glasses pop into my peripheral vision. As usual, I'm a total goner. She always somehow looks out of this world, like magic is surrounding her. I need to stop staring—I *know* I need to just *stop it*—but I feel like an uncool, not-subtle moth drawn to her flame. Quite the apt metaphor for the princess of sky lanterns.

Even though the *li* part of her name means "darkness," she's my light. Has been ever since second grade when my pet hermit crab, Crabby Hermy, died, and she fashioned a coffin for him out of her jewelry box and burned him food for the afterlife. She also insisted that I was not the cause of Crabby Hermy's death even though I was. I tried to get Hermy a friend without knowing that some crab species will fight each other to establish a pecking order. There were no survivors. For the record, she also helped me bury Hermy's friend, but in a different box, and she also burned him afterlife food.

The other part of her name, the *ya*, means "elegant," which . . . she's the best, but she's not the most elegant. It's actually one of the things I really like about her, but I feel like you can't say that. It sounds like criticism—*you're not elegant*—and everything that comes after that sentence would be lost, I'm sure of it. To be clear, she's not clumsy or manic pixie dreamy or whatever, she's just . . . earnest. The kind of girl who tries to sneak shrimp chips into the movie theater, then *tells the employee about them* when he glances at her bag.

I'm not "ya" either. Case in point, when Liya comes closer to me and looks my way, my not-"ya" brain freezes and it takes me so long to work up to a sad wave that my buddy

Chiang has mimed falling asleep by actually *lying down on the ground*. Now, it's grassy and pretty clean, but come on. So dramatic. Maybe he'd understand my hesitation if he knew about the boba incident, but I haven't told him.

Oh man, that was one of the worst days of my life. Not because she threw up on me, but because I asked her out and *then* she threw up. On me. First, I had held up my boba drink and joked, "Who would have ever thought boogers in milk tea would become a national sensation?" And it had landed. Maybe more than it deserved. Liya was laughing harder than I'd ever seen before, and since it was a few months after her nainai passed, she hadn't laughed in a really long time. That—plus the fact that Nainai's death had made me realize I needed to take a chance and do something about my all-consuming crush—had helped me finally work up the nerve to get out the six words I'd been practicing in the mirror for *years*:

"Will you go out with me?"

And then she *threw up*.

If she were more "ya," she would've politely said no, maybe stood up and curtsied, and then left me to wallow in my shame and honey-soaked boba. But no, she had to make the utmost statement by showing how much the idea of us together repulsed her. And it only made me like her more.

Not immediately. I'm not *that* weird. But then, after a little while, well, I don't know. I'm just in too deep. To the point where everything she does convinces me I like her more.

Staying away from her has been so hard—I didn't exactly win the lottery with some of my family, so she's been my found family for a lot of my life—but I also was too embarrassed and hurt and disappointed to be near her. I didn't mean to stay away this long, but now I don't know how to find my way back.

Turns out, it doesn't matter, because Liya doesn't seem to want me back. After I wave, Liya doesn't return it. Sigh. When her father sends me away, I try to convince myself that it's for the best and it's not because he hates me. Because he can't, right? He knows that the Exploding Dumpster Incident wasn't me? And that it was my father, not me, who once threw our trash into the alley so haphazardly it hit their wall and spewed nasty rotten dough bits up and down the side of their store? Or, well, maybe it's about the fact that there are too many possibilities to choose from, and he doesn't know that I'm just as horrified by my father's actions as he is.

Nainai knew.

Guess it's for the best that Liya isn't interested in me, since that would have led to an untenable situation with our families. Not saying it doesn't still suck, but I'm glad I didn't put her in that position.

"What's everyone up to?" I ask my crew—Yong, Chiang, and James (the odd one out, as we joke, poor James). I pray that Chiang won't tease me about my awkward moment with Liya.

"We're trying to help Tin Man find his heart," Chiang joshes, jabbing a thumb toward Yong. Yong is a guy of few words, few emotions, and many video games.

I've grown a lot closer to the three of them during my time away from Liya. Now, as I watch them wrestle, then try to sabotage each other's lanterns, I briefly wonder why. Except who am I kidding? I jump in on the action immediately.

No one said you can only have one found family.

While Yong and James have Chiang distracted, I run over and write **S.M.** on his lantern. Sharon Miao, his crush. I'm doing him a favor. Chiang roars at me and lunges for my lantern, but I snatch it and take off sprinting. My heart can't take Liya being my wish tonight. I don't want to wish for something she doesn't want.

But just because I'm not going to wish for it doesn't mean the moth can ignore the flame. It's in the moth's blood.

So I laugh with James. Then glance at her. Help Yong with his lantern while he writes his wish—to get better at *Call of Duty*—all while listening for her voice. As I'm contemplating my own wish, I see her with Shue Nainai, their heads bent together as if they're sharing secrets. My traitorous heart blooms an inch bigger, ironically because *her* heart is so big.

When they part ways, Liya looks around, and not subtly

at all. For a second I wonder if she's looking for me, but apparently it's Mr. Tang. I haven't seen him in a while because I haven't been able to drink boba the past few months. I feel bad about that because after Liya wiped up the vomit and darted out the door, Mr. Tang had made me a cup of soothing honey green tea while I finished cleaning myself off. Then he sat me down and drank his own cup of tea beside me in complete silence.

From ten feet apart on the grass, Liya and Mr. Tang acknowledge each other, and that's it. But when she turns away from him, there's a twinkle in her eye, one I haven't seen in a while. Wonder what that's about. Whatever it is, it makes my heart beat faster.

Liya breaks away from the crowds. Today feels off, like someone came in and flipped my world on its side. Because Liya and I are usually inseparable at festivals, and our tradition is to send up a lantern together while joking about what we're going to write on our respective sides.

"I'm going to wish for Pluto to become a planet again," I once joked, knowing that she would be riled up at the thought of me wasting a wish on something so random.

After one of her resounding Liya laughs that used to be the best part of my day, she replied, "Well then, I'm going to wish for you to learn how to dream better."

"How about if I wish for us to be on one of the reality shows you love?"

"You would hate that."

"But you wouldn't. So I wouldn't."

"You need to wish for something for yourself," she insisted.

"That would be! I want you to get something you want!"

"Then I guess I'll just have to wish for something you want." And she put down the perfect wish for me, the exact thing I wanted but didn't know yet: she drew Crabby Hermy the Second on the side of the lantern.

In the distance, Liya begins climbing down the stone ledges that run along the shoreline. Not only is today off because she's not with me, but she's different tonight. It's probably because she's still mourning Nainai. I sure am. I don't get along with my father or brother, and my mother is an international flight attendant who is away a lot, so Liya's nainai felt more like family than my real one sometimes. That's why everything is so sideways and upside down and backward—because we should be supporting each other right now, not staying apart.

I keep a closer eye on her as she nears the water, wanting to make sure she's safe. But when I see her glance around furtively, then write on her lantern, I force myself to look away. I don't want to accidentally see. Her wish is her business, not mine. Although, from the way she had closed her eyes before writing, and because of the smile that crossed her face, I'm pretty sure it's about Nainai. And I immediately know what I will wish for.

Like always, it's about her. I want her to find peace and happiness, and to find a way to move on while also holding on to Nainai's memories.

Yong, Chiang, and James don't ask me to elaborate on the three simple words I've written on my lantern: **peace, happiness, memories.** We stand in a reverent circle as we light our sky lanterns and send them off. As everyone watches their wishes floating up, I feel like my heart is rising too, clogging in my throat, then separating from my body and leaving with my lantern.

Under the lit night sky, Liya is glowing. I don't want to say goodbye to the idea of us, but I will—because it's not what she wants, and because I still want to be friends. I will swallow my feelings and find a way to keep her in my life because I can't imagine it without her.

"Goodbye," I whisper. It dissipates in the wind.

3

Radioactive

LIYA

Kai sent off a lantern tonight. *I am not interested in what he wished for, I am not interested in what he wished for, I am not . . .*

As the crowds disperse and the air cools further, I wrap my arms around myself. A shiver overtakes me from head to toe. But I stand there, unmoving, hoping to hang on to the feeling of wonderment another second longer. Before, when the lanterns dotted the sky, I could taste my dreams, but the dark night takes away as quickly as it gives. Sometimes I wish I could bottle up moments and relive them when I need to.

Kai left without saying bye. I try not to, but I find myself thinking about how he should've been part of my wish tonight. He was the one who held my hand during Năinai's funeral, who cried beside me and lit incense and took over my eulogy when I couldn't finish. He had baked a dozen fresh mooncakes filled with Năinai's favorite filling (egg yolk) and with notes inside (his specialty), each with a wish for her in the afterlife. Peace. Comfort. Love. To be reunited with Yéyé. We had written each note together, our eyes filled with tears.

Now it sometimes feels like *that* Kai is a product of my imagination. How could such a small thing loom so large between us?

Once my parents and I are back at home, I busy myself with random little chores: putting my shoes away, getting myself a cup of water, sorting the mail. I don't want to hear my dad say yet again that Kai's family is bad news bears, so I'm hoping my busy hands will fend all conversation off. For the record, I know what my dad means when he says that, and even Kai knows what he means, but just because his father and brother are one way doesn't mean Kai is the same. Năinai knew that. They'd refused to clean up the exploded dumpster, but Kai was out there in the middle of the night, shoveling dough into trash bags. You'd think that would make my father come around at least about Kai, but I think he was mad because I helped. Kai kept insisting he'd do it alone ("It's my family, after all") but I couldn't bear the thought of him out there by himself, suffering, just because of the family he'd been born into. It had turned out to be fun in a weird way, with us goofing around. Kai had kneaded the garbage dough into a bunch of different shapes for me (a flower, a smiley face, a hermit crab) and even though I'd always known he was talented, that was the first time I'd realized his fingers could do anything. I mean, to dough, of course, my god.

My own fingers are currently sorting through the mail, and they linger on a bright neon-orange envelope. That color never means anything good. Road cone—caution! Construction worker in a vest—caution! Carrot—caution, it could be radioactive if it's that bright!

I look around, but my parents have retreated to their bedroom. Since the envelope is addressed to the shop and not one of them (we'd brought our shop mail home today), I open it.

RENT PAST DUE stares at me in big block letters. No, it *glares* at me. Like the jerk it is.

How can this be possible?

My eyes scan the letter, focusing on the bolded characters. **FOUR MONTHS** is what we owe. **TWO MONTHS** is the time we have to pay what we owe plus late fees, or eviction.

EVICTION. That word is so threatening and huge my brain can't wrap around it for a second.

When You Wish Upon a Lantern has been here for fifty-one years. And just like that, it might be over?

The rest of the numbers jumble before me. It's too much. It's too scary. We owe more than sixteen thousand dollars. Which is a number I can't even comprehend. I'm pretty sure the rent has gone up since the last time I accidentally saw some bills in the store's back office. Perhaps significantly.

We owe four months. FOUR MONTHS. That bolded FOUR has teeth, sinking into my dreams and tearing them up. I'm not particularly superstitious, but I can't help thinking about how the number four is unlucky in Chinese culture because the word for four, *sì*, sounds like the word for death, *sǐ*. And as Shue Nǎinai loves to say, we take our homophones seriously.

That little four sends me spiraling. Because this feels like death. Death of my dreams, death of my wish about carrying on Nǎinai's legacy. It's like I finally worked up the nerve to put my wish into the universe, and then the universe decides to crap on it. What a slap-in-the-face reminder that there's no magic in the world. We have to create our own. I briefly wonder: If I didn't help make wishes come true, would the majority of them wither and die?

And that's when it hits me. Not a slap in the face this time but a blow to the chest that makes my breath catch. What if the orange envelope is partly my fault? Once Năinai fell ill, we hardly worked on any wishes. We did a couple, ones that I told her about in the hospital and she helped me brainstorm, but they were few and far between. Then for the past six months, I had barely set foot in the store, let alone thought about wishes.

By taking the magic out of our community, did I doom Năinai's beloved shop that she built from the sky down? I know it shouldn't matter whose fault it is, but my first instinct is to place blame, and it's almost always on myself.

I have to save the store. Not just for Năinai but also for my parents and me. I'm not sure if making some wishes come true will be enough (though I'm still going to do it, not just for the shop but for Năinai), so I need to start coming up with other plans. Unfortunately, I feel helpless because of my lack of knowledge and life experience.

Just do what you can, I tell myself. I repeat those words because I don't want to hear the other ones bubbling up. *I wish I had someone to help me.*

I cram the letter back in its neon envelope and use some water from my cup to try to reseal it. When that doesn't work, I track down some glue. I don't want my parents to know I saw. They already treat me like I'm broken and can't handle anything. And even if that weren't the case, they would tell me not to worry, to let the grown-ups handle it. "Your job is to do well in school." Never mind that it's summer. "The store is our responsibility, not yours." Never mind that I care about it too and it holds half of my memories of Năinai, or that they don't even know about the wish granting.

I hear footsteps from the bedroom to the living room.

"Liya?" my mother calls out. "Do you want to watch our show?" My mom loves reality dating shows as much as I do, but whereas I have a broad taste, she likes to stick to the Chinese ones. Our favorite is *Mama Knows Best*, a reality show from China where the mother "dates" the contestants to choose which ones her daughter will meet. Some may say that's a risky show to watch with your mother (especially when there's already family drama with your crush), but we got into it a long time ago, before I was old enough to realize I was digging myself a hole.

I shove the orange envelope (which suddenly does feel radioactive) into the middle of the mail stack. Then I display everything haphazardly on the counter to look inconspicuous.

"Yeah, of course!" I yell out to my mom. "I'll bring the snacks!"

I grab a bag of shrimp chips off the counter and turn on the electric kettle to steep some chrysanthemum tea, all while asking myself, *How would Năinai save the store?*

Heidi

KAI

I'm up to my elbows in flour, dough, and thoughts of Liya. Okay, maybe I'm up to my ears with that last one. In my defense, I'm making the outer pastry puff for egg tarts, one of her favorites, so it's not *that* unusual for me to be thinking about her. And what's my excuse for when I'm making all the other items in the bakery? Um, she has a sweet tooth?

I place cling film on the countertop, sprinkle it with flour, then plop on the water dough I've just mixed. One more piece of cling film on top, and I begin rolling. Five passes with the rolling pin—never four. Liya won't admit it, but she's superstitious. Not *super* superstitious, but definitely, like, mediumstitious. Just with the number four. So I've gotten into the habit of avoiding it—like if I type four exclamation points on a text, I add or delete one.

I'm not sure if she knows about some of the other superstitious homophones—like *fourteen* in some regions of China being a homophone for "will be dead" or *seventy-four* sounding like "is already dead" or *ninety-four*, "dead for a long time"—but so far it's only been about the number four for her.

After spooning oil dough atop one side of the water dough and folding, I put it in the fridge to chill. Then I switch my focus to making pork sung buns. The dough has been rising for the past hour, so it's now ready to be reworked and the buns assembled.

I have a whole process. In the beginning, Liya helped me use spreadsheets to figure out the best order to do things to optimize my time in the bakery. She printed them out and tacked them to the walls, but it's since become rote for me. It's slightly different during the school year, when my dad and a part-time employee are here when I'm not—and even then, I do most of the baking in the wee hours of the morning before school starts—but in the summers, the kitchen is completely mine.

The front door opens and closes, causing the bell above the doorframe to jingle. We're old-school. I like to think it adds to the bakery's charm. Our tables and chairs are wooden, carved to resemble Tang dynasty furniture. My mom picked them because the Tang style has become what is now widely regarded as "Chinese," and even though it bothers me that the West is sometimes unfamiliar with much of our history, I like the idea of making the customers feel like they've entered another culture and another time. Our yoke-back chairs aren't old or expensive, but my dad treated the wood to give it an antique look. The birdcages and lanterns hanging from the ceiling add pops of color and a more modern streak.

"Out in a second!" I yell to the customer as I cover the partially assembled pork sung buns. I'm the only one here right now since it's ten a.m., before the lunch rush, and there are usually only a few straggler customers who I can easily handle between baking.

I start to wash my hands, my back to the door leading to the front of the store. Suddenly, I'm jerked backward. It happens so fast I can't piece together what's going on—all I know is someone's arm is around my neck.

Oh, it's a familiar arm. Sweet Jesus, no.

A fist rubs the top of my head roughly.

"Ow!" I yell, even though I already know it won't help.

"Did you miss me?" my older brother, Jiao, asks as he continues to noogie me while I'm in a headlock. It doesn't help that he was on the wrestling team in high school.

I push him off with my soapy hands.

"Hey!" he exclaims. "You got my shirt wet!" He looks for a paper towel, but since he's only been back here a few times, he doesn't know they're tucked behind the bags of flour, out of sight.

I grab him one even though I don't want to.

"Can we not do that anymore?" I ask. "I'm seventeen, and you're in college."

Jiao shrugs. "Then you should finally be tough enough to take it."

By the time I finish washing my hands, Jiao has disappeared from the kitchen. I find him in the storefront, popping one of the display pastries—an almond cookie—into his mouth.

"Hey, those are for the customers. I'll get you some from the back." Unlike the rest of my family, I always try to sell the perfectly shaped items first. I save the slightly funky ones for when we're running low. And if something goes wrong—like I can't get the dough consistency just right or the flour is past its prime and doesn't taste exactly how it's supposed to—I start over. I know we're a business and the way I bake bleeds precious money, but I also can't stand serving an item that isn't top-shelf. Liya claims I make the best pastries and puffs and buns, but I keep telling her that the truth is not so glamorous.

Jiao ignores me and grabs a perfect sponge cake from the display. "What, so I'm supposed to eat the second-best ones? Those are for you, Number Two Son."

Sigh. "Can you not call me that? It's bad enough that Dad does." He doesn't call me it to my face—it's similar to how someone would say "my younger son" in conversation to someone else—but of course Jiao, Number One Son, latched onto it and rubs it in my face every chance he gets. It's directly translated from Mandarin, where parents sometimes refer to their kids as *lao da, lao er, lao san,* meaning "oldest," "second child," "third child." My dad chose to translate it to "number one" and "number two" just like his parents did. And because my father loves that he himself was not just the "number one son" but also the prized eldest son of an eldest son, he doesn't think about what it's like for me.

"Okay, then what's another way of saying 'number two'? Hmmm . . . oh, I know!" Jiao gives me a toothy, wolfish grin. "You can be Poop Son. Hey, Poop Son!"

Okay, who would've ever guessed I would miss "Number Two Son"? I hate when Jiao invades my safe space.

"Nice to see you've matured so much after a year of college," I say, closing the display case and holding it shut.

"Poop jokes will always be funny no matter what age you are."

The truth is, Jiao could tell the funniest joke on Earth and I still wouldn't laugh because it came from him. It's gotten to the point where I can't separate the words he says from the fact that *he* said them.

Jiao gulps down the last bite of his sponge cake and leans on the counter as he says, "Can I ask you a serious question?" *No*, I think. "Why do you spend so much time here? I've said it once and I'll say it again: baking is for girls."

Once? He's said it about a million times. Honestly, no good can come from trying to answer Jiao's question, so I ignore it.

The irony is that *he's* the reason I fell in love with baking. Once my mother returned to work and was no longer around to shield me from Jiao, I started hanging out in the Once Upon a Mooncake kitchen, learning from my dad, because it was the one space safe from Jiao—he would never be caught doing something "so girly." I actually hated baking at first because I couldn't get the dough or frosting or puff pastries to obey me, but the more Jiao made fun of me—"Did you lose your balls in the mixer?"—the more I wanted to be good at it as an F U to him. Maybe even to prove him wrong. It's been so long I can't remember if I ever thought I could actually sway his opinion, but in that time baking has become my passion.

And I grew to really love this part of my persona. At first, it sucked when people made fun of me, and even though it still hurts now, I've realized that my view is, if you care that much that I'm a guy who loves baking, I'm perfectly fine with you not wanting to get to know me. In fact, I prefer it. Maybe it also helps that Liya once said that a guy who can bake is sexy. I had interpreted it as a hint toward her potential feelings for me, but obviously I was wrong. Maybe she had been thinking about a contestant from *America's Hottest Buns*, the reality baking show where contestants mix, roll, and frost wearing nothing but an apron.

My mom also encourages my baking. Even though she's not here very often, she still sees Once Upon a Mooncake as her third baby, and she knows I'm its best caretaker. She also loves salted egg yolk buns and claims mine are the ooziest, like when you break into a molten lava cake and the chocolate gushes out. The first time I achieved that with the thick, creamy yolk, I felt like I could finally call myself a baker.

I do feel bad for not making conversation with Jiao after he's been gone for a year—admittedly, a much more blissful year due to his absence—so I say, "Too bad you didn't get back last night—you could've joined us for the lantern festival."

"Blech. That's filled with old people." Jiao shudders. Charming. "I wouldn't have come even if I was home."

The door opens. Saved by the bell. Jiao never has any interest in dealing with customers. He always says, "You're so much better at handling them than me. I'm more of a big-ideas kind of guy. Think of me as Elon Musk, not the Tesla car salesman."

My hope that the customer will make Jiao leave—or at least give me a reprieve from him—evaporates when Liya walks in. My heart leaps into my mouth both from excitement and from dread.

Jiao's eyes gleam. "Ohhh, your girlfriend's here, Poop Son."

I want to chuck a misshapen bun at his head. Liya's eyebrows rise at the words *Poop Son*. Looking at her dries out my mouth, and my tongue suddenly feels huge. *She's here*, my brain says, poking me to attention.

"Heidi," I say like the fool that I am. I had started to say *Howdy* only to realize that I'd never in my life said *howdy* before and it was weird if not said by someone in a ten-gallon hat and large belt buckle, so I tried to switch to *Hi*, only to meld the two.

I kinda sorta wish I could disappear.

"Sofia," Liya says, and I tilt my head at her, questioning. Then I remember the ridiculousness that had just come out of my mouth and I put it together. Classic Liya, not asking me to explain and also making me feel better.

"Simon," I say.

She names a fourth *America's Got Talent* judge: "Howie."

Jiao is staring at us like our ears have sprouted pork sung. Luckily, we have made him so uncomfortable that he doesn't say another word and leaves.

"Sorry he's back," Liya says.

The words mean even more coming from her because no one knows my relationship with Jiao or my feelings toward him better than her.

I nod my thanks, then say, "It's really good to see you."

There's an awkward pause.

I used to have something special prepared for when she stopped by, but she hasn't been here in months. It once was the best part of my day, making her a Portuguese egg tart with a blackened smiley face on top, or a matcha latte with a hermit crab in the foam. Correction—second-best part of my day, after her actual visit.

"I'm so sorry I didn't make something just for you," I say at the same exact moment she says, "Please don't feel bad for not preparing something."

She points toward the kitchen. "I'll take the most unique item from the back. I assume Jiao has been eating the less unique ones?"

With her enormous heart, she has always loved the misshapen food in a Charlie-Brown-Christmas-tree way. And she only ever calls them "unique" or "rare" or "special."

From the back, I retrieve some of her favorites—an egg tart, a taro puff, a lotus seed mooncake—the most misshapen ones. They bring a huge smile to her face. She retrieves her wallet, but I hold a hand up.

"On the house, of course."

She's already shaking her head. "Don't be ridiculous. Lotus seed is the most expensive filling. Please."

We go back and forth a bit until Liya ends it with a joke: "Would we do this if we weren't Chinese?"

"It *is* in our blood."

She places cash on the counter, then changes the conversation so I'll drop it. "I was hoping to place an order today. I, uh, want a Once Upon a Mooncake special. With a personalized note."

Her words make my heart fall. I can't help it. The Once Upon a Mooncake special is a made-from-scratch mooncake, your choice of filling, with a note baked inside. It's inspired by the mooncake rebellion of the Yuan dynasty. As legend has it, in the fourteenth century, when China was ruled by Mongolia, rebel leader Zhu Yuanzhang took advantage of the upcoming Mid-Autumn Festival and the fact that the Chinese would be eating mooncakes that day in celebration. He slipped notes into the mooncakes to coordinate an uprising against Mongol rule, and since the Chinese were the main consumers, it led to a successful rebellion. Zhu Yuanzhang then became the founding emperor of the Ming dynasty. Jiao was obsessed with this story when he was young because it was his main defense when other kids made fun of him for the family business, for being Peeta from *The Hunger Games*, all soft and cowardly. "Mooncakes are a weapon of war!" he used to hurl back at them. "They're offensive, not defensive!" Then the other kids would retort, "Well, Once Upon a Mooncake is a girly name!" Jiao gave up after that.

The mooncake rebellion was Jiao's favorite story, but I was the one who took inspiration from it to create the Once Upon a Mooncake special. We can do any message the customer wants, but we're known for doing heartfelt love notes—admitting a crush, declarations of love, even proposals. Jiao *loathed* how I transformed his beloved war story into love notes, but I was pretty proud—and still am to this day. What's more powerful than love bringing people together?

So when Liya asks about purchasing a special, I already know it's not about me, and the only question I can think of is, *Who is it for?*

"You need a mooncake special with a note?" I repeat like a fool.

"Uh, yeah. It's going to go to . . . Mr. Tang."

"Oh!" I yell this too loudly on account of my anxiety suddenly jolting to relief.

She eyes me suspiciously. "Why do you say that like it suddenly makes sense to you?"

And I immediately begin sweating. "Um . . . I saw you last night, looking for him." Not that any of it makes sense to me yet, though.

"You noticed that? But I was so subtle!"

Her not knowing how *not* subtle she acts is somehow even more adorable than her not being subtle—which is already pretty frickin' adorable.

I say, "You were about as subtle as that time you snuck shrimp chips into the movie theater."

"Oh, so I was really super-duper subtle," she responds with a smile.

I laugh. It feels the way it's always been with us, before. My heart wants to soar but it's also weighed down. As if she heard my thoughts—I mean, maybe she can, she certainly acts like that sometimes—her face contorts slightly, as if remembering the boba incident.

Why had I ruined things? Why did I have to ask her out?

I swallow down the lump of shame and regret clogging my throat. "So what would you like the note to read?" I don't ask the other question gnawing at me: *Will I get to know what this is about?*

"Well, I'm not completely sure yet. It's a little complicated . . ."

With a sigh, she plops down in the closest chair and I come around the counter to sit beside her. I wait, but, nothing. Just her nibbling her bottom lip, her telltale sign that she's nervous. Before, I might've let out a strangled noise as a joke, then begged her to tell me, but I somehow hold everything in. Waiting. Dying just a little. (Maybe Chiang's not the only dramatic one.)

I try to find a way to let her know she doesn't have to let me in on the details if she doesn't want to. As gently as I can—and ignoring my own complicated feelings—I say, "You can always let me know what to put in the note later. I'll rush the order for you when you're ready."

She pauses, her eyes searching my face—for what, I don't know. Then, suddenly, she leans forward as if she's going to tell me a secret. I instinctively lean in too.

"Nainai and I . . ." She wells up and has to stop. I want to reach a hand out and put it on hers, but I don't.

"I miss her every day," I say in the space she's left. "I miss the way she'd show us she loves us by continuing to feed us even after we were full—"

"Oh my gosh, so full!" Liya chimes in, grasping her stomach as if she could feel the sensation right now. A beat later she adds, "I miss the way she would insist we wear winter hats even when it was eighty degrees out because she 'didn't want us to catch colds.' "

"I'm starting to sweat just thinking about it!" I pretend to wipe my forehead as Liya laughs.

Then she waits. Guess it's my turn to share something. My voice is full of emotion as I say, "I . . . haven't been able to eat oranges since she left us."

A lone tear escapes the corner of her eye. "Me neither." Her voice is quiet, a whisper. She grasps my hand. Thank god she made the first move because I wasn't sure if she would want me to, but now I squeeze her fingers back. She initially seems to find strength in the gesture, but after a few seconds, she pulls back a hair—not enough for us to come apart, but the action makes me let go as if her hand burned me.

Awkward. It's awkward now. How did we get here? Oh, right, she wanted to order a mooncake special for Mr. Tang. And she hasn't told me yet what that has to do with Nainai. If it's too hard, I don't want to make her explain.

As I'm about to tell her she doesn't have to tell me anything, she takes a breath.

"Nainai and I used to make the wishes come true, from the lanterns, for the customers. We'd do it behind the scenes, in secret. Together."

Of course they did. I don't know if there was anything they wouldn't do for the community. The idea of them teaming up to bring others happiness fills my heart. I don't want to think about this, but I can't help it—this is exactly why Liya is the light of my life.

Then something hits me. "Wait. So that time I wished for Jiao to stop bullying me so much and suddenly he received an invitation to join the community's new wrestling team—"

"That was us," she admits proudly. "Though, maybe I didn't think that one through. Sorry it made him more, uh, skilled at bullying. But at least he was around less. And Jiao wasn't the only reason a wrestling team was good for the community. That one helped a couple of wishes in one." She smiles, a twinkle in her eye just like Nainai used to get.

I clear my throat, a little choked up. "Well, thank you. That helped a lot, as you already know."

"That's why we did it. And why we started in the first place." Her face is a mix of emotions—pride, happiness, nostalgia, grief. "I haven't granted any wishes since Nainai passed. But . . . I want to begin again, starting with Shue Nainai. She has a crush on Mr. Tang. I don't want to force them to be together, of course," she quickly clarifies. "But I was hoping to find out if Mr. Tang wants to enter the dating world. And if he does, whether he has any interest in Shue Nainai. And if the answer is yes, and he's willing to get to know her, then I want to, you know . . ."

"Play Cupid?" I suggest.

She smiles. "Exactly. Anyway, my idea is to use the mooncake special to see if he's interested, but I'm not exactly sure how to do that yet. But I of course wanted to first make sure you were on board, you know, not that you wouldn't be, of course you would be . . ."

She's rambling. And now she's nibbling her bottom lip again. Maybe she's missed our friendship too. I decide to take the first step, to show her that I'm willing to be just friends. That I prefer it to not being anything.

"Do you, um, want some help? Maybe a partner?" I say lightheartedly.

"A partner in wish granting?" she says quickly before bringing her hand up to her mouth as if she wants to take the words back.

"Yes, exactly. It's okay if you don't. I just think it'd be really fun." And I want to help keep her and Nainai's tradition alive.

Her eyes grow glassy as tears pool. After a beat, she says, "That would be really nice." And then she shoots me a wide smile that shows most of her teeth—my favorite smile of hers because it's the one that means she's truly happy.

Liya's back in my life.

6

Candy Island

LIYA

I leave the bakery quickly because the bubbling emotions are too much and very conflicting. I've been so utterly, crushingly alone for months and suddenly I have Kai back and, in a small way, Nǎinai. After reminiscing with Kai, Nǎinai feels more present than she has since she left us. The resulting joy makes me want to jump up and down (though my Stephanie-Lee-bee instincts keep that in). But there's something else there too.

Guilt, I realize. I'm not . . . replacing Nǎinai, am I?

The guilt has been the most unexpected piece of mourning. I feel guilty for thinking about her too much because I know she wouldn't want that, and I also feel guilty when I don't think about her enough.

As soon as I step into When You Wish Upon a Lantern two minutes later, my mother stops stocking shelves and fixes me with a worried look. "Everything . . . okay, Liya?"

"Uh-huh." Those two sounds have come out of my mouth so much recently they no longer have meaning.

"Do you want to take some time off?" my mother asks hesitantly.

I shake my head. I've already taken too much time off. And now there's a ticking clock over the store's lifespan.

My father's head pops into the aisle. "Liya?" His tone is sharp, the opposite of my mother's. "What were you doing over there?" He says *over there* like I'd just come back from making a deal with the devil in hell.

What, is he spying on me now? I want to call him out on that, but he did catch me red-handed, and it wouldn't do anything to help my case.

I chew on my bottom lip instead of answering. I definitely cannot tell him how much Kai means to me. And I do not want to tell him about the wish granting (Side note: What does it mean that I was okay telling Kai but don't want to tell my own parents?). I also can't help wondering, *Why can't my parents do what Kai just did for me? Why can't we talk about Năinai at all? Why can't we keep her spirit alive?*

"Liya," my father repeats, as my mother says, "Now, now."

I find my voice, small as it is. "Don't you think it's important to keep the peace with our neighbors? For the store's sake, and the community's?"

My father shakes his head. "There's no keeping peace with people like that. We tried and look where it got us. The stench of their rotting garbage hurts foot traffic to our store! People don't want to take their time to browse or even come in! All we're asking for is common decency, and they not only say no, they get angry!"

I see his point, but he also did not ask Mr. Jiang very nicely. Nor is he being fair to Kai, who is on our side.

"Stay away, okay?" he says, but a little gentler now.

With only a brief nod, I take over stocking for my mother. As my parents shuffle off, I try to calm the roiling emotions inside me. They not only can't see how alone I feel, but they're keeping me from Kai. Losing Năinai was painful enough, so why does everything else around me also have to crumble?

I force myself to focus on the joy of filling the candy shelves with my favorites: Pocky, Hello Panda chocolate cream biscuits, Hi-Chew, White Rabbit candies, Tomato Pretz, Yan Yan, and the red-and-gold Lucky Candy that tastes like strawberries and is most popular on Chinese New Year.

We're known for our lanterns, but our store also falls

under the umbrella of Quintessential Random Chinatown Store that carries everything from lucky bamboo plants to Hello Kitty paraphernalia to rice cookers and portable hot-pot cookware.

When I was little, I named all the sections of our store. There was Candy Island (my favorite, of course), Bamboo Forest, Loud Alley (where I used to bang on the pots and pans for fun), Hydration Station (featuring classic Asian drinks like lychee soda and Ramune bottles with the marble in the opening), and the Zoo (our selection of miniature animal figurines that seem to be a feature of many Asian stores).

My phone buzzes, and I shoot straight up, going from squatting in the candy aisle to standing ramrod straight in a few seconds.

It's probably a junk email from a store I ordered something from three years ago or my calendar reminding me my period starts tomorrow, but . . . it could also be a text.

I fumble for my phone, my heart beating so loud I can hear it. More buzzing. Definitely texts.

Kai
How about this
The mooncake note says something
like, someone has a crush on you! If
you're interested in knowing more,
leave a cup in the window when you
close tomorrow night!

Or something else
I don't know

His texts ratchet up the guilt from going behind my parents' back. Not that their feud isn't totally ridiculous, but still.

On the other hand, his messages slightly ease the guilt at replacing Năinai. Because his idea is perfect. It's anonymous, which was Năinai's number one rule, and it's simple. Not to mention, it's also pretty cute (not a rule but a bonus).

Liya
I love it!
We're really taking the Cupid
thing to heart!

Kai
👍

I stare at my phone, waiting for (willing?) another text, but that seems to be it. I consider asking Kai for more details, but then I realize he's already covered everything in his messages. Sometimes I feel like I was born out of time because texting stresses me out. Not that phone calls are better (they're way, way worse), but why are there so many things to be anxious about re: texting? How long to wait before you respond . . . how many times you respond before they respond . . . and the waiting waiting waiting is just so agonizing. In that space, I always go from wondering if I said something offensive (*Do they hate me now?*) to worrying that something horrible happened to them.

Somehow, with Kai, over time, those stresses went away, but now they're all back and ten times worse than before because there's vomit history and layers and new things to stress about.

But then . . . he actually does text again. And it's adorable.

Kai
Do we need a code name
for our plan?
Maybe Operation Cupid?

I think for much too long, not wanting to mess this up. I want to be agreeable, but I also want to be truthful. Five minutes later, I work up the nerve to be honest, replying:

Liya
I love it, but how about
something more covert?

Kai
Good thinking, 008

008?

Lucky number

My thumbs hover. That's pretty cute, except for the fact that I am *not* superstitious. Not really. Not outwardly.

Kai
And before you say it, I know
you're not superstitious

Even though I don't want to, I smile. I forgot how much
he could read my mind.

Kai
So what code name are you
thinking, 008?

My leg jiggles as I try to think of something clever or
funny to suggest. I almost laugh out loud when it comes to me.

Liya
How about calling it Shue-
Tang Potential Clan?

Kai
YOU DID NOT JUST SAY THAT

Too much?

Hilarious—I'm still laughing—but
even less covert, don't you think?

I know
I had to say it though

For sure

In my head I can picture Kai still laughing, the deep

rumbles starting in his chest and bursting out of his mouth, and I wish I could see him for real right now. Making him laugh always feels like the biggest accomplishment even though it's not that rare or hard. I just never can get enough.

I think for a second longer, then start typing again.

> **Liya**
> How about Operation Mooncake?
> Since that's what we're using instead of Cupid's bow and arrow?

> **Kai**
> There it is!
> It's perfect because a bow and arrow's too violent anyway
> Mooncakes are much more the language of love
> Well, and also war, but just that one time

Nothing is cuter than Kai's love of mooncakes. Just another reason why we've found the perfect name for this operation.

I hesitate again over my response, not sure if I even need one but also feeling like it'd be weird not to say anything. I eventually settle on some emojis: Cupid arrow through heart, mooncake, thumbs-up.

The front door of our store opens and closes, setting off

the contraption my father built, which begins playing a few bars of an instrumental version of "Yuèliàng Dàibiǎo Wǒ de Xīn" ("The Moon Represents My Heart"). Kai claims Once Upon a Mooncake is old-school, but nothing is more old-school than that song. My father—who has always dabbled in building things, especially in the tech space—loves that song, yes, but chose it mainly because he was amused by the inherent dichotomy of pairing an old classic song with modern tech. (This is the same man who named me Lí Yǎ because it sounds like the American name Leah and represents my Asian and American sides in two short syllables.)

My mother and I both scurry to the front to greet the customer. I falter (expectedly) when I see it's Stephanie Lee of non-spelling-bee fame and her boyfriend, Eric, who's also a rising senior at my high school.

"Stephanie! Hi!" My voice is one decibel too loud and one note too high. "Hey, Eric," I manage to say normally. "Can I help you two with something?"

My mother returns to the register.

"Yeah, actually, you can!" Stephanie says brightly. She's dragging Eric along, one hand wrapped around his forearm. "We'd love one of your lanterns."

Our over-the-top-on-purpose lantern display is front and center right when you enter, and Stephanie leads Eric directly there. We have display-only lanterns hanging from the ceiling with electric tea lights illuminating them from the inside, and a table of flat, folded, pre-wish lanterns stacked among blown-up photos of our lantern festivals. Depending on the season, I also add other decorations (hearts for Valentine's Day, mooncakes for Mid-Autumn Festival, etc.), and I have rotating display lanterns painted on theme. Right now, the Summer Festival lanterns are still up, which are painted with scenes of sun, sand, and brown sugar boba Popsicles (a special offered at Mr. Tang's boba café from June through August).

As Eric hovers a step behind, Stephanie grabs a plastic-wrapped, folded lantern. "It'll be fun," she says, nudging him in the ribs. "It can't hurt, right? And maybe it'll come true; you've heard all the stories about these lanterns!"

At that, Eric gingerly takes the lantern from Stephanie. "Uh, so, how do these work?" he asks me.

I pick up the lantern left out for demonstration and unfold it. "You write your wish—or wishes, plural, if you want—on the side with a marker, and when you're done, fluff the lantern open by using your hands to air it out, kind of like you do when you're opening a trash bag. It's easier when you're outside and there's wind," I add when the lantern in my hand catches a little and collapses on one side. It's so large that it's difficult to do in a small space with limited airflow. I point to the fuel cell on the bottom. "Light this, starting at the corners. It's easier when you have another person to help you hold it as you light. Then turn the lantern so the flame is down, and hold it here on the wire base while it fills with hot air, like a hot-air balloon. When you're ready, lift it gently and it should rise up."

Eric is eyeing me and the lantern suspiciously. "I guess it's no worse than the Chinese almanac or crystals or something."

"Stop being so negative," Stephanie chastises. "Bonnie used a wishing lantern to wish for Jude to notice her a year ago, and they've been together since!"

I had nothing to do with that one. Bonnie didn't share her wish with me, and even if she had, I'm not sure I would've gotten involved (when I tried to help her with her lantern once, she yelled at me that she could handle it herself, so I doubt she would've wanted me interfering in her life).

Stephanie turns to me. "Can you believe Eric's parents don't support his dream to play basketball in college? He's, like, the next big thing! No one sinks as many three-point dunks as you, baby."

Eric turns red. "I just want them to listen to me," he says softly. "They want me to focus on school, but I can study *and* play. And isn't a basketball scholarship a good thing, even if it means I'll be playing while earning a degree?" He sighs. "Anyway, you don't need to hear my life story. Thanks for this," he says to me as he grabs another lantern off the pile and gestures to Stephanie that it's for her.

Stephanie grins at me. "Date night," she says before looping her hand in Eric's arm again.

"Have fun!" I say as they make their way to the register. "May your wishes find the light!"

In my head, I'm rubbing my hands together again. It may not work (sometimes the wish-granting efforts by me and Nǎinai didn't pan out), but I have an idea for how to at least try something for Eric, as minimal as it might be.

And I would need my partner for this one, because he provides an extra, more anonymous extension of the When You Wish Upon a Lantern reach.

It feels so good to be doing something to try to save the store (all while helping someone else) that it completely replaces the guilt. And the fact that Stephanie Lee doesn't hate me for once accidentally cheering her near-death is the very delicious icing on top.

7

Gouda

KAI

I'm hiding behind a bush with Liya. Repeat, I'm *hiding behind a bush* with Liya. Our knees are brushing against each other and we're sharing the same air and a common goal—to see whether there will be a cup in the window of Mr. Tang's Bubbly Tea in three minutes. Now two.

Liya insisted from the start that we remain anonymous, always, and when I agreed, I hadn't realized it meant concealing ourselves behind some very scratchy shrubs. We're both avoiding the giant metaphorical elephant between us wearing a top hat and tap-dancing. The last time we were at Mr. Tang's was *the last time* we were at Mr. Tang's. I try not to relive the will-you-go-out-with-me-*blech* moment and instead focus on the warm, crouched ball of nerves beside me.

"Are you comfortable?" I ask, trying to give her a little more room. My foot catches on a rock and I teeter forward, scratching my arm on some branches.

"Whose bright idea was it to hide like this?" Liya asks.

"Um, yours?"

She grins. "I know. Sorry."

I laugh.

She nudges me, whispering, "It's happening!"

We hunch down further while peering between leaves. Mr. Tang goes to the window and turns the OPEN sign to CLOSED. Then we hold our breaths. Or, well, I'm assuming she's holding her breath because I am.

Slowly, hesitantly, Mr. Tang goes to the counter, retrieves a paper cup with his Bubbly Tea logo on it—a *B* made up of smiley face boba balls—and places it at the window.

"Ahh!"

"Shh!"

"You shh!"

It's silent for a second, but then I can't hold it in. "He did it! He's interested!" It somehow feels like it's happening to me even though it's not—the exhilaration is that real.

Mr. Tang presses his face closer to the window, looking

left and right, trying to spot someone, anyone, whoever is behind this.

We freeze.

Her left shoe is touching my right.

When he disappears from view, we relax. Her shoe moves away. Even though we don't need to, we're quiet as we duck-walk out of the bush and behind the cover of shrubbery, trash cans, and trees. We keep going until we're no longer in Mr. Tang's sight line.

At the same time, we both straighten with a groan. My calves are *killing* me. "Bakers don't work out their legs that much," I joke. "You couldn't have thought about that before picking our hiding spot?"

"You could've balanced on your hands or forearms instead." She glances at my forearms and, I swear, her cheeks redden slightly.

Okay, she's forgiven. And it turns out she was right to hide, given that Mr. Tang had looked around for us.

"So what do we do next?" I ask.

She nibbles her bottom lip. "Well, it *is* dinnertime . . ."

I had meant about Mr. Tang and Shue Nainai but no way was I giving up this opportunity.

"Yeah, sure, okay." *Take it down a notch, killer.*

"My treat," she adds. "As a thank-you, for rushing the mooncake order."

"Don't be silly, it was nothing." It actually had been a bit complicated fitting the order in so last minute yesterday—and our specials are baked from scratch because it's easier to include the note inside before baking instead of sticking it in after—but I don't want her to know that.

Liya's already marching ahead, refusing to take no for an answer.

I'm about to make a playful jab about her stubbornness when she points in the direction of our usual spot and tilts her head in question. She would've never asked before.

"Yeah, if that's what you want," I say with as casual of a shrug as I can muster.

She nods, and we walk to the restaurant a few feet apart.

Mr. Chen's entire face lights up when Liya and I enter the Noodle Emperorium. For the record, Liya and I both love a good pun, but that's only one of many reasons we love Mr. Chen's restaurant.

"Lai lai lai lai lai," Mr. Chen says in rapid succession, waving us closer, and we obey, following him to a cozy two-person table tucked in the back corner. Our table.

The Emperorium is painted yellow and covered with dragons—yellow because it was the emperor's color, and dragons because they were a symbol of imperial power. Mr. Chen is nothing if not on-brand.

"You two haven't been here in so long!" he exclaims, throwing his hands up in a *what's going on* gesture.

Liya giggles nervously, not saying anything.

My heart experiences a slight twinge as I say, "I know. Sorry, Mr. Chen."

"We're so happy to be back," Liya adds, and I can't help wondering if there's a second underlying meaning to her words. "And we're ready to eat!"

Mr. Chen raises his index finger and shakes it excitedly. "Have I got the perfect dish for you two tonight!" He pulls out a chair for Liya. "Sit, sit, sit, I go make it now!"

"Well, that's new," I muse. Maybe he missed our business and is trying to make sure we come back.

"I'm glad he's just as animated as ever," Liya says.

"Remember that time when—" I start, and Liya's already cracking a smile.

"Oh my god, yes," she chimes in.

We both start mime-kneading imaginary dough with our hands.

"You did so well, no surprise there," Liya says, chuckling, "but my dough looked muddy."

The laughter bursts out of me. *Muddy* is too cute of a way to describe it. Her pasta had looked like it was drowning.

We both mimic Mr. Chen at the same time, waving our hands in the air. *"Aiyah, Liya, what are you doing? We're making noodles, not soup!"*

Our laughter is lengthened by the inside-ness of the joke and both having been there. It was Mr. Chen's first and last noodle-making class that he'd held for people in the community during the in-between afternoon hours when the restaurant was closed. It had been a test run for possibly rolling out classes to the public, but after Mrs. Ahn's break-your-teeth flat noodles and Liya's soupy dough, he had thrown in his white towel on top of the unsalvageable noodles and declared he was giving up.

Liya grins. "Remember how Mrs. Ahn insisted—"

"Man, did she insist."

"—on how you had to boil the noodles for ten minutes, then bake it in the oven for forty? *Forty!* And she talked like she knew better than Mr. Chen!"

"The noodle emperor," I add.

"The emperor of the Noodle Emperorium."

We chuckle.

Liya looks down at her hands sheepishly. "I think Mrs. Ahn and I really did a number on the poor ol' emperor. He started the day talking about how easy it was."

"'Just rou yi rou,'" I mimic, mime-kneading the dough again.

She laughs. "Yeah, that's all, so easy."

Jack, Mr. Chen's son and apparently our waiter for tonight, approaches the table with a steaming pot of tea. "Hey. I know Ba is fixing up our special for you, but what else would you like?"

Liya's eyes brighten. "Ooh, will daoxiaomian go with what he's making? Or will we be noodled out?"

Jack says, "The Noodle Emperorium statement is that no one can be noodled out, ever, but no, it'll go really well. He's not making you noodles."

As the name promises, the restaurant is an emporium, offering more than just noodles, though it is most famous for its made-from-scratch noodles. Daoxiaomian is Liya's favorite. She first fell in love with it as a kid watching Mr. Chen take a giant knife to a hunk of dough held in his hand, angled downward thirty degrees, cutting chunks of it off into the boiling water. When he got in the groove, the knife would fly through the air, the noodle chunks shooting off and splashing into the water so fast you could barely follow them with your eyes. "Magic," child Liya had said. "Therapy," teenage Liya likes to joke, saying how she'd love to be able to do that to work off anger, but can't because her lack of "ya"-ness could lead to lost appendages.

Liya nods at Jack. "Okay, I'll take a pork daoxiaomian, stir-fried."

"I'll have lamian soup with beef." Pulled noodles are my

favorite. Even though I do think it's cool to see Mr. Chen take a giant hunk of dough and twist, fold, and stretch it into long noodles, my love for them is purely about taste and chewiness. Pulled noodles have that perfect balance of giving you a hefty chunk to bite into while also being slurpable. Liya and I usually share all the dishes—we *are* Chinese, after all—but she always ends up having more of the daoxiao and me more of the lamian.

As Jack writes everything down, I ask him, "How's the app coming along?" Jack apprentices with his dad in addition to waiting tables, but his passion lies in programming. Mr. Chen is not only supportive but proud, bragging to everyone who'll listen about how Jack is going to move on to bigger and better things when he applies to college in a few years.

Jack straightens, the excitement elongating his spine. "Shop Frenzy launched a few months ago, and it's been picking up users steadily." His app highlights mom-and-pop restaurants, bakeries, cafés, and stores in your area with specials going on, encouraging users to support local businesses while also offering them deals.

Liya waits for a beat, and I know she's thinking about Stephanie Lee and the non-spelling-bee fiasco, so I quickly say, "Congratulations, Jack, that's fantastic." As soon as I say *congratulations*, Liya smiles and claps.

Jack blushes. "Let me know if you want me to feature

your stores," he offers. "The mooncake special and wishing lanterns would be perfect if you're able to offer a discount on them!"

Liya looks thoughtful for a moment, then uncharacteristically blurts, "Yes! Please! That'd be great!"

Jack manages to quickly move past his surprise at Liya's urgency. "Okay, awesome! I'll text you!"

As soon as Jack leaves, I ask Liya, "Are you okay?"

She nibbles her bottom lip. "Is everything okay with the bakery?"

"Yeah, why?"

She sighs. "Our shop is struggling."

What? That can't be. "Liya, I'm so sorry." I don't know what else to say.

"It's bad. We don't have that much time to fix it. And I . . . I'm worried it's my fault."

"How can it be your fault?" I ask, despite being not shocked at all. She blames herself too often.

As soon as she finishes telling me about her absence from the shop and from wish granting, I instinctively lean forward and put a hand on hers. "You. Are. Not. To. Blame," I say slowly, so it will sink in. "But it still sucks, and we're not going to sit back."

"We?" she says, hopeful.

"If you want. We'll start with Shop Frenzy."

Liya nods, rapid up-down motions.

I fill our teacups with tea, and Liya taps the table twice with three fingers to thank me. It's a tradition my family doesn't do, but I've noticed that all the Huangs do it. The story goes that Qianlong, the emperor of the Qing dynasty, once traveled in disguise to observe his subjects. After he poured tea for his companions, custom dictated they should bow to him in thanks, but they couldn't do this without blowing his cover. So instead, they tapped three fingers on the table, with two fingers representing prostrated arms and the third representing a bowed head. Now the tap translates to a silent thank-you to the person who pours tea. I believe it stems from Cantonese culture, and since Liya's mother's side is from Hong Kong, I'm guessing the tradition started with her and was picked up by her nainai and father too, even though they're Taiwanese.

While sipping steaming teacups of oolong, Liya and I brainstorm ideas until Mr. Chen explodes up to our table with fanfare, clapping his hands and doing a little dance. From behind him, Jack appears with a glistening Peking duck.

Liya and I exchange excited glances.

"Wow, Mr. Chen, you've really outdone yourself," I compliment.

Mr. Chen carves the duck for us, piling the pieces onto a

large serving plate beside julienned scallions and cucumbers. Jack places hoisin sauce and homemade bings—thin flour wraps—on the table.

Mr. Chen points the carving knife toward the latter. "Bing, they're noodles' neighbor!"

He's so cute, Liya mouths to me, and I smile.

"Do you need me to wrap them for you?" Mr. Chen asks.

"I got it," Liya jumps in.

"Ah, you remember your training?" Mr. Chen says with a smirk.

"Yes, sir," Liya jokes, saluting him. She grabs the communal chopsticks and deftly uses them to pluck one bing from the stack. On it, she piles a few pieces of duck, a smattering of cucumber and scallion, and half a spoonful of sauce. Then, most impressive of all, she somehow maneuvers the chopsticks to fold the bing around the filling—right side, left, bottom flap, flip the whole thing onto the remaining flap.

Mr. Chen pats her back. "Good girl."

Liya beams at me.

My mouth might be open. I close it. "I can't believe you did that with chopsticks."

"He taught me during that class after my noodles drowned."

The other piece of it remains unsaid—that Liya has a

thing about germs and doesn't like to touch her food with her hands if she can help it.

When she has folded both of us Peking duck wraps—hers with no scallions—we pick them up with our chopsticks and click them together, toasting. I want to say something, but the words that pop into my head are all too cheesy. And cheese and Peking duck don't really go together, at least not that I know of.

We continue brainstorming ways to boost her store as we eat, and of course I want to help her just for the sake of helping her, but seeing the hope and relief in her eyes when we touch upon a promising idea drives me to come up with as many as I can.

The jackpot idea comes from both of us putting our heads together—almost literally. We're concentrating so hard we're leaning toward each other across the table.

Liya starts the ball rolling with, "I'm thinking that Qixi is going to be the key."

Qixi Festival—sometimes called Chinese Valentine's Day—is not a well-known holiday among many Chinese American communities, but Nainai brought it to life for us and it's grown into a local holiday of note, always receiving write-ups in papers and highlights in Chicago summer event catalogs.

Liya continues, "It's our biggest festival before the

two-month deadline of when we have to pay back our debt."

Two months? She had said it was bad, but I hadn't realized it was *this* bad.

I try to keep my voice hopeful as I ask, "So are you thinking about trying to make it bigger and better?"

"Yeah. And I'm open to anything. It's our best chance to make a decent chunk of money."

I nod, thinking. She nibbles her bottom lip.

After a few dud ideas, I'm staring at the water in my clear glass when it hits me. "Water!" I blurt out.

Her face brightens with optimism and she nods encouragingly. Welp, I have to compose myself for a second because how many people would hear a weird outburst like that and, instead of staring like water had just come out of my nose, get *excited*?

"Okay, picture this," I say, closing my eyes and gesturing for her to follow. "What if . . . we don't just light up the sky. But also . . ." I pause for dramatic effect. "The water?" My eyes open and I'm pleased to see Liya is still eyes closed, imagining. "Water lanterns!" I finish. "Someone must make some, right? If not, maybe we can fashion some on our own?"

Liya blinks open and grabs her phone, thumbs flying as she searches. Bottom lip between her teeth as she scrolls.

After a few minutes, she holds her screen out to me. "Look."

It's a photo of boxy glowing paper lanterns dotting the water's surface. I smile. "They're beautiful."

Liya points at the screen eagerly. "This could be exactly the thing to take Qixi to the next level. But I think that could just be the start."

As the rest of our food arrives and I pick the scallions out of her bowl and put them in mine, Liya takes over, her eyes shining as idea after idea flies out of her. I try to help where I can, but she doesn't need me very much. Those wheels are turning and I'm just along for the ride. It's pretty awesome to witness.

When the check comes, we are *stuffed*. With duck, noodles, and, for me, happiness. (Don't worry, now that the meal is over, cheese is acceptable.)

Liya grabs the check quickly, beating me by a huge margin because I'm weighed down. I groan. She groans too, but for a different reason.

"What?" I ask.

"Nothing," she lies.

"It's not nothing." I swipe the bill from her.

Oh. The Peking duck is pretty pricey.

"It's a blessing and a curse, right?" she says with a shrug.

I know exactly what she means—I love this community and belonging in it, but it does come with complications. Like not having a choice of what to eat and not knowing how much it will cost.

"I got it," I say, but she's already shaking her head.

"This is your thank-you dinner," she argues.

"Split it."

She hesitates.

"Please," I try to insist. I mean, it's her family's store that's struggling. She shouldn't be splurging on me.

She nods ever so slightly. "Okay. Thank you. Not just for that. For all of it."

"Always, Liya," I say, and I mean it. "Always."

I may as well have just handed her a hunk of gouda. But when she smiles at me, all wide and toothy, I remember that she likes cheese as much as I do.

8

Operation Mooncake

LIYA

"So . . . Mǎmá, Bǎbá . . ." My palms are clammy and I'm fighting my desire to run to my childhood When You Wish Upon a Lantern hiding spot (behind the life-size stuffed panda that I coveted until my nǎinai gifted one to me for my sixth birthday). My parents and I don't have a share-all-your-feelings kind of relationship, but we used to talk more. I've never been this nervous before, but we've also never had this many secrets.

The image of the TWO MONTHS from the letter and the bolded EVICTION threat push me to spit it out. "I, uh, have some ideas for the store. Not for any specific reason," I lie, feeling like I have to pretend I don't know. "I just thought it would be fun. To build our brand more."

That wasn't suspicious at all. My parents blink at me, concern etched into the furrow of their brows. Hoping I will be smoother in the details, I barrel on. "Wouldn't it be cool if we also sold floating water lanterns? They would pair so well with the sky ones! Just picture it . . . at our next festival, not only will we light up the sky, but also the *water*." I reach my arm out in a dramatic arc, as if the motion would somehow conjure lit candles on the imaginary lake beside me. I leave out that this had been Kai's idea; I don't want another lecture about his character.

My parents don't say anything, so I keep going, but since I'm through my prepared lines, I start to babble. "Did you hear me? Water lanterns! Think of the amazing photos we could get for our next festival to include in our display and online!"

"Online?" my father says, surprised.

"Yeah, I was thinking maybe we could start a website. I'll do it," I add quickly. "With a free domain name. And we should also feature the store on Jack Chen's Shop Frenzy app. But we need a website to do that so customers can directly place their orders."

My dad's already shaking his head. "So complicated, Liya. We don't need all that stuff."

I (sort of) understand why my parents haven't told me

about the store's troubles, but now they're lying to my face.

"Is this about Năinai?" my mom asks hesitantly.

The distance between us has never felt so huge. How could we have such different interpretations of the same conversation?

"I'll be doing the work!" I say desperately. "You don't have to be involved! Are you worried we'll lose money if we don't sell the new product? We don't have to order that many to start! We'll do a trial run! We can poll our customers!"

My mom holds her palms out in that gesture I hate, the one where she's trying to calm me down. It always does the opposite, riling me up because it feels like she doesn't understand the gravity of the situation.

"*Lí-yă.*" She emphasizes each syllable and says them with exaggerated Mandarin intonations, my version of white parents using the middle name. "I don't think that's a good—"

"We'll order some," my father interjects, punctuating the words to convey that the conversation is over.

Now I'm worried he agreed just to shut me up. What if they had their reasons for resisting, like maybe they think we'll lose money on the new, unvetted item? I suddenly wish I hadn't been so adamant about something I've only dipped a couple of toes in previously.

"We don't have to—" I start. "Not if, I mean, if it's

risky . . ." I'm dying to just tell them I know about the debt. The words are on the verge of forming in my mouth. But this is uncharted territory for me and I'm scared for them to find out I looked through their mail, even if it had been perfectly innocent on my end when I'd done it.

"It's fine," my father says, again with finality.

My mother's pinched face clearly does not agree. She adds, "We'll order just a few at first, for a test run, to make sure the quality is good."

My father nods and they leave abruptly, in different directions, so I can't follow up with anything else. I use that as an excuse for withholding the fact that I already ordered more than a few, sent to Kai's bakery in case my parents said no.

At least I have phase two of Operation Mooncake to distract me today. It's Meet-Cute Day. Or I guess it could be Meet-Disaster Day, depending on so many things out of my control: whether or not Mr. Tang is interested in Shue Nǎinai, whether they'll arrive on time, whether Mr. Tang says anything (unlike Shue Nǎinai, he is a man of few words).

I glance at the clock: 3:12. I watch the second hand tick, tick, tick an embarrassing number of times. My heart thumps in sync, excitement fluttering beneath each beat.

Then, at 3:15 on the nose, the door opens and "The Moon Represents My Heart" plays.

"Liya!" Shue Nǎinai throws her arms open. "My favorite! I'm so happy to see you!"

Punctual as always. I welcome her hug. She smells like cooking oil and flour.

I lured Shue Nǎinai here on the pretense of her winning the Summer Lantern Festival sweepstakes, which was, ahem, a contest that "was in beta testing" and "not very publicized" (or at all). Luckily, as soon as I said "winner," Shue Nǎinai squealed and didn't ask for more details.

My parents are in the back office, probably going over the books, and I have a feeling that they won't come out now that Shue Nǎinai is here. Sad, but also fortunate.

I try to focus on Shue Nǎinai and not peek at the clock. Even though it's not the underlying reason, if I look, I will seem like everyone else she talks to, antsy and bothered. So I force myself to listen to every word, and soon, I get lost in her story. And I'm so glad that I do. Because it reminds me why I so badly want to help her wish come true.

Shue Nǎinai is the embodiment of the word *fighter.* As the youngest of six children, she fought for attention. As a daughter of a rich, land-owning family who lost everything when Communism took over China, she fought for herself and her family to stay afloat, selling her calligraphy paintings on the street and taking every odd job she could find.

When a wealthy American traveler on business in Shanghai bought a crane painting from her, she told him a story despite their differing languages using just her gestures and her brush. He took her to dinner and they made each other laugh continuously, again with minimal talking. After a whirlwind courtship of few words, he whisked her to America. She had dreamed of this as a child, hearing stories of how in America, gold could be found in the streets, but she had never dreamed of love bringing her there.

She had found happiness. She and her husband had two children, one year apart. Shue Năinai was learning English while dreaming of working at her husband's finance company for pleasure, not money, once her children were older.

But then her husband died suddenly. Car accident. All of Shue Năinai's dreams evaporated on the spot. She sold the company out of necessity. She moved to Chinatown out of desperation, to be near people who spoke her first language, and to with provide her with the community she needed. Terrified after her husband's accident, she refused to drive or let her children learn. America turned from a land of golden opportunity into a prison. Shue Năinai was too scared to venture outside Chinatown and was too scared to give her children the freedom to explore. The first chance they had, her children fled, rarely to return.

Grateful for the community that supported her and gave her a home in a foreign land, Shue Năinai now spends her days trying to give back. Trying to care for others the way they cared for her, even when they don't seem to want it.

"Liya," she's saying now, after she told me again about how Chinatown embraced her when she needed it most. "Do you know how lucky you are to be young?"

This was a new direction. I nod even though I only have a vague sense of what her words mean. Then she says, "You don't know what real loneliness is."

Yes, I do, I immediately think. I was loved, but I still experienced moments of loneliness. When I was younger, Năinai and my parents spent most of their time at the store "making sure it refound its footing." They always had excuses (*the economy is bad, Chinatowns aren't what they used to be*) but now I'm wondering if the store has always been stumbling along and I just didn't want to see it. Regardless, even though I cherished my time with Năinai, I did also spend long stretches of my childhood alone. I remember being so bored I would pretend my hands were dogs, with my middle finger being the head and the other four fingers the legs, and my two dog-hands would fight or sniff around and explore their surroundings. (Maybe it was an extension of the three-finger tea tap representing a bowing person.) I mean, if that doesn't classify as loneliness, what does? That's how I found Kai. He used to hide from Jiao in the alley next to the dumpster, and one day my dog-hands sniffed him out. He immediately turned his hands into dogs too, and we were inseparable after that.

Shue Nǎinai doesn't notice my reaction and continues. "Life took a lot away from me and for a long time, I didn't dream. Because my dreams led to heartache. For forty years, I didn't let myself dream, Liya."

I think back to her lantern the other day, her uncharacteristic giggles. It was the first lantern I saw her light that wasn't for her children.

Her eyes twinkle. "Do you know what made me try again? Why I made a wish for myself for the first time in decades?"

I shake my head.

"You." She pats the back of my hand with hers. "You, Liya, who always listens. With both ears and eyes. You ask questions. You're not here out of pity or wrong place wrong time, but because of curiosity, friendship, and interest. And you always tell me to make a wish for myself. So I finally did."

I don't know what to say. Her words are too kind, more than I deserve.

The door opens, interrupting us.

Shue Nǎinai closes her eyes to listen to "The Moon Represents My Heart." She smiles as she says, "Ah, a classic. One of my favorites."

When she opens her eyes, Mr. Tang is standing in front of us. I'm so preoccupied with our previous conversation that I just stare at the two of them, blinking. Forgetting Operation Mooncake.

"Tang Xiānshēng! What a lovely surprise!" Shue Nǎinai's charm oozes out of her. I should take notes.

Mr. Tang, unfortunately, is more like me than like Shue Nǎinai. He thumps on his chest with a fist as he clears his throat. "Uh, hello." His cheeks are slightly colored. A good sign. "Are you . . . shopping?"

I sincerely hope that's not what I look or sound like when I flirt.

"Oh! Dear Liya asked me to come down because I won the Summer Lantern Festival sweepstakes!"

Mr. Tang's eyebrows raise. "There was a sweepstakes?"

I hurry to say: "It wasn't publicized. We were beta testing." It sounds as rehearsed as it is. I pull some more words out of my butt. "I'm hoping to be able to incorporate this now beta-tested sweepstakes in future festivals." Less stilted but equally awkward. "I'll go get your prize!" I blurt out, a little too loudly.

Luckily, neither Mr. Tang nor Shue Nǎinai seems to care about my mysterious contest.

As I disappear around the corner to the lantern display stealthily (actually stealthily—Kai doesn't know what he's talking about), Shue Năinai carries the conversation:

"What brings you here today?"

"Bamboo." Another cough.

I have to stifle my laugh.

Since his divorce, Mr. Tang is always tinkering with his shop: changing decorations, cycling through themes, sprucing up his cups or straws or signs. In classic Chinatown dog-help-dog style, he places many of his orders through When You Wish Upon a Lantern. Earlier today, I had called to inform him that his latest order of table decorations (tiny potted lucky bamboo) was in, and he had said he would stop by around 3:15 to pick them up. I'd made up the sweepstakes and called Shue Năinai as soon as I hung up with Mr. Tang.

"Tables," Mr. Tang tries to clarify.

"Lucky bamboo for the tables in your café?" Shue Năinai somehow deduces. "How fun!"

Mr. Tang lets out a nervous laugh bordering on a giggle.

Okay, I'm sure now. Phase three of Operation Mooncake is certainly going to be a go. I can already see them sitting on a couch in five years, Shue Năinai interpreting his one-word sentences perfectly and immediately. I text Kai, and he responds within seconds with the raised-hands emoji. Wish I could be there, he adds. He's not the only one.

I hear Shue Năinai launch into one of her stories. "Have I ever told you about the time lucky bamboo saved my life? It's why bamboo is my favorite to paint . . ."

Shue Năinai's voice is drowned out by the crinkling of rice paper as I fiddle with the lanterns. But I know this story already. She had been biking once and stopped to buy a lucky bamboo from a man on the side of the street, and right in front of her, a runaway hot dog cart had crashed into a parked car. If she hadn't stopped, she would have been "kaput! Flat as a scallion pancake!" as she always ended the story.

When I return, sweepstakes prize lantern in hand, I take in every word, glance, and movement. I'm used to disappearing into the background, so I've honed my observation skills and gotten pretty good at interpreting minor body language. Like how Mr. Tang's head is tilted toward Shue Năinai's, his eyes focused on hers. He's genuinely listening. With both ears and eyes, as Shue Năinai previously said about me.

My secret job is pretty awesome.

I drop off the lantern on the front counter, not disturbing them, and go in the back to retrieve Mr. Tang's order.

"Everything okay?" my mother asks as soon as she sees me.

"Is that Shue Năinai I hear?" my father says calmly, not looking up, but I notice the extra inflection at the very end signaling that if the answer is yes, he will be very busy.

I nod in answer to both of their questions, giving no

further details. They return to their paperwork, and I can't help glancing around for the neon-orange envelope (or worse, a new one with even scarier bolded numbers). But when my mother looks back up at me, I hurry to grab the pots of bamboo.

"Oh, is Mr. Tang here?" asks my mother.

"Do you need help?" my father asks reluctantly.

"Yes, he's here, and no, I'm fine," I say quickly, kicking the door stopper as I scoot out. I don't want to risk my parents interfering with the totally natural meet-cute moment happening out front.

Once the door to the back office closes behind me, I rest the tray of bamboos on top of the chrysanthemum tea juice boxes. And I wait (yes, occasionally eavesdropping). Eventually, Shue Nǎinai starts to worry about me to Mr. Tang, so I hurry forward and give them their respective items.

Mr. Tang bows his head slightly to me in thanks, then doffs his tweed flat cap in Shue Nǎinai's direction. She giggles. I look away, feeling like I'm intruding.

Once Mr. Tang is gone, Shue Nǎinai picks up her prize lantern and inspects it as if she's viewing it in a brand-new light. "Xīwàng nǐ de yuànwàng zhǎodào guāngmíng," she murmurs to me but mostly to herself because those words have taken on new meaning too. Her wish is beginning to find the light.

When Shue Năinai leaves, she hugs me tightly as usual but also plants a wet kiss on my cheek. "Guāi háizi," she says to me with a smile, and I can't help thinking, *More than you know!*

9

Operation Jeremy Lin

KAI

Focus. Not on Liya, but on the mission tonight. If all goes well, we'll be helping Eric Kao with his parents.

Eric and I played on the basketball team together in junior high, but that's as far as my skills—or lack thereof—got me. At the time, I told myself I wasn't playing in high school because I was putting in more hours at the bakery, but now I've had enough distance to admit the truth.

Anyway, Eric had always been the clear standout star, but he didn't act like it, still being a team player even though it probably would have benefited all of us if he just took the ball and literally ran with it. Then in high school, he hit a massive growth spurt and everyone started calling him Jeremy Lin because he was on his way there.

When a documentary about Jeremy Lin hit theaters several years back, me, Eric, Chiang, and a couple other guys drove forty minutes to find a theater that was showing it. I'm pretty sure Eric had to wipe his eyes a few times during the screening, and now I know why. But it was going to be okay—I could already feel it. Because what I learned during that documentary is going to be what swings this in his favor tonight.

Unfortunately, my dad is kinda the key to this whole operation. And he is—what's the best word? *Unpredictable*, to put it kindly. He's slightly less *him*—grumpy, unresponsive, uncommunicative—when my mom is around, but she's over the Pacific right now and cannot act as a buffer.

"Hey, Ba," I say as nonchalantly as I can while we set up the center Once Upon a Mooncake table for Mahjong. "How was your trip?"

He returned home recently from a long road trip and I haven't talked to him since he got back.

"Pretty good. We're down to a couple thousand vests now," he says proudly.

Probably even fewer because my mother has been throwing them out every chance she gets, but he doesn't know that.

My father is a serial entrepreneur, and not a very good

one. Once Upon a Mooncake is by far his most successful venture—our breadwinner, pun intended. Three years ago, after I took over a lot of his bakery duties, he tried to enter the manufacturing world because of his connections to factories in China. "Uncle Tao has our back!" he would say about his contact, who, for the record, is not actually my uncle.

Problem is, no one was covering our front. My father went around, store to store, in person, and tried to make deals. Since more money could be made from bigger, bulk orders, he started with Walmart and worked his way down. Somehow, he mind-bogglingly managed to get a local pharmacy chain, PharmX, to place an order for ten thousand vests. An *oral* order. For *ten thousand*.

After Uncle Tao sent the vests to us, PharmX backed out of the deal. Since it was oral, my father didn't have any recourse. So, naturally, he thought, and I quote: "Fishermen! Vests!" which translates to, people who fish like to wear vests sometimes. My father ordered *ten thousand* patches with various fish on them—trout, flounder, salmon—and sent *ten thousand vests back to China* so that our trusty pal Tao could sew the patches over the PharmX stitching on the front of the vest.

For the past two years, my father has been taking random road trips, driving around the country, hand-selling fish vests to mom-and-pop stores that, at most, on a very good day, buy four or five. For the past two years, I have had to keep my mouth shut about whether or not the cost of gas is greater than the money made from selling vests. For the past two years, I have received a fish vest for Christmas, my birthday, getting a good grade, when my father was having an especially good Monday. For the past year, my mother has been driving vests to donation centers—and even the dump when the centers say no—because it's easier. On her last road trip with my father many months ago—which was supposed to be a romantic vacation—she had resorted to bartering vests for a hand-crocheted BEACH DAYS ARE THE BEST DAYS blanket we also didn't need, and when she returned home and realized what she had become, she told my father he would be road-tripping on his own from then on.

"Great, Ba, great trip," I say. For some reason, when I'm in my father's presence, his genes find a way to take over and I talk more like him—fewer, less meaningful words just to get the conversation over with. "Heard from Ma lately?"

"Ma's good," he says. I know Mom's time away is hard on him too, but he never talks about it.

I take one of the four trays of Mahjong tiles and turn it over quickly, slamming them onto the table with a *bang* so the tiles won't fall out and will lie on the table backside up, ready for shuffling. It's always highly satisfying. I wait until all four are done to start Operation Jeremy Lin, so the noise won't get in the way.

"So is Kao Shushu coming tonight?" I ask, again as

nonchalantly as I can. Eric's dad was the one who hooked my father up with Uncle Tao of fish vest fame, and ever since then, he's been a regular at my father's weekly Mahjong game.

My father accompanies his nod with a grunt.

Okay, first check mark.

"You know," I say, having to work even harder now to keep the excitement out of my voice, "it's kind of cool that Eric could be the next Jeremy Lin."

My dad's head pops up. He doesn't get worked up about much, but he's a die-hard Jeremy Lin fan. During Linsanity, both of my parents watched every game and would point at the TV and say, "He's Taiwanese, like us!"

I take this as a good sign and continue. "Did you know Jeremy Lin went to Harvard and studied economics? He pursued his dreams but still got a good education. He did it all!"

My dad nods knowingly. "Of course he did. He's the best."

The wheels are still churning behind his eyes after he's done talking, and I cross my fingers that this has been enough for him to—*ha*—take the bait. If I lay it on any thicker, my dad might get suspicious.

I finish setting out the Mahjong accessories—dice, clear plastic pushers, wind indicator—then retreat to the kitchen to plate the game snacks. All the while, my heart is beating hella fast. Is this what James Bond feels like?

On Mahjong night, when the bell above the door dings, it's different than during business hours. Instead of a hopeful customer looking for something to brighten their day, it's one of my dad's overly masculine, grunting friends coming to fill my beloved bakery with cigarette smoke and gambling.

My father's Mahjong game is a holdover from his past life as a bookie. I sometimes wonder if he still does it on the side, just like I wonder if the Mahjong game is really "just chump change" as he claims.

Believe it or not, he turned straighter after having Jiao and me. At my mom's insistence, he closed his pawnshop and started the bakery, which my mother named and decorated when she was too pregnant with Jiao to keep flying. I'm not sure how much money the pawnshop used to make, but I'm quite grateful to my mother that I now spend my days baking instead of deciding how much Grandma's heirlooms are worth.

I hide in the kitchen, thanking my lucky stars for my foresight when I hear that it's Jiao who's arriving. He joined the game when he turned eighteen. Even if I'm offered that honor—which I doubt I will be since Eric's dad and their fourth, Fat Man Lu of Lu's Spice World, won't drop out until they're dead—I don't have any interest.

From the back, I hear Jiao say, "Hey, Ba." Unlike me, he's always like my dad. "Fish vests selling?"

"You know it." My dad is a little more animated with Jiao since they're the same person.

I'm usually gone by now, but I need to see Operation Jeremy Lin through. If my father doesn't bring him up, I have a tray of mooncakes I'll trot out so I can bring him up myself. In the meantime, I focus on getting ahead of my baking schedule for the next day.

After Kao Shushu and Fat Man Lu arrive and they settle into their game, I hit a groove mixing and kneading to the occasional clicking of Mahjong tiles. The first game is completely devoid of conversation. Did I get ahead of myself, thinking this was going to be a piece of mooncake? I should've realized that my dad is happy to remain silent even around his best friends.

I'm about to wipe my hands and start taking the plastic wrap off the mooncakes, but then my dad pipes up in his gravelly voice: "So, Lao Kao, you must be proud of Eric."

"Basketball scholarships on the horizon?" Fat Man Lu asks.

Kao Shushu sighs. "He shouldn't be playing basketball. He won't make it! He should be studying something dependable, like computer science. Or medicine would be better, but he doesn't have the grades for that. He spends too much time on the court."

"Aiyah, what do you mean?" my dad says. Yay, Dad! "Eric could be the next Jeremy Lin! Jeremy Lin studied economics at Harvard while playing for the team and then made the NBA! Now he's representing us on TV! That's every parent's dream! I should be so lucky!"

Never in a million years did I think before tonight that I would one day appreciate the old Chinese social rules of putting down your own children to praise your friends'.

After a brief pause, Kao Shushu hesitantly asks, "You really think so?"

"Eric's a star!" Jiao says, most likely because he agrees with my dad no matter what.

I'm guessing Kao Shushu doesn't care what Jiao thinks. Luckily, my dad and Fat Man Lu chime in: "Yes, a star!" "He's going to be famous! You'll never have to worry about money again!"

Dusting my hands off from flour *and* a wish granting well done, I pull off my apron. On my way out, I grab a victory mooncake. Then I pause, thinking, before deciding to stay a little longer. Liya's for sure long gone from the shop—*bah*— but that doesn't mean I can't do something now so she'll know as soon as she arrives in the morning that I had been thinking about her. As a friend, of course. It's a callback to something we used to do as kids, so it's definitely a friendship kind of thing.

That's how it works, right?

10

Charades

LIYA

By the next morning, Kai hasn't texted to update me on Operation Jeremy Lin. I am most certainly not in my head about it. Not at all. I am not feeling the weight of how much is riding on the successful outcome of our operations. I am also not wondering whether Kai suddenly decided I'm annoying.

I sleep fitfully, waking before my parents. I tiptoe to the kitchen and make myself a cup of Dragon Well tea—the greatest of all the teas, as I concluded a few years ago after Kai and I sampled the entire inventory of When You Wish Upon a Lantern. (We were hopped up for hours and then crashed, both metaphorically and physically, onto the couch in the back office). That was before, when he hadn't become *Kai* yet, when splaying on the couch with him was no big deal.

Instead of sitting at the table and sipping, I find myself drawn to our home "office," a.k.a. the corner of the living room where there's a small desk. It was where Năinai would sit and pen handwritten letters to friends and family close and afar, and thank-you letters to our most loyal customers. Each piece of stationery was spritzed with her signature orange-scented perfume, "to give them a little luck," she would say to me with a wink.

But in Năinai's old age, she could no longer hold the pen for long periods of time (arthritis) and her eyesight deteriorated (cataracts). She rarely sat at the desk. She never complained, but now I wonder if it had been difficult to lose such an integral piece of her identity. She always prided herself on her penmanship and kept up calligraphy practice as long as she could.

As Năinai's health faded, the desk also faded into a gathering of dust and clutter. After her passing, one day I woke up and the desk was immaculate. It had made me sad then—it was too bare, almost sterile—but now I wonder if my father had cleaned it because he couldn't bear to see it so abandoned.

I pull the chair out, the legs scraping against the floor, and after a brief hesitation, I sit. My eyes fall to the top drawer, which has a built-in lock. We keep our most important documents in there: Social Security cards, bank information, passports, etc. My parents have always been paranoid about losing our identities to a robbery (even though that's not the usual way people lose their identities), so it's not a surprise it's locked, but now I wonder if there's another reason.

How bad would it be . . . if I took a look? I know where the key is: under the golden dragon on the mantel that the store won for being the "Best New Business" in Chinatown three years after opening. But . . . I can't. I want to know just how far the debt extends (are we behind on home bills too?), but I also don't want to know. I opened the orange letter innocently, but I can't do this deliberately. And besides, don't I already know? If my parents had money, they would pay the rent. So I already know that our situation as a whole is extremely dire. And I cannot have another secret from them; there are already too many. Add one more and maybe we would never be able to talk to each other again.

Steeling my shoulders, I put the tea down on the worn-out circle in the corner that has discolored over the years from Nǎinai's tea mug being placed there day after day, always filled with oolong tea leaves because she loved it strong, the tea leaves always soaking. I grab a scrap piece of paper and write a to-do list for the store. It's sad and minimal, but it's a start:

<u>To Do</u>
—Continue making plans for Qixi Festival and figure out a way to make it BIGGER and MORE PROFITABLE
—Find more wishes to grant
—See Operation Mooncake through
—Follow up on Operation Jeremy Lin
—Start website TODAY!!!
—Text Jack Chen
—Door-to-door visits to see if any businesses need to place any orders??

I have a feeling Năinai would approve. And sitting here, I feel like she's doing this with me.

I almost miss it at first, because it's been months since Kai and I have done this particular tradition. But I am so freaking happy he brought it back.

I've just arrived at the store and I'm doing a quick check around the aisles to see if anything needs restocking or re-arranging when, out of the corner of my eye, my brain registers that something is different in this very familiar setting.

When You Wish Upon a Lantern has one window that aligns with a window from Once Upon a Mooncake. When Kai and I discovered this as kids, we spent an entire afternoon making funny faces at each other. Then, as teenagers, we started playing charades, drawing from our arsenal of inside jokes for clues. I can't count how many times I was flailing my arms or doing something embarrassing, only to be caught by a surprised customer. The older community members thought it was cute once they realized what Kai and I were doing, but kids our age . . . well, you can guess how that went over. One time, Shang Li, the school's star football player, caught me bending over and making a motion like I was pulling something out of my ass. I was charading "lion" to Kai and was trying to show him my tail, but, well, yeah. Kai had laughed so hard he cried, the jerk.

More recently, before the boba incident, we had started leaving messages for each other on the windowsills. The first time had been when I was too busy setting up for that evening's festival to see him, and all I had time for was to prop a lantern (defective, so as not to be wasteful) in the window with the words "see you tonight!" hastily written on its side. Like I said before, texting stresses me out and I prefer any other mode of communication.

Today, Kai has propped the Once Upon a Mooncake specials board in front of the window for me to see. On it, in chalk, he's drawn a genie lamp and a basketball swishing through a hoop.

I laugh out loud. That's why he didn't text. And this

surprise was worth the wait. The flutter I feel in my chest is a product of the positive progress on Operation Jeremy Lin as well as the revival of an old beloved ritual.

It's almost ten o'clock. Kai should be in the kitchen, working. I have the urge to run over there and see him. I consider texting so he'll at least come to the window, but it turns out I don't need to. Because he knows my schedule as well as I know his.

A minute later, at ten o'clock on the dot, Kai's face appears beside the message board. His grin has such an adorable mischievous tilt I can't stand it.

I mime rubbing a genie lamp and he jumps forward, popping into the full frame of my view. He folds his arms across his chest, then holds up three fingers. As in, three wishes for me.

I think for a second, putting my hand on my chin so he'll know that's what I'm doing. (Charade mode, like riding a bike.) Then I hold up three fingers of my own. He nods, acknowledging that there are three words in my answer. Then I wobble my palm in the air, making the universal "sort of" gesture, followed by two fingers. He nods, understanding that I mean it's actually two words, but I'm going to charade it in three parts. We've developed our own charade system by now.

One finger—first part. Another nod. I pretend I'm a surgeon, scrubbing my hands clean, putting on a mask, gloving up, holding my hand out for a scalpel. When I begin cutting the patient open, Kai gives me a thumbs-up. I move on to the third part. I point at him, the baker, and mime pulling a cake out of the oven and frosting it. No thumbs-up. He doesn't know what exactly he's baking yet (there are probably fifty things it could be). I think for a second and a light bulb goes off in my head. I pretend to put candles on top. Then I light them and blow them out. I get the thumbs-up.

I saved the second part for last because it's the clincher. I consider for a very brief second doing it for real, but of course I'm not going to. I would never. (But the thought crossed my mind in a wouldn't-that-be-wild, what-would-he-do kind of way.)

I pretend to pull my pants down and show him my butt.

Operation moon cake.

Kai is laughing so hard he looks like he's gasping for air. I can't help a few chuckles of my own coming up, but I stifle them so my parents won't hear and come over. When he recovers, he applauds me, and I take an exaggerated bow.

He responds with one word to be charaded in two parts. The first part is the number two. The second: he uses his right hand to pull something long from the opposite side of his torso, up and diagonal. A sword. Then he pretends to pull something down over his face. A helmet. He's a knight.

Two Knight. Tonight. We'll make final plans for Operation Mooncake tonight.

I give him two thumbs up.

After a pause, he quickly makes two gestures: a shake of the head followed by tapping his watch. Our shorthand for "Can't wait."

I point to myself, then hold up two fingers. *Me too.*

Shameful Kai

KAI

Can't wait. Me too. Those words have me humming as I go about preparing the rest of the morning buns. I take extra care with one particular chicken curry bun, my dad's favorite, for our luncheon today. He has lunches—and dinners and Mahjong games and baseball games and horse track days—with Jiao all the time, but for me, we have to schedule it, which only makes them become even more of a thing. I never know what to expect. Sometimes we barely talk, other times he gives me the worst life advice in the world—like, don't play sports or take a big exam on a full scrotum. I wanted to die when he said that, then actually almost did, choking on a piece of bread, when he followed that up with, "Are you masturbating regularly, son?"

My phone dings with a text. My heart beats faster in anticipation, *Li-ya Li-ya Li-ya*. But nope, not her. My heart soars for a different reason.

Mom
Have a good lunch with Baba.
He loves you even if it's hard
for him to say.
And you know I love you.
To the moon and back. I'm
currently in Hong Kong but my
heart is with you.

Dad must have told her about lunch. I'd wanted to but worried I'd be bothering her. She's always so tired during her work weeks that I rarely try to contact her. I just let her call or text when she has a moment.

Kai
Love you too
Miss you
Hope you're getting enough
rest between shifts

You should have your apron on typing that girly message out, Poop Son, I can hear Jiao taunting in my head. When Mom tells him she loves him, he just rolls his eyes and says, "I know."

Mom and I have always been closer—two peas in a pod to parallel Dad and Jiao. Sometimes I wish Mom could be the one who was around more, but no use thinking about that, right?

I masterfully steep two cups of baozhong tea—Dad's favorite—and make a note to replenish our supply with Ming, who owns the Chicago Tea Party store down the street. I buy as much tea as I can from When You Wish Upon a Lantern, of course, but they don't carry the specialized, rarer teas that many of our customers like to pair with our treats.

Hmm. I wonder if that's something I could suggest to Liya to boost revenue at her store. Except that would upset Ming and we shouldn't go there. Right now he brags about how he carries the "real" tea, and there's clearly a line Liya shouldn't cross.

Again, the joys and struggles of a tight-knit community. Speaking of, I wonder if there's some way we can get the community to come together to help Liya's store.

My mind is abuzz with ideas when the bell jangles. For a split second I hope it's a customer, then the guilt floods in.

He's your father, I scold myself as he walks in as if he owns the place, which, okay, fine, he does.

"Hi, Ba," I say.

He grunts. "Items on schedule?"

I nod, then gesture to the display case. He goes over to inspect. Even though I've surpassed the skills of the original

Once Upon a Mooncake baker—thanks, internet, for the wisdom, and Jiao, for fueling my fire—I still hold my breath.

I'm rewarded with another nod. He sits at the table I've set up for us, sipping his tea with no words of thanks or acknowledgment that it's his favorite and I steeped it carefully according to his picky preferences.

I wait until he takes a bite of his bun to take a bite of mine—barbecue pork.

Another nod.

Well, it could be worse. He could be complaining about the taste or texture.

I also wait for him to talk first because I have no idea what to say.

"I'm leaving for another trip tomorrow."

"Oh?"

He nods. Doesn't expand.

"Selling more vests?" I guess.

He shakes his head.

"Really?" I say with genuine surprise.

"Well, I should say, not exactly. There are always some vests in the trunk, and if I'm out, I might as well try. But no, that's not the main purpose of the trip."

He's going to make me ask. I know it's just the way he is, but in moments like these, a teeny-tiny part of me wonders if he's playing a joke on all of us, dying laughing inside while watching us have to deal with him. "What's the trip for, Ba?"

"Leads."

Oh. Goddammit. I should've known. That horse's ass. Literally. Leads is short for Leads the Way, my father's beloved racehorse. And when I say that, I do not mean it in the logical meaning of those words. He doesn't own the horse. He bets on him. Drives around, sometimes a few states away, just to watch him run. His second-favorite child, after Jiao. The true number two son, and a better fit for the nickname *Poop Son*.

I want to know if it's a particularly special race this time, but I cannot bring myself to ask about the horse. He's my nemesis. My father consistently chooses Leads over me, most recently missing my end-of-the-school-year awards ceremony to watch him run—and it wasn't even a final or whatever a big deal is in that world.

But of course, for this, my father offers up the information willingly. "It's the Kentucky Derby of Iowa. Wish your brother luck!"

Yes, he even calls Leads my brother. My barbecue bun suddenly tastes like sand. I obviously say nothing. But I doubt my father really expected me to respond with a resounding *Good luck, Leads!* Or maybe he did. Jiao probably would.

My father puts down his curry bun and clears his throat. *F.*

"Kai . . ." he starts, painfully slow, as my insides seize up.

"Jiao told me you're still not putting out items for silly reasons, like shape."

That tattletale. I shake my head. "I just put out the better items first. Since we have to keep some inventory in the back, why not prioritize them by shape?"

"That's not what he said was going on. Are you throwing away perfectly good food again?"

Come on. Jiao was here for, what, five minutes the other day? He couldn't have seen anything in that time. But . . . he's right. Lucky guess. "I only don't sell the items that taste off."

My father's eyes bore into mine. "The food is spoiled? Or it just doesn't taste perfect?"

I don't answer. Which is his answer.

"You need to stop doing that," he says sternly. "Can't you learn a little from Jiao? He has good business sense."

What about establishing our store as only serving the best items? What about the fact that I'm the dedicated baker, and Jiao doesn't know the difference between flour and baking powder? All those thoughts die a swift death on the tip of my tongue, instantly decapitated by the cool air I suck in through my mouth. Pacifist. That's me. I sometimes hate that about myself. Because in times like these, that word just feels like a nicer way of saying *coward*.

"Okay," says coward me, not even sure what I'm agreeing to. Trying to learn from Jiao? Trying to sell every item I make regardless of quality? It doesn't really matter though. I do this so often I have a nickname for it—*Shameful Kai*.

My father pats my hand and gives me a rare smile.

We return to silence. It's so suffocating I wish my father would just hurry up and finish his curry bun.

Right before he eats his last bite, he asks, "School?"

"Good," I answer immediately. Truthfully, it's more than good—I worked my buns off this year and it paid off—but I don't want to bring that up or that he missed my awards ceremony. He never even asked what I won. Maybe my mother told him, and when he heard it was art related—for sculpting, thanks to my baker hands—he had felt justified in picking Leads over me.

Thank Jesus, Joseph, and Mary, my father finishes his bun. But then he asks for a tea refill.

After another *fifteen minutes* of complete silence during which we both sip our tea and stare at each other and the table, I'm finally free.

Feeling generous since he's about to leave, I wish him a good trip. "Hope Leads wins," I add, because I am Shameful Kai, through and through.

He nods. "Remember—no wasting food." He holds his index finger out at me accusingly, and I want to swat it away. He stands there motionless until I return a nod.

When I'm finally alone, I want to punch some dough or

lie on the floor or scream into a pillow. I look out the shared window into When You Wish Upon a Lantern, but Liya's not there. So I make myself a cup of jasmine tea—*my* favorite—which I discovered the day Liya and I tested the entire When You Wish Upon a Lantern tea inventory, to her parents' dismay and Nainai's amusement. In fact, Nainai had urged us on, claiming "one could not know themselves fully until they know their favorite type of tea." After Liya and I ran around laughing and screaming for three hours straight—poor Nainai—we fell asleep on the couch in the back office. It was the most peaceful sleep I've ever had.

The bell jangles again, and my first thought is, *You couldn't have come sooner, during one of those unending silences?*

I'm expecting a customer but it's a delivery. I sign for the package, confused as to what it is. But when I open it, my day turns around.

Tonight can't come soon enough.

12

Magic

LIYA

"Where are you going?"

My parents used to never ask me that. Probably because they used to barely keep track of me, leaving all the parenting to Năinai, who did ask me, but more for safety reasons. *That's probably why they're asking now*, I remind myself, but I still feel annoyed.

I can't tell them I'm going to see Kai. And it's at this moment I realize that (1) perhaps that's why they're asking, because they don't want me to see Kai, and (2) I don't really have any other friends. What's wrong with me? Is it because I'm too shy and uncomfortable around people? Is it because

I'm no fun to be around? Kai has Yong, Chiang, and James, but I had no one when we weren't talking.

I don't know what to tell my parents. Even though I say otherwise to Kai, I know I can't lie (and I will never admit that to his face, though he probably already knows that I know the truth since, again, I can't lie). Năinai, Kai, and I used to play BS and I lost Every. Single. Time. Năinai would always smile so wide I could see the pink plastic of her dentures as her eyes crinkled with pride. "My Lili, so pure and honest and earnest she cannot even lie for a card game," she'd say, turning my insecurity into a blessing.

But now I'm just self-conscious again. So I busy myself with the cash register, angling my face down as I attempt to lie through my teeth. "I'm going to see Stephanie Lee."

"Since when are you friends with her?" my father asks.

"Oh, she's the one who came in the store the other day, right?" my mother says. Thank goodness. "She's sweet. I heard she's at the top of your class! Good for her!"

Yeah, and that's even without winning the spelling bee in fifth grade.

I hate that there are so many lies between us. But I also don't know what else to do. "I won't be home too late."

"Okay. Is your phone charged?" my mother asks.

With a nod, I leave before they can see the guilt etched into all my features.

I meet Kai down the street in front of the Chinatown senior center. A group is doing Tai Chi on the lawn. Before I can even say hello to Kai, let alone ask about the backpack he's carrying—

"Yoohoo! Liya and Kai!" yells out Yang Pó Pó, Taiwan's proudest ex-pat.

"Shoot," I mutter under my breath.

"What's wrong?" Kai asks, his complete attention on me.

"I told my parents I was meeting Stephanie Lee."

"Oh." The shadow that crosses his face is heavy with all the baggage attached to my statement. "Maybe we should hurry out of here."

As always, he's putting me first even when it hurts him. He does that with everyone, including (especially with?) his family.

We wave quickly to Yang Pó Pó, then book it past the senior center. We keep the pace up since, well, we're in Chinatown and we know everyone here. It's all one sticky connected web. It will only be a matter of time before my lies catch up to me.

"It'll be dark soon," Kai reassures me, but his voice is low and pained.

I nod. "Sorry."

"Nothing to be sorry about."

We walk in silence for a bit, our heads hanging to hide our faces. I'm not even sure where we're going, but Kai seems to have a destination in mind.

"So Operation Jeremy Lin went well last night?" I ask.

His face lights up. "It was mind-blowingly awesome!" he explodes.

I squeal, something I'd never do in front of other people, but it's Kai, and it finally feels like we're back to being us. Best friends. Not completely what I want, but much better than before, I remind myself.

"Tell me *everything*!" I burst out, and we fill each other in on our missions exactly the way I picture James Bond doesn't: with a lot of high fives and jumping up and down.

"I'm not sure it was enough to make something *actually* happen," Kai adds, but I shake my head.

"Every step deserves celebrating. We'll reassess soon and see if we need to do more. Isn't that Mahjong game weekly?"

"Unfortunately," Kai jokes, but he's grinning.

"Thanks for all your help," I say sincerely. I'm not sure if I could've revived the wish-granting tradition if I had to do it alone, and having someone who loved Nǎinai like I did keeps me putting one foot in front of the other. "You're gruper." *Oh god*. "I mean great. Or super. Not both."

Kai smiles. "You're gruper too." Then he groans. "Sorry, mentions of fish still give me nightmares."

I laugh. "Are you guys almost free yet?"

"A few thousand more vests to go."

I pat his arm a few times in sympathy, definitely not noticing how toned it is.

Then Kai does something I haven't seen since we were kids: he turns his right hand into a dog. Before I have a second to think, my hand transforms as if out of pure muscle memory. We stop walking and Kai boops my dog "head" with his.

"Hello, Sniffs the Way," I say to his dog-hand, and Kai bursts out into laughter so loud my body startles. And then I'm joining in, laughing until my lungs hurt from lack of oxygen.

It's not a funny name to anyone else, but to us, those three words hold a history equal parts hilarious and painful. Of course, Sniffs the Way gets his name from the horse Kai's horse ass of a father loves more than him.

"I forgot you named him that!" Kai gasps between laughs. "How could I?"

I don't want to tell him that I keep a list of our inside jokes and there are so many that I often can't remember the reference even with the notes.

"My dad's going to watch Leads this weekend in 'the Kentucky Derby of Iowa.' "

We both dissolve into giggles again.

He continues, "And did I tell you that my dad didn't come to the end-of-year awards ceremony because he was following Leads around?"

I shake my head in disbelief even though I 110 percent believe it. I'd been there that awards night too. I was the nerd who won the math award and felt a lot of conflicting feelings about perpetuating an Asian stereotype while also wanting to be proud of something I'm good at. But I hadn't been able to talk to Kai about any of it because we were still avoiding each other then, something we (ironically) avoid talking about now.

"Sorry, Kai," I say even though it's not enough. I never know what to say about his dad or brother, but Năinai always knew how to make him feel loved. Seen. Appreciated. Just like she did for me. I think Kai is also lost without Năinai.

"It's okay." He quickly shifts topics. "I have to say, there's something about granting these wishes that makes me feel so . . . alive." That look on his face . . . I get it. I feel it. I chase it. "It feels like . . ." He trails off, his hands circling, trying to find the words.

"Magic," I say, my voice low because the topic is sacred.

He nods. "How is that possible? In real life?"

I don't have an answer for him.

His eyes cloud with moisture. "But it also makes sense. You and Năinai changed my life. So of course the two of you changed countless other lives, and all through kindness." I'm completely frozen. He takes a breath. "So many terrible things happen every day and I often want to hide away, lose all hope. And somehow you come along and make me believe in the good of people again."

I can't talk. I'm too overwhelmed.

His body is angled so that we're facing each other, only a few inches apart. "Thank you," he says slowly, as if he wants to emphasize how much he means every word. "For letting me be a part of it. I want to grant a thousand more wishes."

I have not replaced Năinai. She is still a part of this. Because I asked Kai. Kai who loved her. Who would see the fingerprints she left behind.

I still can't seem to find any words, but I don't really need to. Kai already knows. He takes my hand and squeezes it, but almost as soon as the warmth hits my palm, it's gone. It travels straight to my heart and I hold it there as we continue walking in comfortable silence.

A few minutes later, Kai turns and leads us into Hébiān Park (also known as Riverside Park to the non-Chinese community).

I give him a questioning look.

"We need water," he says with a mischievous grin, the one I love, with only the left side lifted. As the name describes, the park sits alongside the south branch of the Chicago River.

"For what?"

Kai unshoulders his bag (which I'd forgotten to ask about) and reaches inside. "We're going to light it up." He pulls out one of the water lanterns I ordered and sent to the bakery.

I squeal, grabbing the lantern from him. "Ahh, when did these arrive?"

"Just today!"

"And you kept it from me until now?"

He laughs. "For only a few hours, to surprise you!"

"Yeah, but had I known, I would've left work immediately!" I'm already running toward the water.

"Hey, wait!" He's struggling to rezip his backpack.

"Come on, come on!" I don't slow down.

I stop by the water and look west at the sky as I wait for Kai. The horizon is pink blush amid cotton candy clouds, with a golden burst so bright I can't look directly at it. It's almost time. I shift focus to the water lantern. As I open the packaging, the instructions fall out. Kai approaches and picks it up.

"Pretty simple," he says just as I come to the same conclusion from my inspection.

It's basically a floating box and a tea light candle. Even without the instructions, it's obvious: unfold the box, light the candle, place it inside, and send it off. I run a finger over the side. "I think we can write on these too," I say. Before I've finished my sentence, Kai is holding a marker in front of my face.

I grab it and, without hesitation, write a wish for our shop on the side.

Kai points to the instructions he's holding. "This says it can burn for an hour."

"An hour? We should've started selling these even sooner! And they won't float away as fast as the sky ones. I mean, it'll be a different effect, but it's kind of cool that these will stick around." My mind is off and running. "Maybe we can hold a much longer festival with these and people will stay into the night. If we add some nighttime activities with more products to sell, that's a whole new untapped market for us."

Kai joins in the brainstorming. "We can light a bonfire, sell items for s'mores or an Asian version of it."

"Or some of your pastries."

We share a huge smile.

Kai asks, "Do you think we have enough time to do all this, plus your other ideas, before Qīxì?"

There's only a week and a few days until the Qīxì Festival will be upon us. Qīxì means "Evening of Sevens," describing how it takes place on the seventh day of the seventh month. Since it's a Chinese holiday, the exact date is usually according to the lunar calendar, but years ago, when Năinai held the first Qīxì Festival for our Chinatown community, she decided to make it July 7. "For ease of remembering," she had said, and also because, like my father, she loved mixing Chinese and American culture.

"I think we can do it if we work together," I answer honestly while thinking, *We have to. We have no choice. This is our best chance at making a big dent in the debt.*

We take a seat on a nearby bench. As we watch the sun paint the sky with pink, orange, and red streaks, we brainstorm ideas, both big picture and unglamorous logistics. Soon, our conversation perfectly segues into Operation Mooncake (and yes, we have to stop for a few minutes to laugh over my earlier charade). We decide to use the Qīxì Festival as the setting for the next and possibly final step of Shue-Tang Future Clan.

"It's perfect," I say, the excitement raising the volume of my voice. "Nǎinai used to tell me how a big part of Qīxì is celebrating marriage and newlywed couples and growing old together. It's why we used to encourage our customers to cast their romance-related wishes if they had any, and why we prioritized granting those first."

Kai's nodding. "Perfect setting to get a new couple together, if you ask me."

As the sun disappears over the horizon, Kai and I stand.

"These better work, huh?" I say as I make my way to the edge of the river with the water lantern in my hand.

It feels like so much is riding on this one tiny box. Well, it's not tiny (it's ten by ten inches or so), but tiny relative to the enormous dreams I've pinned to it, literally. I hope it can hold up under the weight of the wish written on its side.

From his backpack, Kai pulls out more water lanterns as well as some sky ones. "For a fuller effect," he explains.

"You just had some of those lying around?"

He grins. "You never know when you need some help from the universe."

Beside the peaceful waves and in hopeful breathless anticipation, Kai and I take turns writing wishes on the lanterns. I don't ask what his are and he doesn't ask mine, but we already basically know. I write one about my parents and our relationship. One about Kai and his family. Of course, one about Nǎinai and her legacy.

On the last sky lantern, I already know that we will both write a wish on this one, like old times.

He motions for me to go first. "Liya Huang, princess of lanterns"—shoot, I could get used to being called that—"what do you wish for?" He folds his arms across his chest, just like Genie Kai earlier.

I've already written my most important wishes down. I look around, trying to gain inspiration from my surroundings. My gaze takes in the pagoda-style pavilion behind me, then sweeps out and lands on the trees and pathways beyond. So much of my childhood was spent here, at Dragon Boat Festivals, at community picnics, at various lantern festivals throughout the year before we outgrew this space and moved to Promontory Point. In the distance, I hear several ducks quacking at each other.

"The ducks," I blurt out, suddenly remembering. Năinai and I used to come here to feed them when I was a toddler. She couldn't bear to throw away old food but also didn't want me to eat it, so we used to come here when we had some stale rice or old veggies. To reach the rafts of ducks in the water, we used to make our way onto the nine-turn bridge that juts into the river. It zigzags, turning nine times, a replica of the bridges found in Chinese gardens constructed in the Song dynasty. Eyes wide, she used to tell me in her spooky voice about how evil spirits can only travel in straight lines, and thus on an angled bridge, they can't follow you.

"What about the ducks?" Kai asks. "You want some? To eat or something else?"

"God, that's morbid." I think of the Peking duck we ate not that long ago. "No, it's just . . . I feel like I'm starting to lose some things about Năinai. Until a moment ago, I'd forgotten about how we used to come here to feed the ducks. How could I forget that?"

"Lucky ducks. Literally."

"Well, the food was old."

"Still." He takes a step closer and puts a comforting hand on my shoulder. "You're not forgetting. Not the important stuff. And when the smaller things resurface, we can reminisce without the guilt. I'll help you find a way to keep remembering."

I nod. I like that he wants to help. More than that, I like the way Kai's looking at me with pensive, dark eyes that make me feel seen.

As we'd written wishes and talked, night had been seeping in, slow and heavy as molasses. It was dark enough now for us to set off the lanterns, but neither Kai nor I move. I don't want to break the spell first; I want to feel seen for as long as he'll keep looking at me that way.

"I know exactly what to wish for," he says suddenly. The left side of his mouth quirks up and I wait for him to explain, but he doesn't.

"You're not going to tell me?"

He shakes his head. "You'll know soon enough."

"Tell me!" I beg.

"It's a surprise!"

As I say my next sentence, Kai says it out loud with me, having predicted my response perfectly: "But I enjoy it more when I know what to anticipate."

An embarrassed laugh escapes my lips. "Do I really say that that often?"

He nods. "Every birthday, every holiday, every—"

"Okay, okay, I get it."

We smirk at each other. We're still only a foot apart, neither of us having moved since Kai stepped closer to comfort me.

A loud *bang* echoes from the other side of the park. It's so sudden and explosive that my body reacts before I can think. Kai's does too. We're wrapped in each other's arms, trying to shield one another as we attempt to figure out what's happening.

Another pop and sizzle puncture the air, this time accompanied by lights. The gold firework shimmers, a sunburst radiating outward, then dripping down the sky like weeping willow leaves.

Kai's and my eyes lock and our muscles relax once our brains have processed that there's no threat; just a celebration. For me, this kind of fear followed by a surge of relief is usually accompanied by laughter, but I don't feel even a chuckle surfacing. All I can hear is my pounding heartbeat in my ears.

Kai's arms are wrapped around me protectively, our torsos pressed against each other. Our faces are so close. His breath mixes with mine. It's rapid, in out in out, almost as fast as my heartbeat. If I just leaned forward a smidgen . . .

From afar, I wonder if we could be mistaken for a couple on a reality dating show, enjoying personal fireworks in each other's arms. Except for us, it's all reality, no dating.

He lets go first. But as his hands drop back to his sides, his fingertips trail down my arms, sending flutters throughout my body.

"Are you okay?" he asks.

No. "Are you?"

He nods, and I leave his question unanswered.

As we return to our stack of lanterns, I suddenly feel cold without Kai's body heat enclosing me. An unexpected (and embarrassing) shiver runs down my spine. Of course Kai notices.

"Are you cold?" He's already shrugging out of his outer layer (a sporty quarter-zip long-sleeve). It clings to his tee beneath and they both lift up, gracing me with a peek of the V at the base of his abs.

Yeah, I'm definitely not cold anymore.

I shake my head quickly and focus on grabbing as many lanterns as I can.

He pulls his shirt back on (unfortunately).

"Oh wait." He grabs the last blank sky lantern on the ground, which I had left folded up. "Just try to enjoy this one without the anticipation of knowing what's coming, all right?"

He uncaps the marker, twists his body away, and writes quickly while shielding it from my view.

"Really?" I say, feigning annoyance when in reality I'm more excited for the surprise to come.

"Yeah, really. I'm granting this one for you, princess."

Kai's words buoy me so much I feel on the verge of floating into the sky with the lanterns. Thank god he can't see the goofy smile on my turned-away face.

Carefully, we make our way onto the angled bridge and stop in the middle. Since it's windy today, we decide to fluff each lantern as we set them off so we don't prematurely lose one before we've had a chance to light it.

"Which ones first?" Kai asks, pointing at the two types of lanterns sitting side by side.

In my head, I picture what they will look like individually, then together. I picture what it will look like at a festival, with everyone from the Chinatown community there. And I realize that adding the water lanterns will change how the festivals have looked in the past.

"Is it okay to add something?" I wonder out loud. "It would mean the festival would look different from what Nǎinai created. What she saw."

"I get it, Liya. And we don't have to." He pauses, then continues, "But growth is okay. And I think Nǎinai would be happy about this."

I try to imagine it. Yes, if she were here, Kai and I would be running to the water, too eager to wait, and she'd be laughing, trying to keep up with us.

I grab a water lantern and light the candle, gingerly depositing it in the center of the box. Then I lean over the bridge railing, making sure the box is level, and I drop it. It hits the water and begins floating downstream, peaceful and languid. Kai is right beside me, and together we light the rest of the lanterns, both sky and water, and we set them off. Kai's secret sky lantern is left for last, and he of course keeps the wish facing away from me (even after I beg) so I don't see.

There are only seven lanterns total, which is a far cry from what one of our festivals will look like, but the effect still makes me suck in a breath. Glowing islands dot the river and sky, and something about both of them floating, one on air and one on water, makes the scene in front of me feel impossible. Magical.

Kai and I lean against the railing for some time after the sky lanterns are gone, just watching the water lanterns. The boxes glide gently and slowly, a smooth path, while the flames inside dance a chaotic jive.

I'm glad the river will sweep them away before the flame goes out. I don't want to watch the light go out on my wishes.

When the current has claimed most of them, we make our way back to land.

I stop before we leave the park.

"Thank you," I say, two tiny words that hold so much more behind them.

"Liya . . ." His eyes are boring into mine, searching. Three seconds pass. Five. Ten.

"Yes?"

"I . . ." He trails off again, then smiles. "Tonight was really lovely."

I think there's more, but I can already tell he won't be voicing it aloud.

I'm about to ask him what's on his mind when I hear:

"Kai? Liya? Is that you?"

We turn at the same time.

The Court

KAI

Eric and Stephanie are waving at Liya and me as they jog over.

When they reach us, we exchange greetings. I don't know Stephanie that well, but we've had a few classes together over the years. I'm about to ask what brought them out here tonight, but Stephanie's words gush out of her.

"It's so perfect we're running into you, Liya! It worked! Your lantern worked!"

"Already?" Liya asks, surprised. As was I—I'd meant it when I said earlier that I thought Operation Jeremy Lin may need more steps.

Stephanie laughs. "Do you normally have longer time-lines for lantern wishes?" she jokes.

Liya laughs awkwardly—like I said, bad liar. Guess it's on me. I jump in. "This is such great news! What happened?"

Eric scratches the back of his head. Always humble. I glance at Stephanie, who seems to know he needs a little push to say something nice about himself. She gives him a warm smile and an encouraging nod.

"My father. He, uh . . ." Eric's hand drops. Quickly, he says, "He asked me about potential scholarships today. And wanted to talk about Jeremy Lin."

Do not look at Liya right now. One of us has to keep the secret.

Stephanie adds, "He still wants Eric to go to a school that's good in academics, even if it means a worse basketball program, but he's on board!" She grabs Liya's arm and shakes it. "He's on board!"

Her enthusiasm is infectious.

"Huge congrats, bud," I say, thumping Eric's back.

Liya nods frantically. "That's so great. We're so happy for you."

"We're celebrating tonight!" Stephanie says, waving a now-burnt-out sparkler.

"Was that you earlier, with the firework?" I realize.

Eric grins. "Yeah. Got that from a teammate years ago

and for some reason I've been saving it—not sure why—but then today it became so obvious. Like something had told me all that time ago to save it because it knew this was coming."

Stephanie nudges Liya with an elbow. "That same something that controls lantern wishes, am I right?" I'm not sure how much she believes it, but Eric's face is wide with wonderment.

A thousand more wish grantings—that's what I want. And yes, I wished for it on one of the lanterns Liya and I sent off earlier.

Stephanie asks, "We're heading to the court. Wanna join?"

The court is what everyone from school calls the biggest food court in Chinatown that's open late—meaning, it's where all the teens go to hang out at night over good food and drink. Our version of the diner, if you will.

Liya looks at me, and I try to gauge whether she wants to go since I know she won't answer first. I tilt my head slightly, trying to tell her I'm game for whatever she wants.

Stephanie giggles. "Look, they have their own secret language."

"Sorry," I say. Then I try to find a way to give Liya an easy out. "Liya, do you need to get home or do you have a little more time?"

"So sweet," Stephanie coos.

"I'm in," Liya says.

Is she really though? She looks a little disappointed. But

we're already walking in a haphazard group, Stephanie and Eric in front with Stephanie's hand looped through his arm, and me and Liya behind them, a few feet apart.

At the underground food court, we've taken full advantage of our setting and ordered quite the hodgepodge feast. We're waiting to hear our numbers called from five different counters, so we divide the tickets among ourselves so we won't miss any. As I predicted though, Liya hears them all and is the one who jumps up and retrieves each dish. It's a mix of her feeling awkward and not wanting to join in on the conversation plus her just being good at stuff—remembering numbers, paying attention. Adorable stuff.

Our table is covered with pickled cucumbers, grilled squid on a stick, cold noodles in spicy peanut sauce, dumplings, and a rou jia mo, a.k.a. a Chinese hamburger, which Liya is currently cutting into fourths.

Eric grabs a toothpick from the holder on the table and spears a pickled cucumber. "You all know it's unusual to have toothpicks everywhere, right?"

Stephanie, who's sitting next to him, swats his wrist. "'Unusual' is all about perspective. This is our norm."

Eric moved to Chinatown in junior high after growing up

in the northern suburbs, and his viewpoint often made me realize how rare my experience is, growing up in a mostly East Asian community where our practices are "normal."

"I mean, it's nice, especially for my dad," Eric says. "He won't go back to Graeter's, the best ice cream place on Earth, because he's mad they don't have toothpicks there. Who needs a toothpick after ice cream?"

"Good thing you moved here," Stephanie says while poking his side, implying a second meaning.

As they playfully nudge each other back and forth, Liya talks so quietly it's like she only wants me to hear. "Why *are* toothpicks more prevalent in Chinese culture? Are we bigger on clean teeth?"

Stephanie had to lean in to hear Liya but she apparently did, replying, "Or maybe we're more likely to use them as utensils." She jokingly gives Eric a pointed look.

Liya appears pleased that Stephanie seemed to enjoy her comment, and her shoulders relax a hair.

We dive into the food, happy murmurs and noises erupting periodically. The rou jia mo is *chef's-kiss* perfect—crispy flatbread hugging minced lamb seasoned with cumin and pepper and other delicious things I can't quite tease out. The crunch of the bread is so satisfying, and the burst of flavors that follows is pure heaven.

Liya hesitates before grabbing her piece of the hamburger with her chopsticks, using them even though it's less convenient. I shoot her a warm smile, hoping it'll make her feel more at ease. When she dishes herself some noodles, I immediately pick the scallions out for her and transfer them onto my plate. She gives me a look at first, worried Stephanie or Eric will judge her, but I keep going—I don't want her to force herself to eat them just to fit in.

"You two are so cute," Stephanie says, watching our routine.

We both turn red and fidget in our seats but don't say anything.

Is Liya going to barf again? Which is worse, boba barf or lamb and squid barf? Probably the latter. Thanks, Stephanie.

Oh well. I'm still glad Stephanie and Eric are here. Because I'm enjoying their company and the breadth of our smorgasbord—which would've been difficult to achieve if it had been just Liya and me—but most of all, if they weren't here, I'm not sure Liya would've stayed out after the lanterns, especially since she had lied to her parents.

Oh wait. She said she was with Stephanie.

I start laughing out of nowhere. Stephanie, Eric, and Liya turn to stare at me. Crap—probably because it sounds like I was laughing in response to Stephanie's you-two-are-so-cute comment, which, I also kind of want to laugh at, but in a sad sorta way.

"Sorry." I swallow the last of the chuckles with a gulp of water. "I was just thinking about how funny it is that Liya told her parents she was hanging out with you tonight, Stephanie, and now she is. Funny how things turn out sometimes."

Eric nods knowingly, the same expression from earlier appearing on his face.

Nonchalantly, Stephanie asks, "Oh, do they not approve of you two dating?"

She has no idea what a big can of worms she just opened. Except instead of worms, it's a potential geyser of lamb and squid.

Liya's shaking her head.

"We're just friends," I say, trying not to let on how those words are cracking my heart open. Or something a little less dramatic.

"What?!" Stephanie blurts. "Seriously? Then what was up with that ridiculously romantic lantern lighting we witnessed? We waited so long to interrupt because . . ." She flails her arms a few times, trying to illustrate the *because*.

Eric chimes in. "And you two talk without saying anything. And you say *we*: '*We're* so happy for you.' It took Steph and me *months* to get there."

"*No*, it was months for me, a *year* for you," Stephanie clarifies. "But you're forgiven."

Eric grins, then kisses her cheek.

She's appeased. "Anyway, sorry, didn't mean to make it uncomfortable."

"Too late, babe," Eric jokes beneath his breath.

"But why *aren't* you two together?" Stephanie pushes. "I mean, seriously. I bet you two have even moved past the first fart already, am I right?"

Eric forces a laugh that dissolves into coughs.

"What?" Liya bursts out. "Is that a thing for people?"

Eric shakes his head. "I'm pretty sure it's a purely Stephanie thing."

Stephanie leans forward. "Well, okay, here's the thing. It *shouldn't* be a thing. Everybody farts. But even with the progress we've made with feminism, bodily functions, whatever, we still have so far to go. *Some* boys in our grade—not the ones here, though, I hope—still don't know this. So after my elementary school boyfriend freaked out and dumped me after I let out a toot on the playground, I don't know, it traumatized me so much I was terrified of farting in front of another boyfriend. Then one night, after Eric and I had been dating for like eight months—which included a *lot* of farts held in; my butt cheeks were so toned then—Eric took me out for five-ninety-nine all-you-can-eat shrimp."

"Oh no," I say.

"Oh yes," Stephanie says emphatically. "So many farts. Followed by Diarrhea City. We really bonded that night."

Eric shrugs. "I still think it was a good deal. Only five ninety-nine!"

Liya is staring with her mouth slightly open. When she sees me looking at her, she closes her jaw, her cheeks flushing slightly. Then she surprises me by asking, "That brought you two . . . *closer*?"

Stephanie smiles. "Oh, hell yeah. We told each other 'I love you' just a few weeks later."

Eric nods as he stuffs his face with noodles, clearly not affected by the memory of Diarrhea City.

Meanwhile, Stephanie is *relentless*. "So, Liya, you've farted in front of Kai, right?"

No, just vomit so far. *On* me.

Liya's red again.

Can we talk about literally *anything* else?

Eric laughs with his mouth open, his chewed food on display. "Don't worry, she's like this with everyone."

Is that better or worse?

"What colleges are at the top of your list?" I ask Eric.

Annnd nothing but net. My question successfully turns the conversation and we focus on Eric's promising future for some time.

As we're demolishing the last few bites and the conversation reaches a natural lull, Stephanie leans forward again.

"I'm sorry about your grandmother, Liya. She was the

sweetest. Every time I came in the store with my parents, she'd give me a treat—candy or a juice box or a toy. Always free. As a kid, I loved your store more than any other place!"

Liya's entire face glows. I'm guessing mine does too. Nainai treated her customers like family. And she was who I learned customer service from. She's why I put out the best products and don't sacrifice quality to save money. Despite my father's criticism, I'm incredibly proud. And this reminder of where my practices come from makes me vow on the spot to forget what my dad said and always do what I feel is best for Once Upon a Mooncake.

But When You Wish Upon a Lantern is struggling, an unwelcome voice says in the back of my head.

No. The family model is how all the Chinatown businesses run, except for maybe Once Upon in the past, before I got involved. They can't all be struggling, can they? I'd rather make Nainai and our community proud than my father and Jiao.

Liya blinks away a few tears. "Thanks, Stephanie. That means a lot."

After more hugs and another round of congratulations to Eric, we part ways.

"I can walk you home," I offer to Liya.

"Uh . . ."

Right, the lie to her parents. "I can walk you to your street," I amend.

"Thanks, that'd be nice."

We stop and grab dessert drinks—papaya for me, taro for her—and our walk is mostly slurping for the first few minutes.

"Sorry about the . . . you know, what Stephanie said," I say because I'm a masochist. My brain is yelling at me to STFU, but the words spill out anyway.

She squirms and sips loudly, and for the first time maybe ever, I can't read her face.

"Thanks for not throwing up," I joke, trying to lighten the mood.

"What?" She whips her drink away from her lips so quickly it startles me. She looks genuinely confused.

"Never mind," I say quickly, trying to defuse.

"Oh," she says, understanding filling her eyes. "Because I'm drinking boba right now."

It's my turn to be confused. Did she forget that she threw up on me because I asked her out?

She pokes my side. "As long as you don't make me laugh so hard I snort one up my nose, we're good."

Wait.

Our eyes lock, and I try to ask her the question in my mind with my eyes: *Was that the only reason you threw up that day?* But for the first time, my question doesn't come through.

"What?" she says again.

I search her eyes for one more second, then give up. "Nothing."

We return to walking in slurpy quiet.

Is she pretending I didn't ask her out that horrible day out of pity? Or . . . ?

What a heavy dot dot dot.

I'm pretty sure I know when she's lying. I mean, did she ever win a single BS game? And outside of games, even in the rare moments she slipped a lie through, she would admit it almost immediately, like the shrimp chips at the movie theater.

There had been no hint of deceit on her face—no wrinkle in the corner of her mouth, no difficulty meeting my eye. Only confusion.

But it's not like I could just ask her. So I shove it all down—deep, past where Jiao's taunts and noogies are festering. Then I slap a bright smile on my face and change the subject.

"Stephanie was quite something, huh?"

Liya beams. "It's funny in retrospect." Her eyes turn pensive. "Maybe it's kind of interesting that she's so opposite of all my instincts." She laughs. "Some instincts of which developed indirectly because of her!"

My smile widens. I'd always told her she didn't have to worry so much about the spelling bee incident, but I'm glad she could see for herself that Stephanie doesn't care.

Liya seems to be thinking out loud as she says, "I guess one great part about talking to her is that you don't really have to worry about what you say, you know? She probably isn't the kind of person to judge you or make fun of you. We should hang out with them more."

Could that mean she didn't mind all the comments about us dating?

I don't have time to ponder that because we're already reaching her street. Why do we have to live in such a small neighborhood? I love it most times, but not right now.

She stops underneath her street sign as if that's the magical point that will prevent her parents from seeing. Adorbs.

She faces me. "Thank you."

I'm not exactly sure what she's thanking me for, but I automatically say, "Of course, anything. Anytime." *Jesus, Kai.*

She tilts her head to one side. "Is there an ETA on that last lantern wish, the surprise?"

Oh shoot. I'm glad she reminded me. Gotta get on that. "Soon," I promise, giving her a lopsided grin. Maybe I'm playing this up too much and she'll be disappointed, but I don't think so.

"I can't wait."

After a brief pause, she holds up two fingers—two words. First word, she flashes me a thumbs-up. Second word, she mimes taking out a sword and closing her helmet.

Good knight.

I return her good-night in charade fashion. And I watch her walk away into the darkness, taking my heart with her.

14

Inner Beauty

LIYA

Stephanie's words consume me. They're all I can think and hear as I come in and answer my parents' questions (mostly with one-word answers to minimize lie detection). Then I retreat to my room.

Kai and I aren't past the first fart, but everything else Stephanie said about us was true. Did that . . . mean anything? Is it possible that what I'm feeling isn't one-sided? Yet, on the other hand, does any of it matter given our feuding families?

To distract myself, I marathon-watch *Inner Beauty*, a reality show where couples go on a series of dates that consist solely of talking to each other while behind screens with voices altered. The show came about after a viral study claimed that the more you like someone's personality, the more physically attractive you found them. After several of these talking-only dates, if the contestant is interested enough to continue a relationship, they press a green button. If they're not interested, red. Regardless, they get to meet, and after a face-to-face date, they have the opportunity to change their previous red or green decision.

I like that the show stresses inner beauty and getting to know each other first, but it's also dismaying how many people change from red to green after seeing what the other person looks like. There's less of the opposite (green to red after not being physically attracted to someone), but it still happens more than it should. I obviously watch for the people who fall in love (both hit green and stay green).

I think I'm drawn to reality shows in general because they're real people. The magic I feel when I grant someone's wish . . . I feel a small piece of that when I see people's dreams coming true even through a screen. And it applies to many reality shows, whether it's winning a talent competition or finding their person.

Inner Beauty is entertaining enough to keep my mind off Kai, but then . . . it veers too close to my reality.

I've been loving this particular episode so far because the two guests (Janie and Jesse) are hitting it off exponentially like they were meant to be, two peas in a pod, soul mates. I'm shipping them harder than I've ever shipped another reality show couple, and to my relief, they both hit the green button.

And my heart soars right up out of my chest when Janie is shown in a separate prerecorded shot talking about how for the first time in the show's history, she knows who the other person is. She and Jesse are childhood best friends, and when she heard he was going on the show, she reached out to the producers and told them she's in love with him. They decided to bring her on, but without telling Jesse.

I stop breathing as Jesse emerges from his screen to see Janie running toward him. His face is pure shock, and then . . . disappointment. My face mirrors his as my soaring heart turns to lead.

I'm gripping my laptop screen as Jesse says, "What are you doing here?"

Poor Janie. I want to hug her. Undeterred, she declares her feelings for him while sharing story after story about how he's been there for her through the years (after her parents divorced, when she found out her high school sweetheart was cheating on her) and how it was always him, she just couldn't see it before.

Jesse's pinching the spot between his eyes. When he looks at her, his gaze could turn water to ice. "Why would I come on this show if I felt the same way?"

Janie's losing her confidence. "Because you didn't know how I felt?"

Jesse sighs. "You're living in a fantasy world, where The One has been under your nose the whole time, the friend you just needed to look at in a different light."

"Don't you dare make fun of my love of rom-coms right now."

Their words grow barbs. Each one escalates the fight even more. I don't want to see the rest but I have to. So I watch as Janie points out that he hit the green button, only for Jesse to land the final blow. He accuses her of manipulating him, using her knowledge from their history to an unfair advantage.

The credits roll as their relationship crumbles.

In the background, Jesse's final words are full of anger and pain. "Why would you do this? Why did you have to ruin our friendship?"

The screen darkens and my stricken face suddenly reflecting back at me makes me jump.

Hastily, as if my life depends on it, I Google them. Only to find out that their friendship indeed did end, Janie wishes she never went on the show, and Jesse has a new girlfriend he's flaunting all over social media.

I slam my laptop shut. I wish I could unsee it, but I'm also grateful for the information. My friendship with Kai is more important than anything. I've seen the other side. Lived it.

For our first few weeks apart immediately after the boba incident, I was focused on my embarrassment. But then, when the reality of our distance began sinking in, it felt like I couldn't catch my breath. And during Qīngmíng Festival (the day the Chinese honor their ancestors) when I visited Nǎinai's grave for the first time since her passing, without Kai . . . I couldn't breathe at all. I had cried silently, trying to hold it in, following my father's lead. He didn't let anyone else in on his grief. But for me, it was too much. I was consumed by that feeling where you're gasping for air because you've cried too long and hard. It somehow felt just as crushing as Nǎinai's funeral, except at the funeral I had Kai sharing my pain and holding me up when I couldn't.

Not having him for those few months was . . . like missing a piece of myself. Painful enough that I never want to risk losing him again. And Kai is not just my support system but also my living, breathing, loving conduit to Nǎinai. Losing him means losing her even more than I already have.

I think back to the night of the Summer Lantern Festival when I let go of my wishing lantern and made that secret wish I was too afraid to write down. *I don't want to feel alone anymore*, I'd said to myself. I can't go back to that.

I don't care about the *we*s or how I feel or what Stephanie thinks. I cannot lose Kai. No matter what.

15

Hobbies

LIYA

The day after the court and, more important, Janie and Jesse, Kai of course notices that I'm being weird (which I am, I totally am). I tell him I'm just stressed planning for the upcoming Qīxì Festival, which is not a lie. Not only have I bit off more than I can chew with all the ideas I want to implement, but the event has to be a smash because we have less than two months to pay our past-due rent. Or **EVICTION**. That threat keeps me in high gear regardless of how tired I feel.

Once Kai is convinced, he continues texting and charading like nothing has changed, and soon I'm falling back into our friendship like it's a warm hug, Stephanie's words success-fully forced into oblivion.

The week leading up to Qīxì is packed with research, logistics, phone calls, asking favors, and an ungodly amount of work. I've been learning so much about Qīxì that it's boggling my mind why we didn't try to grow this festival sooner. Or any of our other festivals, for that matter.

I no longer worry about changing Nǎinai's vision because I finally feel what Kai had said: I'm simply expanding, all while helping the store and giving more to the community. And Nǎinai would be proud. In some ways, it still feels like I'm doing this with her because as I talk to community elders about what Qīxì means to them, it's stirring up treasured memories of Nǎinai that had been lost to time.

Shue Nǎinai: "As a little girl, the Cowherd and the Weaver Girl folktale was my *favorite*. I used to take my mother's shawl and pretend it was the weaver girl's magic one that helped her fly into the heavens! You know the Qīxì Festival is in honor of them and dates back to the Han dynasty, right? The Han! That's more than two thousand years ago!"

Nǎinai used to tell me that folktale as a little girl before she even brought our Qīxì celebration to life. Niúláng Zhīnǚ. As a kid, those were just sounds that went along with the story I knew, but now that I'm older, I realize those words are not just what we call those characters in the story, but a description of who they were: a cowherd and a weaver girl. A story of star-crossed lovers (literally) about a fairy who falls in love with a human man, but they cannot be together because Yù Huáng Dàdì, the ruler of heaven and also the fairy's father, forbids it. There are many versions of the story, but the one Nǎinai told me was that the weaver girl, as punishment, became a star in the sky, and out of pity, the ruler of heaven turned the cowherd into a star as well. But he banished them to opposite sides of the heavenly river. On Qīxì, one day a year, a flock of magpies forms a bridge to help the two lovers reunite for a single day, their stars coming together. The raindrops that fall are the tears of the separated couple, raining down to Earth from the heavens.

The story used to make me cry (and cry and cry). The idea of two people in love, not able to be together? It broke my heart. So Nǎinai always tried to shift the focus, telling me they were tears of joy, and that Qīxì Festival was a celebration of love. I used to only be able to focus on what a jerk the ruler of heaven was, and that his "pity" gets him no credit in my book since he caused the problem to begin with. Nǎinai would laugh and tell me it was a fair point that was true for the gods of many religions, not just Yù Huáng Dàdì.

"It's an old story," she would say as she dried my tears with a rolled-up tissue. "From thousands of years ago. Things are better now. You will not have to choose between family and love." Strangely, the resurfacing of this memory brings a new, unexplained, ominous feeling.

Yang Pó Pó's connection to Qīxì was more heartwarming than I, an American-born, could have guessed: "Oh, Qīxì, wonderful Qīxì. I love that your nǎinai brought that back to us. It's rarely celebrated in the US! In Taipei, when I was little, my family and I used to eat good food and go out and look at the stars. To this day the only stars I know are Niúláng and Zhīnǚ and the magpie bridge. Did you know it always rains in Taiwan on this day? Spooky! Here, the first time we had a festival, aiyah, I felt like a child again. I remember it like it was yesterday. When we all gathered to look at the stars, it hit me that we were looking at the *same* stars I looked at back home as a kid. And it made the world feel so small, like I was still close to home even though I was really on the other side."

When I had told Yang Pó Pó some of my ideas to expand our celebration, she had squealed and waved her arms in the air. "How can I help?" she asked, which gave me one of the many ideas I've been working hard on this last week.

I'm exhausted. Running-around, a-million-things-on-my-mind exhausted. But it will be worth it (I hope). Because it's all starting to come together, and Yang Pó Pó's reaction reminded me why I'm doing this. And it's the same reason I grant wishes.

So far, I'm proud of what I've created. The Qīxì Festival

has such incredible history but seems to have lost its importance and many of its traditions over time. Granted, my Googling showed that the traditions evolved every dynasty, but to me, this just meant there were that many more possibilities to choose from for how we celebrate today. Unfortunately nowadays it seems that in Asian countries, it's become similar to what Valentine's Day is here: a corporate holiday where restaurants and greeting card companies try to capitalize on customer spending. Guess it's fitting Qīxì is now sometimes called Chinese Valentine's Day. But our Qīxì? Will be completely unique. I've borrowed traditions from ancient China, from modern-day Taiwan and China, and from Qīxì-adjacent festivals in other parts of Asia, including the Tanabata festival of Japan, Chilseok of Korea, and more.

As for getting the word out about all the new Qīxì activities and offerings, I relied on an advantage (and sometimes disadvantage) of being in a small community: gossip and news travel fast through the grapevine. The disadvantage comes two days before the festival when the grapevine reaches my parents and they sit me down at the dinner table (a very bad sign always but especially now that we haven't been talking).

"Liya . . ." my mother says, her voice dripping with concern.

"Are you okay?" my father asks.

For the first time in a while, yes. I feel like I'm doing something important. For the store, for our community, for Năinai. "I'm fine."

In the silence that follows, my thoughts spiral. *Please talk to me about her. Please offer to at least help me. Please tell me about the debt so we can work together, the way it should be, and maybe I can finally unload this weight a little.*

"We . . ." my mother starts but trails off again.

"We think you need a hobby," my father says matter-of-factly.

I'm pretty offended. "What is this actually about?" I ask, failing to keep the frustration out of my voice, because this—*this*—is important enough to warrant a sit-down conversation, ahead of everything else we haven't talked about?

"We just . . ." My mother is talking so slow I'm having a hard time staying patient. "We think . . . you know, it would be good for you."

I waited that long for *that*?

My father, on the other hand, speaks quickly in a no-nonsense tone. "You need interests other than the store."

Have they given up on When You Wish Upon a Lantern?

"I'll think about it," I say, only to end this conversation. I don't mean it in the least.

But my father keeps going: "Working at the store and watching reality TV shows don't count as hobbies, Liya."

I stand and leave. And immediately retreat to my room to finish up Qīxì plans.

16

Surprises

KAI

Even though Liya seemed okay immediately after the court, she was a little strange the next day. I was, of course, worried that she was weirded out by everything Stephanie said, especially because I could tell it was more than just Qixi stress like she claimed. But I obviously let it go.

Luckily, it passed by the end of the week, and then we quickly fell back into our friendship groove. And now, holy moly, have we been busy. Balancing the regular bakery tasks with the additional preparations for Qixi has been no easy feat. I know Liya is even more swamped than me so I don't complain, but some nights I'm so beat I fall asleep the second my head touches the pillow. I used to think that saying was so exaggerated, but now I know—it's real.

I have a couple surprises I'm working on covertly. One of them is the secret wish I wrote for her on the lantern at Hebian Park, and the other is something special just for Qixi. Sure, Liya likes enjoying the anticipation, but I can't resist seeing that gleeful, gobsmacked look in her eyes when I surprise her.

I thought granting wishes for the community was the best feeling in the world, but it can't even compare to helping Liya's wishes find the light.

17

Qixi Festival

LIYA

When July 7 arrives, I'm a mess of emotions: excitement at seeing my hard work come to fruition; apprehension that something will go wrong; desperation to show my parents that this is much more important than a simple "hobby."

Poor Kai has been running around tackling all the tasks I need help with. I haven't heard from him in a little while and I'm beginning to worry I've stretched him too thin, but then he asks me to meet him at the festival early. I'd already been planning on being there hours ahead of the official start time to set up, so it's no problem for me.

I'm at Promontory Point hanging signs on tables to

label each "station" when Kai arrives carrying two enormous totes.

"There's more in the car," he greets me.

I want to cry (what is it with me and this day?). "I can't believe you did all this for the festival. Except I can. Thank you." The words don't feel like enough.

Kai—"Humble, gentle Kai," as Năinai always called him—blushes and brushes it off, saying, "It's nothing."

I channel Năinai and say, sincerely, to make him feel seen, "It's a huge deal. Thank you. I couldn't have done this without you."

Kai bites his lip, then smiles, his cheeks still pink. "I think we're going to make a lot of people happy today."

He gestures to the bag in his left hand, which has a signature red-and-gold Once Upon a Mooncake special box on top.

My heart skips a beat. "Operation Mooncake, phase three!"

Kai leans over and pulls out a paper bag from beneath the box. He motions for me to reach inside.

"Does this have to do with the surprise? The secret wish you wrote on our last lantern?" I ask.

"It's *a* surprise, but not that one."

I keep myself from asking him when that surprise is coming by channeling all my excitement toward the one in front of me. Inside the bag, I feel a thin, crisp food item. "Oh my god," I say when I realize what it is. I had asked him to make these, but after I pull the qiǎo guǒ out of the bag, I understand the surprise part.

It's so amazing I'm speechless. How does he continue to impress me when the bar is already so high?

Kai scratches the back of his head. "Do you like it?"

"Like it? Kai, you're a *genius*."

When I learned that in ancient times the Chinese made qiǎo guǒ, or fried thin pastes, to celebrate Qīxì, I asked Kai if he'd be able to dig up a recipe and make it. I'd read that the tradition was to mold the sweet, fried dough into different shapes (namely, stars, or Cowherd and Weaver Girl), but I hadn't told him that part because I figured it would've been hard enough just to figure out this new pastry in a week. But of course Kai, my star baker, had also somehow learned of this tradition and made perfect, beautiful, stunning Cowherd and Weaver Girl qiǎo guǒ.

"I can't even . . . this is . . ." I'm still speechless. "Kai, I'm just . . . Thank you."

Humble, gentle Kai surfaces again to say, "It was nothing. It's just eggs, milk, flour, sugar, and sesame seeds."

"Kai! You made Niúláng and Zhīnǚ!"

He accepts the praise this time. "The holiday didn't seem complete without them."

I nod in agreement. *This holiday wouldn't be complete without you.* I need to get a hold of myself. It's just the magic of Qīxì getting to me (right?).

"Sorry they won't be piping hot when everyone gets here," he apologizes.

"Kai, stop. It's perfect."

And then it somehow becomes even more perfect. He reaches into the bag and hands me a very misshapen one, wrapped in tissue paper for me to hold so I don't have to touch the food. I take it and chomp right in, eager. I groan and he beams. The best compliment you can give a baker.

As I devour my special qiǎo guǒ, Kai empties the second bag onto the table. Water lanterns. I bulk ordered them a week ago and sent them to the bakery behind my parents' back. Together, Kai and I experiment with how to display them.

"You know," Kai says, "I read somewhere that releasing wishing lanterns on the water is a modern tradition of Qīxì in some places."

"No way!" It feels like stars aligning (and not just Niúláng and Zhīnǚ).

"Well, I read it on some random blog."

"That's good enough for me. It makes me feel better about pushing my parents on this item." A little. I'll feel even better if they sell well tonight.

After we finish the display, Kai reaches into one of his bags to retrieve a gift-wrapped item. A mischievous grin graces his face, then morphs into one of pure joy, with both sides lifted and all his (beautiful) teeth showing.

"The surprise from the secret lantern wish," he says, holding the present out to me.

I barely keep it together as I tear into the red glitter paper. This time, the tears do fall.

"I wished that you wouldn't forget," he says as I clutch the gift in my hand.

I'm holding a notebook covered in hand-painted oranges. I swear I can almost smell Nǎinai's citrus perfume.

Kai's voice is just above a whisper. "I was thinking that you can write down your memories of Nǎinai so you don't have to be scared of losing them."

I hug the notebook to my chest. "It's perfect." The gift is perfect, the qiǎo guǒ are perfect, he's perfect. "These are just Niúláng and Zhīnǚ's tears on my face," I joke.

"That's not how it works," Kai teases. "It's rain, not real tears." And I love that we share this story, a culture, a childhood.

The festival hasn't even started yet and I already feel the magic of Qīxì.

I try not to stare at Kai's forearms as he carries over more totes, his legs as he squats down, his fingers as he delicately hangs decorations.

Luckily (or *un*luckily), there's so much to do that there

isn't time to fantasize. Before I know it, people are trickling in. My parents arrive with more lanterns, the rest of the wish writing supplies, and the other items for sale: cold beverages and snacks; blankets for those who want them for stargazing later; flashlights and battery-operated hand-held lanterns; and crafts on theme with the holiday, like star folding paper. I've also asked for a suggested $10 donation for enjoying the festivities tonight, and there's a donation box decorated with twinkling lights to place on our table.

I quickly shift a sign to shield the water lanterns from view as my mother turns in a circle to take in the setup. "Wow, Liya, this is quite something."

It took me an hour to drag in enough tables for all the stations I've prepared: wish-making station with lanterns (obviously), a qiǎo guǒ station (of course), a lantern riddle station (dēng mí, more traditionally a part of Mid-Autumn Festival or Chinese New Year but no reason why it can't be a part of today too), a wheat emporium table that will feature Mr. Chen and his noodles (inspired by Korea's Chilseok festival where they eat wheat flour noodles), and a craft table where Yang Pó Pó will teach patrons how to make her paper creations (inspired by Japan's Tanabata, where they make origami and other paper objects). Each table has a sign and is adorned with knickknacks that tell you what you'll find there: fairy lights around the wish-making station, images of Qīxì Festivals throughout the years for the qiǎo guǒ, plastic bundles of wheat around Mr. Chen's, and samples of Yang Pó Pó's creations around the craft table. The paper lanterns I cut out of construction paper and wrote riddles on are decoration enough for the dēng mí station and took me a whole afternoon to create. Everything is glued down or weighted somehow to keep things from flying away, which took almost as long as dragging everything in.

The tables are set up in a large circle, and the patch of grass in the center will be perfect for the additional activities I've planned that will take place throughout the evening. (And each activity has a suggested donation to participate, though it's not required.) I've set up chairs in the middle for the activities and also in case people need a place to take a break or eat their snacks.

"Kai helped a lot," I say loudly so my father will hear. "And he spent all week making treats."

My mother sighs. "He shouldn't have." Her tone implies she means the words literally. I'm tempted to call her out, but I also don't want to fight right now.

"Well, he's *selling* the qiǎo guǒ, isn't he?" my father interjects.

"Well, yes, of course"—Why shouldn't the bakery get to make money too? We sell the lanterns, don't we?—"But he donated other treats for prizes and . . ." *Operation Mooncake*. "You know, stuff," I finish weakly.

My father doesn't seem impressed. He takes another

look around. "You didn't have to do all this."

Would it be so hard for them to just say *Good job*? I'm doing this for us, for the store, and they can't even muster a little appreciation? Should I just tell them I know?

"Liya Liya Liya!"

Yang Pó Pó has arrived. I leave my parents so I can thank her for volunteering her time and skills, to help her get settled at her table, and to be around someone who appreciates my efforts.

The event is a huge hit so far. The younger kids are loving the lantern riddles and perhaps loving the candy prizes even more.

"Hey, Bao," I say to the son of Fat Man Lu as I grab a red paper dēng mí. "Here's my favorite riddle. What's yī jiā yī?" I ask, saying *one plus one* in Chinese.

"Èr!" he exclaims, holding up two fingers.

I nod. "Very good! Here's another fun answer: Wáng."

He frowns at me, not understanding.

"Let's write it out together." I flip the lantern to the back and write the number one in Chinese (a straight horizontal line). "Now, when writing Chinese, instead of writing right to left, we go . . ."

"Up and down!" Bao says, triumphant.

"Yes!" I write a plus sign underneath the one, followed by another Chinese *one* below that. "If we smoosh this all together . . ." I extend the vertical line of the plus sign to connect it to the horizontal lines above and below: 王.

"Wáng!" Bao exclaims.

The character that results is both the last name Wang and the word for "king," and it's one of the first words children learn in school because it's easy to write.

Bao immediately runs to his mother and asks, "Mā, what's yī jiā yī?"

And my job is done. Nǎinai told me that joke when I was four years old, right after I learned how to write Wáng, and for two years I ran around constantly asking her, *What's yī jiā yī?* Nǎinai always somehow answered with delight, even the thousandth time.

Kai catches my eye from the qiǎo guǒ station and uses a finger to write *Wáng* in the air. I grin at him. Of course he knows child Liya's favorite joke. Bao runs to him and asks him the riddle. Kai asks Bao what the answer is, then asks him to explain it. Bao's delight is palpable even from here as he flips the lantern over and shows him the *Wáng* I wrote on the back.

Our first non-station activity, trivia, is a huge hit with the adults and teens. It's such a simple idea but given that the bulk of trivia happens at bars, the senior citizens and teens especially get into it. They're also playing for lantern coupons (buy three, get 10 percent off) and the grand prize, a Once Upon a Mooncake special, your choice of filling and message.

The star of the trivia round is Stephanie. The girl is on fire, answering things that I know only because of Wikipedia.

"What are the names of the stars that represent Niúláng and Zhīnǚ?" I ask from the middle patch of grass. I'm surrounded by thirty or so people, with many more forgoing trivia to spend time at the stations.

Stephanie's hand shoots into the air first. "Weaver Girl is Vega of constellation Lyra, and Cowherd is Altair of constellation Aquila, and today's the day they come together in the Summer Triangle!" Stephanie yells from her front-row seat. Eric puts his arm around her shoulder and pulls her close, proud.

Around the same time, Yang Pó Pó yells the answer in Mandarin from her craft table. I'm not sure if she raised her hand (and technically she's not even really participating), but since she's graciously been at her station this whole time, I hand a coupon to both her and Stephanie.

I flip to the next note card. "What are qiǎo guǒ made of?"

Daniel, the French-Chinese fusion chef, answers correctly as he thoughtfully chews the qiǎo guǒ he's consuming.

"No fair!" Fat Man Lu yells out from the fancy lawn chair he brought.

"All's fair in food and trivia!" Mr. Chen yells back, standing up for his fellow restaurateur.

"I'll allow it!" I declare with more confidence than I'm used to. Perhaps all this is getting to my head. I certainly feel different today.

Everyone, including Fat Man Lu, chuckles.

By the last question, Stephanie and Fat Man Lu's wife, Meili (a.k.a. Bao's mom), are tied.

"All right, it's down to this one," I say, feeling like the host of *The Bachelor*. *Ladies, gentlemen, the last question tonight.* Stephanie wants the Once Upon a Mooncake special, I can feel it. (An anniversary gift for Eric, perhaps?)

I clear my throat. Stephanie and Meili lean forward. Bao does too, clutching the red lantern riddle so tight it's crumpling.

"What female domestic skill was most commonly associated with Qīxì in ancient China, often being the skill they prayed for, and that was tested in Qīxì contests?" Uncharacteristically, I add, "It has luckily fallen out of fashion and is no longer the most important skill for a female."

Stephanie's eyes meet mine. She doesn't seem to know. Meili is distracted by a crying Bao, who is shedding big fat tears over his rumpled lantern.

Kai runs in and scoops Bao up, taking him to the craft table to make a new one.

Stephanie raises her hand hesitantly, then guesses, "Needlepoint?"

After hearing Stephanie's answer, Meili throws her hand up and yells, "Cìxiù!"

Fat Man Lu gestures to his wife. "The winner! Cìxiù is the more correct term!"

"Mandarin doesn't make it more correct," UIC grad student Kenny retorts.

Meili argues, "Cìxiù is embroidery, which is more accurate than needlepoint."

People start talking at once, creating an uproar, and panic rises in my throat. I personally think Stephanie's answer was good enough (Wikipedia isn't 100 percent accurate, but they used the word *needlepoint* too). *And* Meili came up with her answer second.

But I hate confrontation. I also have been raised to be deferential to people older than me.

"Two winners! Congratulations!" I hear from the direction of the craft table. Kai is standing there with a smiling Bao, new paper lantern in hand, and a giant, calm smile on his own (gorgeous) face.

The chatter pauses, and as soon as the words sink in, everyone claps for Stephanie and Meili.

"Stop by the bakery anytime!" Kai adds.

I hesitate, then rip the Once Upon a Mooncake coupon

in half so I can give each of them a piece.

I save Stephanie for second so I can whisper to her, "I think you had it."

"I know, right? C'mon!" She's not as quiet as I am. In fact, it almost feels like she *wants* Meili to hear.

"You impressed me. How do you know so much about this holiday?"

Her usually playful face softens. "Jeannie loved learning about Chinese stuff—holidays, lesser-known traditions, differences between regions and dialects—so for a lot of the time when she was stuck in bed and couldn't do much else, we learned about it together." Her younger sister, Jeannie, was diagnosed with leukemia at age four and passed away two years later. Stephanie had been in junior high at the time and it had wrecked her, her family, and the community.

I'm about to say *I'm so sorry* but then I realize that she's not grieving as she's telling me. She's remembering. Her eyes are tinged with a tear or two, but they're also nostalgic.

I don't want to say the wrong thing, but I'm also more comfortable with Stephanie after the other night. So I follow my gut and instead share a story about Jeannie, because that's what I would want to hear about Nǎinai. "Jeannie was such a sweetheart. I remember her go-to item at the store was that Japanese boxed bubble gum that came in different flavors, and her favorite was the orange but she felt bad giving me the ones she didn't like, so she always tried to give me her favorite. So I lied and told her my favorite was grape even though—"

"Ugh, grape is the worst one!" Stephanie's laughing now. "I remember you doing that! I suspected it at the time—you aren't the best liar—but Jeannie believed you. So pure of heart."

A silence follows that's somehow both heavy and light-hearted at the same time.

"Hey." She playfully pushes my shoulder. "Good hosting skills today. Better than Phil Keoghan or Ryan Seacrest or Jeff Probst. You were a Cat Deeley today."

I know reality shows are popular (they have to be, given the ratings), but in my experience, no one ever wants to admit to watching them unless it's ironically, like they only watch them to make fun of them, or they just happened to see an episode once by accident. So I'm surprised for a moment. But of course honest Stephanie would have no problem telling me how she really feels. I envy and admire it.

For some reason I don't fathom, I respond, "Reality shows are kind of a hobby of mine." The words dredge up the shame I'd felt earlier when my parents said it, and I hate myself for repeating them.

But Stephanie just laughs and says, "It's more than a hobby for me. It's, like, my life."

I beam. Widely, maybe even embarrassingly so.

"You know," Stephanie says, "the Galentine part of Qīxì

was also a big thing. The holiday was the one day girls in the past—like, *past* past, dynasty past—could get out and do stuff, so a lot of times girls would hang out and have fun. We should do that sometime."

I grin. "Yeah, we should."

We exchange phone numbers.

"Or we can do it with the boys too," she says, throwing Eric a flirty smirk. He blows her a kiss, she pretends to catch it, and then she runs toward him, leaping into his arms.

I swallow down the pang of jealousy searing my throat like heartburn. I try not to, but my eyes are pulled to Kai. A part of me somehow always knows approximately where he is as if my subconscious keeps tabs on him in my peripheral vision. He's currently busy at the qiǎo guǒ table surrounded by eager customers and Chiang, James, and Yong. They're part helping him serve and part messing around. Somehow, like he can sense me looking, Kai lifts his head and our eyes meet. I wave. He smiles.

Then I wave him over. It's time for Operation Mooncake's next phase.

Last week's research had turned up that in ancient China, as part of the Qīxì celebration, single folks would come out at night holding lanterns to try to meet a potential match. Of course I had to make this a part of our festival, and I had to make it a key in Operation Mooncake.

I printed out flyers for the festival as a whole but made a few dozen that highlighted the Lantern Singles Match and sent them to all the single people I knew in the community. And of course, Shue Nǎinai and Mr. Tang received personalized invitations.

As the time for the Lantern Singles Match approaches, Kai and I finish arranging the chairs in the center in two parallel lines, facing each other. A few eager participants are already beginning to hover. One of them is Shue Nǎinai.

"Liya, my favorite, how is my hair?" she asks me as she takes a seat.

Her full-blown perm hasn't moved the entire time I've known her. "Beautiful," I say with a smile.

She wrings her hands. "Is this lipstick too much? I feel like a clown." She puckers her pale pink lips, and it's so cute I want to go track down Mr. Tang this instant.

"You look perfect," I tell her sincerely.

When the gathering group hits double digits, I start the event, explaining how it will work. Essentially, it's speed dating plus construction paper lanterns with suggested topics of discussion written on them.

It's a little cheesy, maybe even derivative of the worst kind of reality show, but I think it's cute and, more important,

I think it will work. Operation Mooncake is the top priority during this event. Mr. Tang needs a little nudging and my hope is that the paper lanterns will help them talk about *real* topics (unlike many reality shows). Perhaps it's weird and not how a normal date would work, but what's normal anymore? Tinder? Catfishing? I stand by my plan.

As a relationship noob, I did have some trouble coming up with the questions, but yay internet. I covered everything from deal breakers to what a typical Friday night looks like to which side of the bed (I didn't even know that was a thing). And while I did briefly consider finding a way to incorporate first farts, I didn't.

After I finish my explanation, the seats fill and people start chatting. Mr. Tang has arrived late and is far from Shue Năinai at the moment, but that's exactly why I planned the rotating "dates."

Kai joins me off to the side. "Hey, partner," he says softly so only I can hear.

That word makes me grin. "Operation Mooncake is in motion," I say, matching his low volume. I quietly tell him about how, after everyone took their seats, I backward inducted to figure out who I needed to give what lantern to so that by the time they finish rotating chairs and lanterns (clockwise for the first, counter for the latter), Shue Năinai and Mr. Tang will have the lantern topic I planned for them: *Tell your partner what you hope your future will look like.* I know Mr. Tang needs a huge push, so I didn't hold back.

Kai looks impressed. "Good work."

As the stopwatch beeps, Mr. Tang's current partner, Mrs. Bing, grabs his sleeve to try to get him to stay.

"Okay, everyone move along," I say, hoping she'll get the hint. She does not look happy.

"Didn't plan for that," I whisper to Kai.

Four speed dates later, Operation Mooncake is officially a go. Kai and I walk casually around the chairs so we can eavesdrop on Shue Năinai and Mr. Tang.

Two minutes in, he's doffed his tweed cap to her, and Shue Năinai has asked him about his future, but he's struggling to respond. Shue Năinai smartly jumps in and answers the question first. As Mr. Tang nods and listens, she tells him how it's taken her so long but she's learning to dream for herself and she hopes her future will be full of happy new memories. She doesn't come out and talk about a relationship or finding someone, but she alludes to it perfectly. (I consider jotting down some notes in my oranges notebook, but I don't want Kai to see.)

When she's done, there's a long silence. Then Mr. Tang clears his throat. He opens his mouth, but nothing comes out. He tries again. Still nothing.

"Happiness," he eventually says. "That sounds nice. I want that."

Come on, Mr. Tang.

And finally, *finally*, he begins opening up. Just a smidgen, but it's progress. He begins telling her about how the divorce had been a shock to him.

"Shoot." Kai points to my stopwatch. "There's only a minute left."

I have to improvise. They need just a little more time.

"Oh no!" I say, a decibel too loud. "The, uh, timer broke! Everyone, keep going! Kai, can you help me fix this?"

We turn our backs to the chairs and fumble clumsily with the stopwatch.

"Hey!" a voice rings out from one of the chairs. Mrs. Bing. Her seventy-year-old frame has sprung out of her seat and she's pointing a finger at me. "It's not fair that Shue Năinai gets more time with Mr. Tang! We either need to rotate now or I get extra time with him too!"

Twenty-five-year-old Gus Chiu feigns hurt from his seat across from Mrs. Bing. "What am I, chopped liver?"

Mrs. Bing opens her mouth wide and laughs once, displaying the silver crowns on her molars. "Hah, sonny, if you're really gonna give me a chance, I'm willing."

Gus quickly changes his tune and holds up two hands in defeat.

"It's always the same," Yang Pó Pó pipes up from the craft table. "More women our age than men so we fight over the crumbs we have."

Poor Mr. Tang. He's no crumb.

Shue Nǎinai straightens in her seat. "Unlike you, Bing Jiě, I'm not interested in *every* man my age. I like Mr. Tang because of his big heart and attention to detail."

Mrs. Bing leaves Gus behind and tries to shove herself next to Mr. Tang. "Same here, same with me. Big heart, details." Her words jumble as she focuses on trying not to spill out of the chair she's forcing herself onto, the one that is still half-holding young graduate student Kenny.

"Jesus," I exhale.

Kai and I run over and try to restore order. It comes only after I miraculously "fix" the timer.

As everyone continues to rotate, I see Shue Nǎinai and Mr. Tang peeking at each other periodically. Kai flails a little every time he catches one of their sneak peeks. I do the same. My heart might explode any second.

Once everyone has had a chance to speak with each prospect, the activity naturally winds down and people begin dispersing. Some linger, gravitating back toward the person who piqued their interest most, and I'm over the moon(cake) when Shue Nǎinai and Mr. Tang find their way back to each other, sitting on two chairs off to the side for more privacy. I don't interrupt, letting their conversation pick back up.

Unfortunately, a few minutes later, I see Mrs. Bing waddling over. Come on, Mr. Tang, make a move. Shue Nǎinai already put herself out there—it's your turn!

But I see him blushing and looking away and hemming and hawing. Shue Nǎinai is traditional when it comes to courtship (she hasn't dated in over forty years), so I know she won't make any more moves after what she already said.

They need help. They need me.

Before Mrs. Bing reaches them, I hurry forward and announce, "If anyone agrees to a date at the end of this, they'll receive a free wishing lantern to set off together later tonight!"

Everyone cheers.

My hope is to appeal to Mr. Tang's stingy side. His frugality is legendary in the community, and, thank goodness, his eyes lit up at the word *free*.

Shue Nǎinai gives him a hopeful look, which is just enough to push him to the finish line.

"Well," he says, coughing once, twice. "It'd be a shame to give up that offer, don't you think?"

Shue Nǎinai nods. It was enough for her. "I'd love to have dinner."

I want to squeal but can't so I grab Kai's hand and squeeze my squeal into his palm. He returns it.

Now that Shue Năinai has said yes, Mr. Tang beams widely. Since I've been eavesdropping, I'm about to grab a lantern to gift them when—

"Actually . . ." Mr. Tang clears his throat again. "Now that I know your answer is yes, I don't need the free lantern. I will buy one for us. I didn't ask you on a date to get the free prize . . . You *are* the prize."

Mr. Tang! Who knew?

Shue Năinai looks like she's about to fall off her chair. "Tang Xiānshēng! Whoo! What are you doing to me?"

Kai holds his palm out subtly behind his back. I don't know what he's doing at first, but then I understand and I give him the smallest most secretive high five ever. Since we're still within eye and earshot of the newly formed Shue-Tang Clan, we'll have to hold off celebrating until later.

"Poor Mrs. Bing," Kai whispers to me.

"I got it."

I walk over and talk to her, trying to hint that she can put a wish out in the universe tonight if she wants. Once she catches on, she claps her hands and tells me, "I want to wish for a companion—romance or friendship. And I want to make it official," she adds, then scurries off to my parents behind the lantern table.

"We're going to have so many wishes to keep track of after tonight," I say to Kai excitedly once she's out of hearing range.

And then an idea hits me. I take the oranges notebook out of my bag. Carefully, I open it to the first page and write WISHES at the top. Underneath, I write

Mrs. Bing—friend or boyfriend

Half can be for memories of Năinai, and the other half for keeping track of our wish grantings.

Kai's smile stretches across his entire face. "Let's collect as many wishes as we can tonight."

As the sun begins to set and everyone begins pondering water or sky lantern, this wish or that, Kai and I split up to assist people with their lanterns and listen to their wishes.

The older generation is especially open to sharing tonight. Mrs. Zhao is devastated that her grandchildren only speak English and she can't communicate with them. Mrs. Suen misses her children and grandchildren who moved to the East Coast and is sad that she can only talk to them on the phone or see photos. Mrs. Ma misses her family back in Asia and is distressed that it's so expensive to call them. Mr. Kwok wants to spend more time outdoors but doesn't like to do it alone.

But we learn wishes from people of all ages, the youngest being little Sam Tong. "A dog!" he whispers much too loud in my ear, and it's so cute I can't even be upset. And Vivian Law, a seven-year-old whose family moved here a year ago, shyly whispers in my ear that she wants to see the place her grandpa keeps talking about, where he grew up.

My oranges notebook and my heart are filling up. The former with wishes and the latter with joy. And my heart soars even higher when I see that the water lanterns are flying (floating?) off the shelves (er, table).

My parents don't say anything about it at first, but when we run out of water lanterns before the sky lanterns, my father wonders out loud if it was a fluke because they were just the shiny new thing.

"Well, if that's the case, then we need a shiny new thing every time," I retort. He's not amused.

He's so not amused that he says forebodingly, "We'll talk about you ordering these behind our backs later."

Crap.

I mean, I get it, but what about the fact that I was right? What about all the additional revenue I brought in today? As long as I help our store, I don't care about the cost to myself. Bring it on, Bǎbá. I still wouldn't change a thing.

I'm now listening to Serena Lum vent about how she is excited about her promotion but isn't sure what she's going to do with the new long hours and her poor dog, Jilly, at home. I listen intently, trying not to get too distracted by Shue Nǎinai and Mr. Tang stocking up on sky lanterns in my peripheral vision. The adorable scene of him carrying as many as he can and Shue Năinai following happily behind further convinces me that today was worth all the effort and even my parents' criticism. And I vow to devote myself to each new wish I've written down in the notebook.

As I bustle about, busier than usual because people want help with the new item, I bask in the compliments.

"Aiyah, Liya, the sky *and* the water?" Yang Pó Pó gushes. "This is even better than the lantern festivals in Taiwan when I was a kid!"

"Thanks for adding the water lanterns," young mom Eva Lin says as I walk by. "My Ting Ting is beyond excited to set it off tonight, as am I!"

"You've outdone yourself today, Liya," Sung Ăyí tells me with a pat to my shoulder. "Thank you for bringing so much of our culture—both old and new—to life."

If my heart soars any higher, I will be floating among the sky lanterns.

When the sun is setting, I usually try to find a moment to appreciate the pinks and oranges streaking the sky, but I'm too busy today to glance up for more than a couple of seconds at a time.

Then . . . oh, and then.

The sun disappears over the horizon. Excited murmurs ripple through the crowd. Everyone is dying to see what the added water lanterns will look like. We welcome the arrival of the dark night with bated breath.

One by one, mini flames are ignited throughout the park. Dots of hope, excitement, and everything good in this world. Someone lifts their sky lantern into the air, setting off a chain reaction. More and more fill the sky. Water lanterns are dropped into the lake. Most of them line the eastern shore, where the water is calmer, and they float and bob, dancing a heartfelt waltz while their partners above alternate between graceful and energetic depending on the wind.

I hurry to take photos for marketing purposes. I've asked Linda (granddaughter of Yang Pó Pó and head of the photography club at our high school) to take pictures for us, but I want to take some of my own just in case something goes wrong. Re-creating something like this is expensive, so better safe than sorry.

Soon the *ooh*s and *aah*s that fill the air are not just from our community but others at the public park. They begin wandering over, asking questions, and before long, a line of new people forms in front of the lantern table. I snap as many photos as I can of the sky and water, then hurry to help out. I don't meet my parents' eyes as I teach the newcomers how to fluff up the sky lanterns, and when several of them ask when the next festival will be, I proudly direct them to the now up-and-running (albeit minimal) website I've set up. I also tell them about our ongoing promotions on the Shop Frenzy app (again, recently up and running). Several of them are delighted when I leave them with, "May your wishes find the light," and they repeat the mantra back to me. Pretty quickly, we're sold out of sky lanterns too.

Now that all the merchandise is gone, for the first time today, I allow myself to take a second. And the timing is perfect. The visual that the sky and water lanterns create together is breathtaking. Mesmerizing. I stand in silence, in complete awe, drinking it in. Feeling the magic around me. It's my favorite part of lantern festivals, when the world feels tangible and possibilities are endless, and the bridge to the universe seems open for one brief moment in time. Just like the magpie bridge connecting Niúláng and Zhīnǔ.

I wish Nǎinai could see this. I wish my parents could enjoy this with me. I grab a flashlight and find myself searching for Kai.

I locate him on the north side of the park, at the bottom of the stone ledges, near the water. He's helping Bao with his many, many lanterns.

"Now, this one is for more video games," I hear Bao saying as I approach. "And this one is for more stuffed animals."

Kai is lighting each lantern, then he and Bao are lifting them off together.

Before I reach them, I hear frantic footsteps behind me, then see Meili Lu rush past me.

"There you are! Bao, you scared me half to death! You can't run away from Māmá like that!"

She scoops him up, covering his head in kisses, then thanks Kai, telling him she's got it from here. They leave hand in hand, likely to find Fat Man Lu.

"Spoiled rotten, that one," Kai jokes as I approach.

"One can never have too many video games or stuffed animals at that age."

"Or Pocky," he adds.

"At any age for that one."

He smiles at me. "Hey," he says, like he's just taken his first deep breath all day.

"Hey," I parrot back, more shyly than I mean to.

"Congratulations on a killer event today," he gushes. "Went off without a hitch."

"Except for that pesky timer during the Lantern Singles Match," I joke, and he laughs so hard I can't help but join in.

"Man, my adrenaline is still pumping from that! I feel like . . . like the words don't exist that can accurately describe how that felt, bringing them together. Gah, we did it, Liya!" He holds his hands up and when I raise mine, he high-fives me a bunch of times, over and over in excited bursts.

Then his smile fades. "I'm so glad it worked out but I'm also a little sad it's over, you know?"

"There are plenty more wishes to grant," I promise, holding up the notebook.

"Yeah," he says, his face lighting up. The hope and

optimism infused in that one word buoys me. "You're so amazing, you know that? Shue Năinai and Mr. Tang, this event . . ." He sweeps a hand out in a grand gesture.

I feel my cheeks flush. "It was nothing."

Kai laughs. "I get in trouble when I say that, so you have to accept my compliment!"

I grin. "Annoying, isn't it?" We chuckle together. "I couldn't have done it without you today, Kai. Speaking of which, do you want to help me with the last part of Qīxì?"

Kai nods eagerly and we make our way back to the crowd.

Once we've gotten everyone's attention, I tell the Niúláng Zhīnǚ story, focusing on their constellations and what we're looking for in the sky. Throughout the day, I'd placed star maps around the festival so that people would have a sense of what we would be looking for. While I talk, Kai goes around to hand out the printed images to anyone who wants them as a guide.

All eyes are directed toward the sky. Families are using the blankets they brought or bought from our table so they can lie back and search for Niúláng and Zhīnǚ. There are murmurings here and there, in pockets, but it also feels like everyone is bonded by a shared goal.

"It's like *Where's Waldo!*" little Ting Ting shouts, and people laugh.

"Except there are Waldos everywhere," Mrs. Bing complains. "How are we supposed to know which stars are *the* stars?

Maybe it'd be easier if I had someone to look for them with me."

Mrs. Bing's wish is already at the top of my list, but I make a mental note to work on it soon (partly because I feel bad and partly because I'm scared she'll try to interfere with Mr. Tang and Shue Năinai if she stews for too long).

I glance around, making sure everyone is content before I go looking for Kai again. He never reappeared after handing out the star maps. Most handheld lights are now off so people can see the stars better, and in the dark, it's almost impossible to find him. I briefly use my phone flashlight, trying to keep it away from people's faces so as not to disturb them, and eventually I hear Kai calling out my name. I follow his voice to where he's sitting on a purple blanket.

"I know this blanket," I say as I sit next to him. As kids, we used to pretend it was the magic carpet from *Aladdin* and we would "go on magic carpet rides," visiting different parts of the world. I run my hand over the familiar, now-worn surface. "It's more frayed than I remember," I muse. This very blanket held so much magic to me—it wasn't this old back then, was it?

Kai sways side to side, just like he used to when we pretended to be flying through the air. Nostalgia washes over me. I join him for a brief second. When we lie down, it almost feels like I'm transported back to simpler times, when my only job was to have fun.

I take a deep breath and for the first time today, I truly relax.

18
Magic Carpet

KAI

I'm lying next to Liya on our magic carpet. It almost feels like we're children again, carefree, without any confusing emotions to get in the way. *Almost*. Because unlike child Kai, teenage Kai is currently stressing about things child Kai never would. Like how her face is kinda sorta dangerously close to my armpit. I put on deodorant today—didn't I? Let's see . . . washed my face, shaved, got a little nick and needed to put some ointment on, and then, okay, yes, I put on deodorant. But that was *many* hours ago. Yong, Chiang, or James would've said something to me earlier if it was bad, right?

Right??

"Oh jeez, yeah, I see what Mrs. Bing means now," Liya says, forcing my thoughts away from my pits. "I just see a huge mess of dots."

"I found them!" a voice calls out from nearby.

"I knew you'd find them first, Yang Po Po," Liya calls back.

Yang Po Po comes over to us, a flashlight lighting her way, and we sit up so we can chat with her.

"Liya, precious Liya. Wah, you not only made me feel close to home tonight, you brought it here. Yet you still made it feel like my American home at the same time. How did you do that?" Yang Po Po takes Liya's hand in hers. "Thank you for this. I feel like I am somehow complete. My two homes are here." She places her free hand over her heart.

The glow from Yang Po Po's flashlight illuminates how much the words mean to Liya.

"Today was perfect," Yang Po Po finishes. "Except . . ." Liya grows worried. Yang Po Po drops Liya's hand and points to the sky. "It didn't rain! It always rains in Taiwan! Why are Niulang and Zhinu not crying today?"

Relief washes over Liya's face. With a chuckle, she jokes, "Sorry, Yang Po Po. I'll do better next year."

Yang Po Po throws her head back and laughs. Then she squeezes Liya's shoulder, once. "Just perfect. Beautiful. Your parents should be so proud. Nainai would have been."

She totters off, humming an old Chinese song to herself.

The light disappears with her and we're once again swathed by the dark night.

Liya lies back and I follow, this time angling my torso so my armpit is farther from her face.

"Yang Po Po didn't tell us where Niulang and Zhinu are," I say.

"Just as well. I want to find them myself."

We search in silence for a bit, my eyes growing more accustomed to the dark by the second. The stars now appear a little brighter than before, and I'm noticing a few that I hadn't earlier.

"Got 'em," Liya says triumphantly ten minutes later.

"Where?"

"Are you sure you want me to show you?" She pokes my arm. "What happened to you being better about surprises than me and not needing to know immediately?"

I laugh. "This is different. Just show me." I'm seeing the stars clearer now, but it just means the big hot mess of dots is bigger and messier.

"Okay." She leans closer to me, pointing. "It's kind of hard because of all the city lights, but do you see the three stars that are brighter?"

I follow the direction of her finger but again, I just see a smattering of dots. Maybe some of them are brighter, but not a distinctive three.

"Um . . ."

Her head comes closer and she gently uses one hand to tilt my face in the right direction, which, coincidentally, means tilting it more toward her. She gestures again, this time talking about triangles and diamonds and constellations, but I barely hear what she's saying. I'm not even looking at the sky.

When I don't respond, she turns toward me, and our faces are *millimeters* apart.

I freeze on account of my nerves.

Then, suddenly, I'm frozen from fear. A bright light is shining directly into our eyes. I can't see. I can't think. My only thought is that I want to protect Liya, but I'm not exactly sure how.

19

Roller Coaster

LIYA

The first thing I feel is Kai's arms in front of me, protective, trying to shield me from whatever the threat is.

The first thing I hear is Kai yelling "Hey!" in a more threatening tone than I've ever heard from him (the closest was the time he yelled at Bobby Lee for making fun of my bowl cut in third grade).

All I can see is too-bright light, even after the source is redirected elsewhere.

Kai and I both hurry to sit up, with Kai maneuvering his body so it's between me and the threat.

Which, after my eyes adjust, turns out to be . . . our fathers?

"Liya, what are you doing?" My father's eyes look as frantic as his voice sounds.

"Kai!" Mr. Jiang barks, and Kai immediately shrinks back. "You disobeyed me!"

The flashlight in Mr. Jiang's hand is now angled toward the ground, giving just enough illumination for us to see how upset they are.

Kai and I scramble to our feet, him getting up first and extending a hand to help me.

"Get away from her," my father commands, grabbing the arm that Kai is holding on to and yanking me toward him instead.

"I'm not a yo-yo," I say with much less conviction than intended.

"What were you two doing?" my father demands just as Mr. Jiang yells at Kai, "I had to haul my ass down here after hearing from Fat Man Lu that you're giving away free goods! What did I say about free?"

Surprisingly, Mr. Jiang's comment is enough to distract my father, who pivots and retorts, "He was selling qiǎo guǒ all night! You probably made a fortune off our event!"

So now it's our *event*, I can't help thinking.

Mr. Jiang ignores my dad, still focused on Kai. "First you don't answer your phone, then I have to drag myself away from the Mahjong game to come down here—and tonight's a windfall; Moneybags Chu is filling in for Fat Man Lu—and *then* I couldn't find you! I had to ask *this one* for help!" He can't seem to bring himself to look at my dad as he jabs an irritated thumb in his direction.

My father doesn't address Mr. Jiang's comment as he turns to me and demands, "And what the hell was going on? You shouldn't be doing *that*—canoodling—with anybody, but especially not him." His voice is dripping with even more anger now.

"We were just looking for Niúláng and Zhīnǔ in the sky!" I exclaim. It's making my blood bubble that I'm getting in trouble when I wasn't even doing anything. (And if I were, was it really that bad?)

I add, "Just because you have a silly feud with the Jiangs doesn't mean I can't be friends with Kai."

Now it's Mr. Jiang's turn to be distracted. "Feud? *You're* the one constantly ranting and complaining about the smallest—"

"Smallest?" My father's yelling now, matching Mr. Jiang's decibel. "You're the worst neighbor possible!"

Mr. Jiang's hands ball into fists. "You're the weirdo who seems to always know what's in my garbage!"

"Only because you aren't capable of putting it where it belongs!"

Mr. Jiang raises a threatening index finger. "Now, you see here, I've told you once and I'll tell you again—the alley is *for trash*. That's why we *put our trash* in it. Not all of us need our dumpsters to be sparkling clean—do you insist your toilet be immaculate enough to eat off of?"

My father's face flushes red. "You make our lives harder and have never lifted a finger to help!"

"I gave you a fish vest!" Mr. Jiang yells.

Yes, but he gave everyone in this community a fish vest. And as far as I know, no one actually fishes except for Old Man Pan, who provides the local restaurants with his weekly catch.

"You tried to *sell* me fish vests!" my father throws back. "For three times more than you probably paid for them!"

"How dare you! I offered you an exceptional deal! A steal! How could you say no when you stock those ugly knockoff T-shirts from China?" Their novelty makes them popular among our non-Chinese customers. Our bestselling one has a knockoff Nike swoosh, a hair thinner than the real one, sitting above the words *It Just Do*. "You're the bad neighbor for not stocking our product!"

I have no idea what to do. Or say. All the animosity between them has been festering for so long that the wound has burst open, spurting pus everywhere in a split second. Or a less gross metaphor . . . it's like the roller coaster we're riding has been climbing until this moment when we were sent over the crest and into free fall. Now could we find our way to a more level part of the track or would we keep falling?

My father answers that question with just four words: "You have no honor."

I grasp Kai's arm. But my father's just getting started.

"And you're shady, rude, and inconsiderate." My father turns to me. "I don't want you around Kai anymore, Liya. I forbid it. If I see you two together, you'll be, what's the word? *Grounded.* No phone, no store, no TV."

Has my heart stopped? I can't breathe. I want to tell him how unfair that is, how much I need Kai in my life, but what good would that do? It would only make him watch me closer. He's always told me to stay away but never with the threat of consequences before.

"You don't think my son is good enough to hang around your daughter?" Mr. Jiang bellows. "*My* son? He's the best!"

It's funny how this is the first time I've heard Mr. Jiang say anything nice about Kai.

My father and Mr. Jiang begin yelling at the same time, their words crashing together and becoming indiscernible. Concerned bodies just visible in the dark as shadowy blobs are beginning to make their way toward us.

Kai and I both move at the same time. We grab our fathers and pull them apart.

I'm so embarrassed by what my dad said. Yet I can't seem to get the words *Stop it!* or *You're acting like a child!* out.

I can't hear what Kai is saying to his father. But he's

clearly trying to calm him down. And as I watch him talk calmly while holding his ground physically, all I can think is, *How can my dad not see how good he is?*

Kai ushers his father away first. He calls out "Sorry" to me and my dad even though he didn't do anything wrong and my dad certainly hasn't earned an apology.

We share one last look before he turns away. The helplessness in his eyes sends a shiver down my spine.

I was wrong. Completely wrong. We're not the Hatfields and McCoys. It's worse. We're Niúláng and Zhīnǚ.

It's an old story, Nǎinai had said when I'd cried about the forbidden lovers. *You will not have to choose.* Now I know why it felt so ominous revisiting that memory earlier. Because deep down I knew Nǎinai was wrong. Maybe it had been true when she was around, but everything has changed since she left. That's when Kai and I became stars. And now, our own Yù Huáng Dàdìs have forbidden even our friendship, without as much as a special day to come together. Nǎinai had been our magpie bridge and without her, we are forever star-crossed.

How can our story be over when it has barely begun?

It didn't rain today, but I feel like it's raining inside my soul.

20

Shameful Liya

LIYA

After a wonderful, hard-earned day, the fight sucks all the magic out of Qīxì.

All my father says once Kai and Mr. Jiang are gone is, "I mean it, Liya. Stay away." And then, "Come help clean up. There's a lot to do."

My blood is one degree from boiling. For the next twenty minutes, it slowly heats up more, with everything my father does annoying me, even the way he collects the decorations without much care (we're going to use them again!).

My mother can't meet my eye. Just as well; I don't want to look at her either. She wasn't there for the fight, but I'm sure my father told her. Or perhaps she overheard. I wouldn't be surprised if *everyone* did.

Later that night, after we've cleaned up and returned tables and chairs to the store in silence, I'm on the verge of exploding. I decide to count the money we've made in the hopes that it will make me feel better.

I've only reached the fourth twenty-dollar bill when my father comes over to the register and takes the bills from my hands.

"I'll finish this," he says coldly, not meeting my gaze.

I stare at him standing in front of me, passing bills from one hand to another while illuminated by the harsh fluorescent store lighting. The magic of our store is evaporating.

I want to know exactly how much we made and how much there is left to go. I want him to know that I did this without them, and with Kai, the person he wants me to stay away from for no good reason.

His silence annoys me enough to say, "Bǎbá, you're being unfair to Kai." Even though he can't see how good he is, the person he respected most did. So I use it. "Nǎinai loved him. And you know it. Don't you trust her judgment?"

That stops him, his hands pausing as his jaw tenses. "His family . . ." he starts but trails off.

"Just because his father and brother are one way doesn't mean he's the same."

My father shakes his head, slowly at first, then gaining resolve. "Yǒu qí fù bì yǒu qí zi. Like father, like son. You know who taught me that? Nǎinai."

The Chinese idiom churns my insides. Yes, I'd heard those words from Nǎinai. But in a positive light, about how my father's loyalty came from her and his tenacity from Yéyé, and how I had inherited those traits as well.

"You're twisting her words."

"Everything goes both ways, Liya," my father says dismissively. "I'm just trying to protect you." His eyes bore into me. "Stay away from Kai. I *will* follow through and ground you. No phone, no store, no nothing. Okay?"

I don't answer. If I'm not at the store, who will fight for it? But if I don't have Kai, who will fight for me?

"O-*kay*?" My father's voice has taken on an ominous edge. It doesn't happen often, but when it does, it scares me.

"Okay," I lie. I understand Shameful Kai more than ever in that moment.

21

Shameful Kai, Again

KAI

"Jesus, Kai, really?" Jiao scolds me once my father and I are back at home. Of course. "Stop upsetting Dad so much."

My father gives him an appreciative pat on the shoulder, then turns his dagger eyes on me. Again, of course.

What did I even do wrong today? I only gave away like five things! What about the pile of cash we made? The one I dumped into my father's lap a few minutes ago, which only earned me a grunt. Not to mention *they're* the ones who used our garbage to treat our neighbors like garbage, then yelled at *me* whenever I said or did or shoveled anything.

I perpetually feel like I can't escape them. I mean, sweet

Jesus, their embarrassing schemes follow me everywhere I go and their complete lack of empathy just cost me the only person I care about! Maybe it would be different outside this tiny community, but no, here we are, in the middle of it, our income relying on the very people my family doesn't give a crap about upsetting.

At least, unlike Liya's dad, my father is a man of few words. But, sigh, *of course* he chooses this moment to snatch his tongue back from the proverbial cat.

"Stop hanging around that shagua's daughter."

You can't tell me what to do. What right do you have, swooping in now, years too late, suddenly wanting to be my father? If I have to choose between her and you, it's her. You're the shagua.

All the words, as usual, die a swift death, filling the already-at-capacity graveyard in my head.

My dad and Jiao are staring at me in that way I hate, like they can't fit me in with the rest of our family. The distorted, wonky, stepped-on puzzle piece—that's me.

Shaguas, both of them. Fools.

I didn't feel so out of place when Mom was around. She and I fit together, and she was the nexus connecting me to Jiao and Dad. But right now, no one is on my side. No one in this living room will defend me. And without Mom, I can't wedge myself into the rest of the puzzle.

"Sorry you went all the way down there," someone says.

I say. Because I am a Shameful Kai coward who blurts things only when they're words that will hurt me, not them.

My father nods, supplicated by my apology, and he leaves the room first. The left side of Jiao's mouth quirks up in a smug smile, and he pounds me on the back way too hard before jogging after my dad.

I'm left alone. All I can think about is how this is their fault—I'm getting judged for their actions. And how unfair it is that Liya's father can't open his mind enough to realize that the day I was born, there was a freak hurricane and the apple sometimes *can* fall far from the tree.

Nainai knew. But Nainai's gone.

I go to the kitchen and knead dough until my arms grow numb enough to numb my mind.

22

Gutey

LIYA

There were already so many secrets between my parents and me, but now there's an additional obstacle: anger. The Qīxì blowup was the final straw and now I can barely look at them.

I'm also angry at myself and wish I had reacted differently. I punish myself at night thinking through all the things I *should* have said to stand up for Kai, for me, for us.

But obviously I wouldn't have been able to actually say any of those things. Even now, with all the anger, I'm still not texting Kai for fear of my parents finding out (and not, for once, because of my dislike of texting). We see each other in passing because of our neighboring stores, but I'm scared of my father catching us in the alleyway chatting or charading through the window. It already feels like I'm grounded because I don't have Kai, but I still don't want to get caught. Because I cannot risk getting banned from the store. And because I cannot risk my father saying more hurtful things to Kai.

Or to Mr. Jiang. Kai's father is usually pretty absent from the bakery, but I spot his salt-and-pepper head through the window today. (Just because Kai and I are not charading doesn't mean I don't frequently look over there hoping for a sneak peek of my favorite baker.) Then I get a glimpse of Jiao's taller, stockier frame too.

My anxiety skyrockets. Are they punishing Kai for giving away too many free goodies? Are they watching him? Are they getting in his way and driving him up the wall? Definitely yes to that last one; Kai is very particular about his routines, and for good reason since it takes a lot to keep the place running smoothly.

The shelves near my window are immaculate and fully stocked that morning.

Kai is keeping his distance too, and even though it's exactly what I'm doing, my heart hurts the few times he meets my eye through the window without a charade. Or a smile. Just a brief tick of his chin, not even a full nod. I know he's probably worried about upsetting my father and also preoccupied with his unexpected company, but it still feels awful.

On this side of the window, When You Wish Upon a Lantern isn't anywhere near as busy as I would like, with just a few stragglers here and there. I have no idea how much of a dent we made with Qīxì. I think it was significant, but the amount we owe is also such a big number (why is rent so freaking much?). We don't have another festival in the next few weeks, so I brainstorm ideas for increasing business and wish grantings. Since I'm coming up empty on the former, I focus on the latter. At the very least, I'm doing *something* to help the store while, I hope, bringing a little joy to someone's life.

But without Kai, granting wishes suddenly feels impossible. No magic in sight. How am I supposed to find a companion, romantic or otherwise, for Mrs. Bing? I can't force someone to hang out with her. And I don't want to do it, not really, not after her behavior at Qīxì (no one messes with Shue Nǎinai!). And getting little Sam Tong a dog? I couldn't manage that with my own parents as a kid (hence the dog-hands)—how am I supposed to convince his?

Collecting these same wishes with Kai, I had felt so excited and hopeful, but now I want to lie down on the floor. I don't know why, but I decide to tackle the hardest one first—the dog—almost as if to prove to myself that I can do all of them.

I call nearby animal shelters, inquiring whether they're

looking for volunteers to walk the rescue dogs. The first few say no, several say extensive training is required since volunteers do more than just walk the dogs, and one says yes but I still need some training sessions to learn how to limit the transfer of diseases between the animals.

That . . . does not sit well with the part of me that dislikes touching the food I eat. I'm not *not* a dog person (like I said, I wanted one when I was a kid), but maybe now I realize that I don't love them enough to make up for possible ticks or their fondness for sniffing each other's butts.

I've never had to ask myself this before, but how far am I willing to go for a wish granting?

Since I don't have any other ideas, I decide to call the shelter back. I schedule a training session for later in the week. Sam Tong, you better *really* want that dog.

After I hang up, I feel a small sense of accomplishment. But I also feel very alone. I'm alone in the store, I'm alone at home even when my parents are there, and now I don't have Kai. Perhaps spending time with dogs will also be good for me, personally (despite their butt-loving noses).

When Stephanie texts me later that day asking if I want to hang out, I jump at the opportunity and fire off a much too eager text ending in (by accident) four exclamation points. I wish I could delete one or add another but it's too late now. I wonder what Stephanie would say if I told her about this quirk of mine, which leads me to panic about spending time with someone I don't know that well. Someone whose misfortune I once enthusiastically clapped about.

Stephanie
Sleepover at my house?

Okay, not just spending some time with but an entire night. I hesitate for a second. But I need to get out of the house and I really want to get to know Stephanie better.

Liya
👍

I just hope my parents believe me when I say I'm hanging out with Stephanie Lee.

They do believe me, but not until they call Stephanie's mother to double-check. I feel like a delinquent, and even though I *have* lied to them before (and, in fact, using this exact lie), I'm offended.

I pack the cutest pajamas I can find: little snowflakes on them, gifted to me by Meili Lu in a Secret Santa one year. But then I stress over whether it's weird to wear them when it's summer.

Calm the eff down, I tell myself. *It's Stephanie, not Cat*

Deeley. Then I remember that Stephanie loves reality shows *and* Cat, and I feel a little better.

My parents make me bring something over to Stephanie's house. As always, I'm embarrassed. At times like these, I wish we had a bakery instead of the store because then I could bring over pastries, which are normal and usually welcome. But my parents have a stockpile of gifts in the basement for exactly these purposes, and they are completely random, totally weird items like postcards from a museum or a promotional calendar from one of our vendors or a decorative plate you can't even put food on because it could poison you.

Today, it's a tissue box cover that makes it look like a square teddy bear. Something you have no idea if the receiver wants, and it's just so bizarre.

"Thank you, honey," Stephanie's mom says to me, nothing but appreciation in her voice (I need to learn from her). Sometimes I wonder if everyone in the community knows and talks about our strange gifts behind our backs like they talk about Shue Năinai's long-windedness.

After a quick hello to Mr. Lee, who's watching television, Stephanie and I retreat to her room. Posters of K-pop groups are tacked to the wall with Scotch tape, some of them haphazard, which makes me want to straighten them. In the corner sits a collection of Gutedama items (stuffed animals, a water bottle, notebooks, and pens), clearly set up on display.

I pick up the pillow Gutedama on her bed, which depicts the anthropomorphized egg yolk lying atop an egg white base.

Stephanie grins. "Everyone always goes for Gutey first."

"He's just too huggable."

We plop down, me onto a beanbag in the corner and her onto the bed.

"Spotty Dotty used to be my favorite Sanrio character," I tell her.

She holds up her hand for an air five, which takes me a second to catch on to, but I eventually figure it out. "Hello Kitty is overrated, right?" she says.

"Non-Asians used to make fun of me for liking Hello Kitty and then suddenly, it became cool."

Stephanie rolls her eyes. "Just like seaweed and sushi and a bajillion other things."

"Gutey isn't mainstream yet though."

"Key word being *yet*. Everyone's going to fall in love once he gets out there."

He's an egg yolk with a butt crack, I want to point out but don't.

Stephanie sprawls atop her bed, stretching. "I love him because he reflects my attitude on life. I know he's supposed to be a lazy egg yolk who doesn't seem to care about anything, but I interpret the meh-ness to mean, just be yourself because if anyone doesn't like it, *meh*."

I want to channel that for myself but it feels so foreign.

We order pizza and eat in her room while watching reality shows on her laptop. She introduces me to *Date Roulette*, where the roulette wheel determines if the couple will embark on the most extravagant, luxurious date ever (think private jet to Italy for dinner), or the worst, most taxing date (think a dinner of bugs followed by babysitting for newborn septuplets). The show claims that the worst dates are actually better for your relationship since they make you overcome an obstacle together, though I'd still prefer the ten-course meal prepared by the world-famous chef, thank you very much.

After Stephanie shows me her favorite episodes, I ask her if she's seen *Mama Knows Best*. When she shakes her head, I give her a short elevator pitch.

Immediately she says, "Okay, we are so watching that!" She turns the laptop to me so I can pull it up.

I scroll through, knowing exactly where I'm going. "My mom and I love this episode, and you're going to appreciate it too, I think. One of the mothers in it is just like Ong Ăyí from the flower shop. We couldn't stop laughing!"

"You watch this with your mom?" she asks, incredulous.

I squirm a little. "We've been watching it for a long time, starting back when boys still had cooties."

"Maybe that's why she feels so comfortable objecting to you and Kai. Or, I guess, maybe it's more your father."

I squirm even more. "Oh ha, you, uh, heard our dads at the festival?"

"*Everyone* did." She gives me a sympathetic pout.

I flop back onto the beanbag chair, suddenly exhausted.

My eyes are fixed to the glow-in-the-dark stars on Stephanie's ceiling as she says, "I wanted to hang out tonight, of course, but I also wanted to make sure you're okay."

That was nice of her. But I also feel a little like a sad-sack project.

"Thanks," I say after a moment. I wonder if I should elaborate, maybe answer her question of whether or not I'm okay. But I can't.

"How come we didn't hang out more before?" she asks. "We've known each other since, what, first grade?"

I chew my bottom lip. *Because until recently, I steered clear of you, convinced you hated me over the spelling bee incident.*

I can't admit that to her, but I do tell her something else embarrassing I may not have admitted if not for Gutey staring at me with his *meh* eyes. "I'm glad you invited me. It's my first sleepover." The words sound so pathetic coming out of my mouth, like I'm confirming her view of me as a sad sack. "I mean, just, you know, this is nice." Oh god, that was even worse.

Stephanie sits up ramrod straight in bed. "We have to play Truth or Dare."

I don't answer, but she's already off and running,

figuratively and literally, hurrying over and plopping on the floor next to me on top of an oversized pillow.

"I don't know . . ." I say hesitantly. It feels like a nightmare coming to life, the inability to get out of a question you don't want to answer. Or worse, doing something you don't want to.

Stephanie presses her palms together and begs me silently. Then not so silently. "It'll be fun!"

"You just want to ask me about Kai," I half-joke.

She grins. "Duh. You can also pick dare, you know."

I shake my head. "I can't. You must know that. This game for me is just Truth."

She stifles a chuckle, then points out, "You'll get to ask me questions and dare me to do stuff too." I still haven't explicitly said no, so Stephanie suggests, "I can go first. I pick Dare. No, Truth. Truth."

I think for a second, then decide to use this as an opportunity to both apologize and get an answer to a question that's been eating at me for too long: "Did you hear about the clapping bee sting incident in fifth grade, and were you upset at me about it?"

She blinks at me a few times. "I literally have no idea what you're talking about."

At first, I feel relief, but then, a confusing mix of emotions floods in. I've been obsessing over this for six years for . . . no reason? It even affected how I act in public! And it turns out, she didn't even know about it? What does that mean?

"Okay, your turn," Stephanie says. "What are you talking about, and why do you look so weird right now?"

Before I've finished telling her, she's already laughing. "Why would I be mad about that? It was an honest mistake."

Again, how had I let that one incident affect me for so long? What else am I harboring that is a way smaller deal than it is in my head?

Even though this has gone as well as I could've hoped, I'm embarrassed. So I ask, hoping to change the subject, "Truth or Dare?"

"Truth."

I ask something I want to know but would never have the guts to ask otherwise: "When did you know you liked Eric, and were you ever afraid you'd lose your friendship if you two didn't work out?" Stephanie's and Eric's families were good friends, their fathers both working at the local bank, and they knew each other for a little while before they started dating.

Stephanie leans over and pokes my calf. "Any specific reason you want to know? Huh? Huh?"

My cheeks grow hot.

She flops back down on the pillow. "I didn't really know I liked him at first. But I don't know, he was cute and he asked me out and I thought sure, why not? It wasn't until a few months in when I noticed how considerate he was and how much he made me laugh that I really started to see him. And then things kept progressing and progressing, and as I said before, that shrimp night really bonded us. If he could still want to kiss me after seeing that, he's a keeper!"

Her words shock me. A few months? It makes me feel a little ridiculous that I've had such strong feelings for Kai for so long and we're still just friends. But then again, their friendship clearly wasn't that close based on what she said; she barely seemed to know him before.

Stephanie has a gleam in her eye and I'm dreading what's coming as I say, "Truth. Obviously."

"Kai. Spill it."

"That's not a question," I protest.

"It so is. Answer."

"He's my best friend. That's all."

Stephanie lets out a long, exaggerated sigh. "*Please*. That's not all you want him to be."

I shake my head in full denial. It's not like Truth is contractually binding, right?

"Liya, you know I've seen you two together, right? And even if I haven't, Kai is a *hot baker*. He's a cinnamon roll who can *make* cinnamon rolls."

I can't hold it in any longer. I've never had someone who I could squeal with about these kinds of things, and

Stephanie's words open the floodgates. "I know, why do I find his baking skills so sexy? I can't stop looking at his forearms. They bulge when he kneads dough. And those veins!"

Stephanie lets out a noise that is part squeal, part hyena. "That's what I'm talking about!"

"Have you ever seen *America's Hottest Buns*? They bake in nothing but an apron."

"Holy crap, we're watching that right now."

As I pick out an episode for us (the one with the male model who can't frost a cake but can flex one pec at a time to music while he tries), I think about how I admitted the truth to her and didn't die. In fact, it feels like a massive weight has been lifted.

With a giggle, Stephanie says, "Kai should go on this show."

A flare of jealousy sparks in my chest. "Maybe a different reality baking show."

"Hmm, I wonder why," Stephanie teases as she shoots me a knowing smile. I can't help but chuckle.

By the time the episode ends, we no longer need Truth or Dare to talk.

"So what's keeping you and Kai apart?" she asks.

"Physically, our parents." I sigh. "And besides that, I don't even know if he's interested!"

"Oh, he's interested. You two haven't even tried?"

"I don't want to hurt our friendship. He's the most important person in my life right now."

I tell her about Janie and Jesse, and of course Stephanie insists we have to watch the episode immediately. I don't want to, but I'm curious enough for her thoughts that I agree.

"Whoa, mama, am I shipping them," Stephanie murmurs as Janie and Jesse bond over their first few behind-the-screen dates.

"I know, right?"

When they both hit the green button, Stephanie cheers, just like I had. Then, when everything falls apart, her face grows thoughtful. I'm watching her watch the show. She doesn't betray her thoughts, and all I can see is her wheels churning beneath.

When the episode finishes, Stephanie looks at me and says with full confidence, "That won't happen to you and Kai."

"How do you know?"

"Because Kai likes you too."

I don't know how much I believe her. All of it is too scary to think about. "Doesn't matter anyway after what happened with our parents."

We talk about that for a while, about Kai's family, about how my father has the completely wrong perception, and about how I feel totally stuck.

I tell her, "I don't know how to communicate with my

parents anymore, like Năinai was needed for us to hear and see each other." Then without pausing or taking a breath, I blurt out, "The store is struggling—I don't know how much longer we can stay afloat—and they haven't even talked to me about it. I'm trying to do what I can, but they're not only refusing to help, they're in my way!"

Stephanie doesn't seem surprised by this information. "You know, I hear a lot of the Chinatown businesses are struggling."

That makes me sit up so I can see her face clearer. "Really?"

She nods. "I think the rent is increasing for everyone. The gentrification of surrounding areas is driving the price up."

I take a mental walk through the neighborhood, trying to see if there have been any signs of struggle I missed before. Mr. Chen! He insisted on making Kai and me that Peking duck special, then charged a pretty penny for it.

Does that mean Once Upon a Mooncake could be struggling? No, Kai would tell me. Especially after I trusted him with our store's debt.

"What do we do?" I ask Stephanie.

"I don't know, but if I can help, just let me know how."

I consider telling her about the wish granting and asking her to brainstorm with me, but something holds me back. As much as I like and trust Stephanie, it's not about that. The wish granting was a special thing between Năinai and me, and now it belongs to me and Kai. Even though I'm struggling, I'm not ready to bring her into it yet.

"Thanks, Steph, that means a lot." For some reason, the nickname just comes out of my mouth naturally, and she doesn't object.

"No problem, Lili."

For a second I consider telling her that it's Năinai's nickname for me and no one else uses it, but I like it when she says it. It felt wrong coming from my dad, who refuses to acknowledge Năinai's existence in any way other than stealing her nickname for me, but this is different. A way to keep the nickname alive. And instead of feeling sad, it feels a little like a warm hug from my grandmother.

I smile. "We still have to watch *Mama Knows Best*." The episode with Ong Ăyí's doppelganger is still open and waiting on Stephanie's laptop.

"Ahh, yes, I love watching overbearing moms and aunties when they're not mine!"

As I hug Gutey to my chest and let the problems of others drown out my own, I'm grateful for tonight while simultaneously wondering what would have been if I hadn't let my fear of the Great Spelling Bee Incident of Fifth Grade control my life.

What if I was doing the same with the Boba Tea Catastrophe of Junior Year?

23

Poop Son

KAI

Nine hundred fifty-one. Nine hundred fifty-two. Nine hundred fifty-three.

Sigh. I have been counting in my head to stay calm for the last, well, nine hundred fifty-four—now fifty-five—seconds. I know, I know, it doesn't sound like an over-the-top amount of time, but I also didn't start counting until I was one teeny-tiny infinitesimal step away from completely losing it.

My father and brother have been in the bakery with me for the past three years—I mean, three hours. If I thought they were bad the last few times they were here, well, past Kai, have I got news for you. Together, they are exponentially worse.

Their presence alone was suspicious enough, but they also showed up with a mission, which on the surface appears to be, *How can we piss Kai off the most?* But beneath the surface, they're trying to "improve" the bakery, emphasis on the air quotes because at the moment, Jiao is trying to change our charming, Tang-dynasty-meets-modern-day theme into man cave.

"The bakery *needs* a big-screen TV," Jiao is saying, already measuring the wall. "Then we can be open on game nights." He turns back to the counter. "And we should offer beer on tap. Local ones. Cool brews."

I somehow manage to hold it together as I say, calmly, "That makes *no* sense. It's completely out of left field, we'd need to get a liquor license, and we're not even open at night."

"Exactly," Jiao says. "The space is unused for so many hours in the evening! Wasted money. This can be a bakery during the day, then . . ." He drumrolls on the counter. "At night, a bar! A speakeasy. One that you need a password to get into. We'll earn back whatever the liquor license costs in no time."

"But then you can't play Mahjong here." I'm grasping at straws.

My father grunts, the first time all day I've gotten any kind of agreement from him. Of course. Mahjong night is the most important thing on his calendar—unless Leads is running.

Jiao waves a hand. "Fine, speakeasy will be closed on the nights there's Mahjong."

"I think Mom would be upset about all this," I argue, my best defense.

They ignore me—probably because they know I'm right. So I try a different avenue. I look directly at my penny-pinching dad as I say, "All of those things require a lot of money up front, money we may never see again."

My dad is so cheap—*how cheap is he?* My dad is so cheap that when he travels to see Leads, he won't book a hotel because they're always "too expensive." So the night of, he'll drive around from hotel to hotel trying to haggle a better price, thinking they'll "come to their business senses" when they're face-to-face with him. Of course, that's not how hotels work, so he usually ends up sleeping in his car.

Jiao tries to shut down my argument. "Hey, Ba, remember when I took you to Dave & Buster's? They're hugely successful. A ten-billion-dollar company!"

That cannot be true. But I know better than to try to argue with Number One Great At Business Son in front of my dad.

Jiao finishes, "If we follow their lead, nothing can go wrong!"

My dad begins examining the bakery in a new light. Please, God, don't let it be in a Dave & Buster's light. But of course, there may as well already be an orange-and-white sign out front because my father gestures to the corner of the store and says, "Maybe we could get an arcade machine in here."

"How about board games?" I suggest, excited about that one. "They would keep people here longer, ordering more, and they don't take up too much space, and—"

Jiao cuts me off before I can say, *they fit with our cozy family theme.* "Board games aren't cool. No."

"Dave & Buster's doesn't have board games," my father says, legitimately confused by the conversation.

Jiao continues pushing, "We definitely need the TV. It's a tax write-off so we're losing money if we *don't* do it!"

Jesus. How am I related to them?

"I think the bakery is perfect as is," I say as confidently as I can muster. "Mom decorated it and wouldn't want all these changes." They still ignore me, so I blather, "And besides, why change something that isn't broken? Business has been very steady."

We were slammed with customers this afternoon—all of whom I'd taken care of since Jiao is still the "big-ideas guy."

"Not steady enough," Jiao argues. "And especially not steady enough for all the freebies you've been giving out, not that we should *ever* be giving our goods away—that's, like, lesson number one in business."

Again with the freebies. I didn't even give out that many! Wait. I think about my dad's obsession with the wasted and free food, their presence here, Liya.

Reading between the lines, I ask, "Is the bakery struggling?"

"Rent has increased," Jiao says.

My father makes his *don't talk about that* grunt.

So we *are* struggling. Rents increasing also likely explains why When You Wish Upon a Lantern has fallen on hard times too.

I have bigger concerns I should be focused on, but I find myself responding to my father's grunt with, "You told Jiao before me?"

The only thing I'm possessive of in this world is the bakery, which is almost like a piece of me. But with my family, I constantly have to defend my ground, stake my claim, remind them that I am the heart and soul of this place, not "baking is girly" Jiao.

My brother rolls his eyes. "He's always going to end up telling one of us first unless he tells us at the same time when we're together. And we're hardly ever together."

Thanks, Jiao, I didn't know that. *So* not the point.

"Ah, but we are together now," my father says in a surprisingly wistful tone. But then he ruins it. "Isn't this nice, my boys together? We're just missing Leads."

He and Jiao chuckle together, then dive into retelling Leads's latest victory.

I find myself staring out the window, hoping for a glimpse

of Liya. She was around earlier, but now her shoulder-length hair and cat-eye glasses are nowhere in sight. Just as well, for her sake. Sometimes I don't blame her father for wanting her to stay away from all this.

24

Operation Bagel

LIYA

It's been a week since the sleepover at Stephanie's, and I am not in the best of places. I miss Kai, I'm still mad at my parents, I'm deeply worried about the store, and today, my attempt to grant little Sam Tong's wish has not gone according to plan.

After days of training at the animal shelter (days!), I am finally deemed ready to take a dog on a walk. I pick Bagel, a dachshund, because how can you not love that adorable hot-dog shape? And I thought maybe a smaller-sized dog would be less daunting for both me (the newbie volunteer) and Sam's parents (who live in an apartment).

I plan Bagel's walk for a time when the Tongs would be in Hébiān Park. More specifically, for when, according to his summer camp's website, Sam would be finishing up a Capture the Flag championship. I assume, since he's only six, that one of his parents will be there to pick him up.

I "run" into them pretty smoothly (I think, if I do say so myself), and Sam of course falls in love with Bagel immediately. There are nuzzles, hugs, and face licking.

But instead of gazing lovingly at her son rolling around in the grass with Bagel, Mrs. Tong's eyes narrow. I can't quite read what's going on in her head.

"Okay, Sam, that's enough, we have to go!" she calls out.

When Sam and Bagel return to our side and he hands me the leash, I decide to continue with the plan since I'm not completely sure what Mrs. Tong is thinking. Quickly, I explain that Bagel is a rescue dog without a home and that they can adopt him if they wish.

"Canwecanwecanwecanwe?" Sam begs, squishing Bagel's face against his.

Even *my* heart is about to burst, but Mrs. Tong is somehow unfazed. "No, Sam, I'm sorry. We've talked about this."

My heart crashes and burns next to Sam's.

Sympathy creeps onto Mrs. Tong's face, but she remains otherwise steadfast. "Okay, Sam, say goodbye to the dog. We have to go."

"His name is Bagel!" he shrieks. Tears pour down as he rubs his nose against Bagel's, two wet noses smooshed together.

"Thank you for making him fall in love with that dog," Mrs. Tong hisses at me. "We can't afford one, and you just forced me to break his heart!"

My heart is even more shattered than Sam's as I watch Mrs. Tong pick him up and carry him to the car, with Sam wailing the entire way.

What have I done?

I've broken Sam's heart and pissed off his mom, and now I have another wish to grant on top of Sam's and all the others in the notebook: I have to find poor Bagel a home.

Why did I have to pick the hardest wish to do first on my own? What kind of dodo does that?

After I drop Bagel back at the shelter (yes, I left my heart behind with him), I return home and somehow my day worsens.

Perhaps because of the festering anger, I snoop around. In Nǎinai's desk drawer, I find a radioactive envelope postmarked a few days ago, and this time, the words FINAL NOTICE are stamped on the outside.

With my heart beating so fast I can hear it in my ears, my finger quickly slips underneath the edge of the flap and slides toward the sealed part. But the paper cuts through my flesh.

"Ow!"

I squeeze my finger with my thumb, trying to curb the pain.

It has to be a sign. And thank goodness for it. Because now that I have a second to think, I realize I can't cross that line. Last time was an accident, but this would be deliberate. No, I have to find out some other way how far we still have to go.

I nestle the envelope back in its spot and slam the drawer shut.

Then I don't know what to do with myself. I pace, I turn on the TV, I get myself a snack but, let's face it, I'm a jittery mess. Those two words, **FINAL NOTICE**, are eating away at me. I've made up my mind about not snooping, but the temptation is ever present, calling to me.

I have to get out of here.

I had asked for the day off so I could initiate Operation Bagel, but I decide to go to When You Wish Upon a Lantern anyway. Even if my parents can't use my help directly (which they definitely can, regardless of what they say), I can at least work on saving the store. Perhaps I can convince them to show me the books or give me some other useful information.

At the very least, maybe I'll get a glimpse of Kai.

My parents are still lying to my face and standing in my way.

I try to ask how much revenue Qīxì brought in and whether we should start thinking about the next festival. Their response? "Don't worry about it."

How am I supposed to do anything when I'm up against this? I have the urge to punch or throw something, but I squeeze it down real small and bottle it up so I don't explode on the spot.

I decide to start planning for the next festival even though it's not for a few weeks, on the fifteenth day of the seventh month on the lunar calendar. The Ghost Festival. Zhōngyuán Jié. The day when the deceased visit us, similar to the Day of the Dead in Mexico.

Even though as a community we don't celebrate Qīxì according to the lunar calendar, we do for Zhōngyuán Jié. Nǎinai mainly did this to space it out from Qīxì, because that way the Ghost Festival falls mid to late August (August 12 this year). That will be cutting it close to the due date, but it's also our next best opportunity to rake in a larger chunk of revenue.

The first addition to this year's festival will obviously be water lanterns. And when I learn via Googling on my phone that a Zhōngyuán Jié tradition is to light water lanterns to create a path for lost spirits, it feels like fate. And it buoys me up, past my frustration and fear, and finally, I focus.

As I'm losing myself in Ghost Festival research, the door

opens and "The Moon Represents My Heart" sings from the worn box at the front. I run over, much too eager, hoping for a paying customer.

"Liya, my favorite!" Shue Nǎinai wraps me in a hug and I revel in it longer than usual.

She notices and doesn't let go as she asks, "Everything okay?"

I pull away and nod quickly. "Of course! Just happy to see you."

She's touched but there's still concern in the furrow of her perfectly shaped brows.

My father had come out after hearing "The Moon Represents My Heart," but when he sees it's Shue Nǎinai, he hurriedly says, "Oh, hello, Shue Nǎinai! Lovely to see you! I'm sure Liya can help you today! I'm, ahem, busy in the back. But again, so lovely to see you!"

Is being a bad liar genetic?

But I'm glad for the privacy. Especially when Shue Nǎinai says to me (quietly so my father won't overhear), "Is he still being a baby?"

I'm not sure whether she and Mr. Tang were still at Qīxì when everything went down or if she just heard through the grapevine, but it doesn't matter. I blurt out, "I wasn't even doing anything with Kai! We were just looking for Niúláng and Zhīnǔ together! As friends!"

"*Just* as friends?"

First Stephanie, now Shue Năinai? "Yes, just friends," I say, exasperated.

"Why?"

"What do you mean, why?"

She narrows her eyes at me. "Liya, give me a little credit. I've seen you two together."

My mouth goes completely dry. I can't find any words.

Then she says, "He looks at you like you are the sun and moon and stars."

I blink at her. Once, twice. "Are you . . . sure?"

She laughs, two quick chortles from deep in her throat. "My vision is terrible, but I can see better than you, it seems."

"But I threw up on him."

That doesn't faze her in the least. "So?"

"So!" I want to throw my hands in the air but don't.

"So what? You'll laugh about that in the future. Together. When you're in a serious relationship with someone, you see them at their worst and it's okay."

"We weren't in a serious relationship. Not romantically. And it wasn't okay. After it happened, we drifted apart for a while." The devil on my shoulder was rearing its ugly head.

Shue Năinai clucks her tongue. "You know as well as I do, that is out of character for Kai Jiang. Give him the benefit of the doubt. Instead of speculating, *ask* him, *talk* to him about what happened, what he's feeling."

I absentmindedly nibble my bottom lip.

The twinkle returns to Shue Năinai's eye. "If Mr. Tang can do it, so can you, Liya."

Mr. Tang . . . Mr. "bamboo" and "tables" . . . did do well, but he also had a little help from yours truly. Though his declaration at the end of the singles event was all him.

"That was really sweet of Mr. Tang, at Qīxì," I say, and it's all the invitation she needs to gush to me.

As I listen to her updates about all the time they've spent together since (drinking tea in his shop, going for walks, having dinner at various restaurants in the neighborhood), my heart is happy for her but also beating so loud I swear I can hear it.

I smile and laugh in the right places as Shue Năinai tells me about how she's helping him redecorate his boba café. I dutifully show her some possible store items for centerpieces. But she knows me, and she knows how her words have affected me, because before she leaves (sans purchase, but with a promise to return), she leans toward me.

"Time is precious, Liya, even when you are young. And in case no one has ever told you, things feel like a much bigger deal at your age. But that will go away."

Not necessarily. "What about my father? And Mr. Jiang?"

I ask. They're the definition of making things too big a deal.

For a second I hope she'll tell me the feud isn't as bad as it feels right now and will resolve itself soon, but she sighs, dragging my heart down with her exhale.

"Family . . . can be difficult," she says slowly. "But don't give up on them."

My chest begins to fill with the smallest bit of hope.

She pats me on the hand twice. "The Moon Represents My Heart" plays her out of the store.

She looked so happy today. Happier than I've ever seen her.

When the song ends, my father emerges from the back.

His voice is calm but his words are threatening. "Don't forget what I said."

At first, I'm not completely sure if he's talking about what I think he's talking about, but then he follows up with, "About Kai. I mean it, Liya."

My cheeks flush from embarrassment at him over-hearing (eavesdropping on?) my conversation with Shue Nǎinai. Then anger takes over. How can he be that freaking stubborn?

The timing of his words almost feels like a warning from the universe: Don't even try to go after what you want, because it's futile.

25

Dumpster Fires

KAI

This week has been a dumpster fire. And I mean that figuratively and literally—Jiao set fire to the dumpster a few days ago. How, I have no frickin' clue. I just know I was the one who had to put it out. Mr. Huang showed up halfway through, not to help, but to scream at me. Luckily, Liya wasn't there that afternoon to witness any of it.

Jiao and my father have been showing up every day, all the livelong day, and I'm now convinced that their mission is indeed to piss the hell out of me. They have an ongoing bet over who can do it better, I'm sure of it. And they're both winning.

Today, I arrive thirty minutes early—partly in the hopes of having some quiet time to bake and partly because I need the extra time to catch up—but Jiao and my dad are already here. When I'd left the house it was quiet, but I thought maybe they were out having their favorite guys' breakfast of "meat, meat, meat"—actual direct quote.

Jiao doesn't set the dumpster on fire today, but he does manage to fight with me about everything from the display case to the cash register to the frickin' smell of the café, which he thinks could be improved by spritzing the scent of some herb that Fat Man Lu promises will make people hungry. "It certainly makes me hungry when I smell it," Fat Man Lu had said, which was enough to convince Jiao to buy a year's supply. Doesn't matter that I think it smells like feet.

In the afternoon, after running out of things to "fix," Jiao and my father circle back to the tables. They rearrange them over and over until Jiao bangs one straight into the wall, creating a giant hole that is, of course, the first thing you see when you enter.

I grab my phone and pull up the number for Mr. Du, our neighborhood contractor who does everything from drywall to asphalt. But before I can hit call, my father runs over and snatches my phone from me.

"Waste of money," he scolds.

"We could cover it with an arcade machine," Jiao says

so quickly I wonder if he rammed the table into the wall on purpose.

My father shakes his head. "I looked into it. Too expensive."

Jiao is about to suggest a big-screen TV. I'm so sure I'd bet money on it, which would sadly make my dad proud. But before Jiao can open his mouth, my father makes his *come on* grunt, and the two of them leave. I don't care where they're going—I just bask in the reprieve.

When they return, I realize that I should have known where they went. Peeking out of the shopping bags in their hands are sanders and spackling knives.

No. Not this again.

"You don't know how to spackle, Ba," I try to point out.

But my father doesn't want to hear it, arguing, "You also said I didn't know how plumbing works when I fixed our toilet."

Yes, the toilet that now screams every time you flush it like it's dying a long, excruciating death.

Jiao jumps in. "Yeah, thanks to Dad, that toilet doesn't overfill with water now, costing us extra on our water bill every month."

There's so little water I have to use up an entire pumice stone cleaning it every day, but, okay.

There is no task that scares my dad, but he lacks finesse, and a lot of his attempts are half-assed. And often, by the time the project is done, it would've been cheaper to hire someone else.

Case in point, I know it's futile, but I still have to say it: "Isn't that just as expensive, maybe more so, than hiring Mr. Du?" I gesture to the tools they've just lugged in.

"Shut up, Poop Son, you don't know anything," Jiao says.

My father just ignores me. "Okay, Jiao, do the thing."

My brother opens YouTube and clicks on the first How To Spackle video.

I can't watch this.

I retreat to the kitchen to catch up with the baking. Because even though it doesn't seem like it at the moment, this is a bakery. Jiao and my father have been getting in my way so much I've been off schedule, which hasn't happened in years.

An hour later, I'm mixing sponge cake batter when I hear the bell jangle. I hurry to wash my hands and run out there, faster than I've ever done before, because I've recently learned that Jiao is right—he can't greet customers, but it's not because he's the "big-ideas" guy. It's because he's a jerk and gets the names of our customers wrong even though half of them are people he grew up with.

When I enter the front of the store, I'm overwhelmed. Too many things are going on.

First, I am completely distracted by the crap job Jiao and my father have done. Yes, the hole is gone, but there's so much spackle that there's a protrusion from the wall as lumpy as a cat trying to hide under a rug. It's worse than the hole because at least a hole is recognizable and patrons will understand it was caused by an accident, but that giant eyesore looks like we're trying to hide something horrible.

The blob is so god-awful it momentarily distracts me, but then my peripheral vision begins taking in the rest of the room. A delivery person is at the door, but I'm not expecting anything today. My father is signing for the stack of mid-sized packages like he knows what they are. Jiao is already unboxing them, using the jagged edges of a key to tear through the tape.

The world slows down as he unfolds the top flaps of the box and reaches inside. It could be any number of horrors—video games, a beer tap, a fryer so we can make onion rings and french fries—but it's somehow even worse than I could imagine. Because I never imagined my brother and father doing *this*, even with the low bar they already hold in my mind.

They're wishing lanterns.

I'm in disbelief at first.

"What are those for?" I ask, like a shagua, because there's really only one answer.

"We're going to start selling them," my father says evenly, like it's not a big deal at all.

"What?" My voice has risen so high I almost don't recognize it.

Jiao elbows my father. "I told you he'd be annoying about this."

"Kai." My father's tone is all warning, no mirth.

I'm shaking my head. "Even you two wouldn't do this."

"Do what, Poop Son? It's just a business decision. Strategic. Nothing personal."

My father echoes Jiao's statement. "Kai, this truly was a purely strategic move. I promise it's not personal."

That's not even the point. I push back. "What kind of thought even went into this?"

Jiao shakes his head at me like he can't believe how little I know. "It's been keeping our neighbors in business, so why *wouldn't* we sell them?"

"Because we're a bakery!"

Jiao shrugs. "One-stop shopping. Look at Walmart and Target and Costco."

My father nods. "Jiao knows business."

Sweet Jesus, I don't know whether to cry or laugh.

"Where are we even going to put them?" I ask, looking around our already cramped space. It's not the best argument, but I will take anything that will make the ridiculousness stop.

Jiao and my dad look at each other. They haven't even thought about it!

"In the window!" Jiao declares triumphantly. "A window display! So everyone walking by will see!"

Can steam come out of my ears? I might explode. Or implode. Any second now.

My father must realize they've pushed me past a certain line because he stops emptying the packages and comes over. "I don't want to burden you with unnecessary things, so I haven't told you the extent of it, but the bakery is really struggling. To the point where we need something to stay afloat. And when Jiao suggested selling wishing lanterns here, it was like I'd been hit by lightning. They were selling so well at that festival I showed up at to keep you from giving away too much food. This is the Hail Mary we need."

Of course it was Jiao's idea.

I think about how Liya would never sell specialized tea so as not to step on Ming and Chicago Tea Party's toes. I try again. "What about our unspoken community rule? About how there are certain lines we don't cross out of respect for our neighboring businesses?"

My father scoffs. "Respect? You want to talk about respect? That shagua hasn't treated *me* with any! What do we owe them?"

"This will sink our business," I argue. Not to mention theirs, but my father doesn't care about that. "The community will be so angry at us for doing this they'll stop supporting us."

My father shakes his head. "It's a dog-eat-dog world, Kai. Everyone else will follow suit. We all came here for the

American dream, and we got it, but it's slipping through our fingers. The neighborhood is changing, and we're starting to get driven out. To survive, even this community will start stepping on each other's backs to get a leg up."

I refuse to believe it. "Even if other people do that—which they won't—*we* don't have to."

Jiao looks at me like the pain in the butt he sees me as. "Do you want to eat or do you want to feel good about yourself?"

There has to be another way.

My father is puffed up with pride over Jiao. "Such good instincts. You're going to do so well when you take over the bakery."

The blood drains from my face.

"What?" My voice is so squeaky I'm anticipating a joke from Jiao about how kneading dough made my balls crawl back into my body.

But he doesn't, too incredulous over my surprise. "What do you mean, what?"

I somehow find my tongue. "Ba, you're really leaving everything to Jiao?"

My father looks at me like I'm the one spouting nonsense. "Well, what did you expect, Kai?"

Well, what *did* I expect? Just because I poured my heart and soul into this place, just because I was the one running it day in and day out, what did that entitle me to? As Jiao always says, he's the big-picture owner and I'm the employee. After all, the big cheese isn't the one in the kitchen sweating over whether the baos are fluffy enough.

I feel like Poop Son, through and through.

I retreat to the kitchen—to hide or cry or yell, I have no idea, but I find myself standing over the sink, my palms against the cold counter, my eyes locked onto the faucet head. I can't move. I watch a water droplet form at a snail's pace, then drip into the basin when it hits critical mass. And I watch it happen again. And again. I make a mental note to not tell my dad about the drip lest he "fix it" and make it so that it takes all my strength to turn the faucet on.

Except what do I care now? Let him fix every last thing in this place. It'll be Jiao's problem, not mine.

Jesus, this hurts. How is it that I've just lost a piece of me, and yet I feel like it's my own fault? My father was right—I should have known. But given how much Jiao hates this place, how he constantly complains it's too girly, how *he doesn't even know how to bake*, I just assumed he wouldn't want anything to do with it. That he'd dream bigger, wanting to open a casino or a Dave & Buster's franchise. How did I fail to see he would just turn the bird in his hand into his man cave dream?

His voice calls out to me from the front. "Kai, you know you have a job here for, like, forever, right?"

Under his thumb, as his employee. At an unrecognizable place with sticky floors, cigarette smoke, and gambling.

Never.

Just the thought of the bakery turning into that makes me want to crumple to the floor. Symbolically, I rip my apron off and throw it across the kitchen. I march to the front, not sure if I'm going to leave without saying anything or if I'm going to finally let them have it for once. But, welp, it doesn't matter because I don't have a chance to do either.

I'm stopped in my tracks by the giant wishing lantern window display that has gone up. Of course, *this* they manage to do quickly. I almost forgot about the lanterns with everything else, but now I'm reminded there are dumpster fires everywhere.

"Please take that down," I plead. "Let's talk about it first."

"We already did, Poop Son."

I'm reaching the end of my fuse. What then? I'll blow up? Beg? Cry?

The bell over the door jangles.

Liya enters. I almost wish she were storming in, a cloud of anger around her. But it's worse. Her mouth is open and her face is completely, utterly hurt.

She looks from the display, to me, then back.

My mind goes blank.

26

Betrayal

LIYA

I had a lovely morning. I met Shue Năinai for boba at Mr. Tang's Bubbly Tea. I glowed almost as bright as Shue Năinai as I watched Mr. Tang fuss over her while preparing his favorites for us to try. Hopped up on caffeine reminiscent of the time Kai and I sampled the When You Wish Upon a Lantern inventory, I decided to take a detour back to the store so I could pass by Once Upon a Mooncake. Just to get a glimpse of Kai. I was still keeping my distance, but I hadn't stopped thinking about my previous conversation with Shue Năinai.

Then . . .

Walking by the bakery's window display of wishing

lanterns, I did the first double take of my life. It was one of those surreal moments where my eyes first subconsciously registered a familiar item, and then my brain caught up and realized the item wasn't in a place it belonged.

My head turned back, then my body stopped short and I was twisted for a second until I straightened myself out. But I couldn't straighten out what I was looking at.

A tower of wishing lanterns was piled in the bakery window. Some of the lanterns weren't fully inflated and many were stacked in a way that would damage their neighbors and cause them to have trouble lifting off—meaning, this wasn't done by Kai. The sign in the window that read ON SALE! MAKE YOUR WISHES COME TRUE! also wasn't Kai's distinctive blocky handwriting, but did that even matter?

Now, as my eyes take in the entire display once, twice, three times to confirm I'm not hallucinating, I find myself walking through the door. It's almost as if my feet carry me of their own volition. I'm not sure what I'm going to do, but I have to know more information, see Kai's face.

All three of them freeze when they see me.

Is this real? How could you do this? Too many questions float through my head. The one that makes its way from my brain to my mouth is the worst one: "Really?"

Kai's face is completely blank. Which annoys me. He has nothing to say?

Jiao laughs. Laughs! I shouldn't expect anything else, but I'm still shocked.

"Hate to break it to you," he says with a smile, "but you don't own wishing lanterns. You didn't invent them. We're not doing anything wrong."

Kai seems to finally return to his body. "Will you please shut up?"

For the first time since I've known him, Jiao is fazed. "What did you just say to me?"

"You heard me." Kai turns his back on them to face me. Gently, he asks, "Do you want to go talk? In private?"

Numbly, I follow him to the kitchen, aware of Jiao and Mr. Jiang's eyes on me as I go. I feel my nose starting to burn and I know the tears are creeping up, but I try to force them back.

Kai pulls out the stool for me (the only place to sit) and leans against the counter beside me.

"This is messed up," I say even as Jiao's words repeat in my head. *You don't own wishing lanterns. You didn't invent them.* I mean, technically, he's right, and we don't have any recourse. But come on. "They're your family," I continue, my tone more accusatory than I thought I was capable of. "Can't you get them to . . . not?"

Words are suddenly very hard.

"I'm trying. Really, Liya, I am. I was begging them when you came in."

"Well, try harder! You know we're already on the brink of closing. Please, Kai, you know more than anyone why this is so important. You can't take away any business from us—we won't make it!"

"I know, I know. I'm doing my best."

A charged moment passes between us, and for once it's not a good one.

I know he'll try his best, but it doesn't feel like enough, not when Jiao and Mr. Jiang are involved. So I blurt out, "They walk all over you all the time and you let them. You never say what you mean." *Maybe not just with them either.*

Frustration takes over his features. "You think I don't know that? But I would never let that get in the way of something as important as this. Don't you know by now I would do anything for you? That I always put you first?"

Yes, but . . . "Just because you want to help me doesn't mean you can." I don't have any faith that Kai will come through on this. And all I care about right now is getting those lanterns out of the bakery. "Come on, Kai, even when you told Jiao to shut up just now, it was in the nicest way possible." *Will you please shut up?* he had said.

"But I told him to shut up, didn't I? Don't I get any credit for that?"

"It's not about credit, it's about *fixing* this mess!"

"Liya, I can't fix it in one second. You know what they're

like, especially with me. Give me a chance to think."

"Just tell them! Tell them they're horrible! Tell them if they do this you'll never talk to them again!" I know it's too much but I can't stop.

Hurt takes over Kai's face. "You of all people should understand it's not that easy."

"What's that supposed to mean?"

"For all your judgment about my relationship with my family, you aren't communicating with yours either. Why don't you just tell them, Liya? Tell them you know about the store, and work *together*. Grieve *together*. Your dad isn't like mine—you can talk to him, and you can help each other get through all this."

"Easy for you to say, on the outside looking in. I could say the same to you. Have you stood up to them this week? I've seen them through the window. Things are different in here." I gesture to the layout of his once-immaculate kitchen, now cluttered and reorganized by someone who clearly doesn't know how to bake. Not to mention that disgusting *thing* out front that looks like a monster is climbing through the wall. "Why did you let them make all these changes?"

"I *tried*. And all I got in return was my father telling me that Once Upon a Mooncake is going to Jiao."

Ba dum dum. Joke's on me, trying to get him to feel bad for me, only for him to come back with the ultimate clincher.

"Sorry, Kai. I can't imagine how it—"

"It's fine."

He doesn't want to talk about it. With me. That's new. I don't know what to do with that. I'm feeling terrible, wanting to apologize and backpedal and be there for him, but then he says, "But at least I *tried*, Liya. You haven't even tried to tell your parents."

And then he keeps going. "Have you ever thought that maybe your efforts to save the store aren't working because you only have half of the information? You haven't even tried to get the whole picture from your parents. You think you're doing everything you can but you're not."

He's right, but I'm embarrassed and livid that he dared say it to me. "You don't go after what you want either," I retort. Definitely not with his family, and if Stephanie and Shue Năinai are right, not with other things too.

Something flashes in his eyes. "I do more than you. Isn't our friendship important to you? You haven't fought for us at all! Your father hates me and you just go along with what he wants even though you don't agree. You let him say all those horrible things at the Qīxì Festival!"

"Is that what this is about?" I ask. "Is that why your father is doing this? To get back at my dad for what he said?"

Kai grows exasperated. "I was trying to talk to you about something personal."

"You don't think the lanterns are personal? Why else is your dad doing this?"

Kai sighs. "We're struggling too. It sounds like a lot of businesses here are."

Betrayal enters my tornado of emotions. "What? How could you not tell me that? Why would you hide something like that from me unless you were a part of it? What are you going to tell me next, that you're going to be granting wishes behind the scenes for Once Upon a Mooncake now? Were you just getting closer to me and Nǎinai to learn our secrets?"

As soon as the words leave my mouth I want to snatch them out of the air between us. But it's too late. I already released the arrow, and from the pained look on Kai's face, it's a bull's-eye hit.

27

Alone

KAI

How dare she. *How dare she.*

Liya's words ring over and over in my head: *Were you just getting closer to me and Nainai to learn our secrets?* It was already unfair of her to put all of this on me, especially when she knows what my family is like, and now *this*?

Yeah, Liya, that was my glorious evil plan. In first grade, I knew you and your nainai would one day have an amazing idea our bakery would want to poach, so I became friends with you just because of that.

I'm so offended—so deeply, utterly betrayed to my core—that I lose the ability to function, like I'm a robot and my circuits have just shorted.

I come back to when she speaks.

"Kai, I—"

And I cut her off. Immediately. "Save it. I hear you loud and clear." *That even after everything, you somehow don't trust me.*

I can't look at her. I can't look at this kitchen.

I run out the back door, past the dumpster, down the alley, and turn onto the sidewalk. I don't slow down until I'm at Hebian Park.

She doesn't follow me.

Everything she said was true—I do let my family walk all over me and I don't say what's on my mind—but for me to entrust her with these secrets, with my most shameful weaknesses, and to have her throw them back at me?

You did the same to her, a voice says in my head.

But she did it first.

I am a petulant child throwing rocks.

I know how devastating seeing those lanterns must have been for her. I also thought she would know that I'm on her side. And then, when she lay bare my greatest shame and used it against me, I don't know, I couldn't handle it. It's like I disappeared from my body and my defenses went up.

I look around me at the water, at the joggers, at the parents with kids enjoying their afternoon.

I don't know where to go. Once Upon a Mooncake isn't mine anymore. I'm no longer welcome at When You Wish Upon a Lantern. I flop onto a bench and watch the river rushing, gushing, passing me and everything else by, devouring whatever is in its path, just like my father and brother.

I am completely alone.

28

Pop

LIYA

All of this had been festering too long. The secrets, the tension between families and within, the suppressed emotions . . . everything had been suppurating beneath the surface for months. And when Kai threw those accusations at me, the pus bubble broke. Green goo everywhere. I took things out on him because I didn't know where else to channel it. Now it smells gross, I feel gross, and I've messed everything up.

I do feel awful for the last thing I said to him, but when I tried to apologize he shut me down. And in the aftermath of all the barbs we hurled at each other, I'm angry. His words had cut deep. The irony was just now sinking in that holding someone's heart means wielding the most damaging weapons for it too. We knew exactly where to strike so it hurt, and I was still reeling.

Now I'm standing in the Once Upon a Mooncake kitchen, alone, for the first time ever. It doesn't feel familiar anymore, not with all the utensils and ingredients in the wrong places. I want to storm out, maybe over to Jiao and Mr. Jiang so I can tell them how I feel, but . . . I can't.

I look around the kitchen again. Without thinking, I grab the flour and move it over in front of the paper towels. And I return the rolling pin to where Kai likes it, the shelf right below the smoothest, most level part of the counter.

Then I leave, my only stand against Jiao and Mr. Jiang being the slamming of the back door.

Năinai's Wish

LIYA

All those times as a kid playing with my dog-hands alone was nothing compared to the next few days.

I'm so angry at first. The image of the wishing lanterns in the bakery window is burned into my retinas and I see it when I sleep, eat, watch TV. And all the barbs Kai and I flung at each other only cut deeper each time I replay our fight in my head.

Eventually, the anger burns itself out and I grow numb. When I look at myself in the mirror as I brush my teeth or dry my hair, the face staring back looks the same but I don't recognize myself anymore.

Everything feels like it's closing in. I'm numb but I also can't breathe.

How did I get here?

All of this started when we lost Năinai. She was the glue holding everything and everyone together.

Except . . . it wasn't as simple as that. We lost the glue and then we all started keeping secrets. It began in the hopes of tiptoeing around each other's feelings, but perhaps that was precisely the problem. I accused Kai of not knowing how to communicate with his family, but, as much as I don't want to admit it, he was right: I haven't been able to communicate with my parents either. It's so easy to judge when it's someone else, isn't it?

The secrets are why I can't breathe. As upset as I am at Kai for saying it, he might have been onto something. Is the store doomed until my parents and I come together?

I guess an equally important question is . . . What do I possibly have to lose at this point?

It's easier said than done.

Days later, I'm still tiptoeing around my parents.

I remember when I was a kid, I used to climb all over my father. There's a photo I love of me sitting on his shoulders, looking at a picture book as he reads a wǔxiá novel. Most of the time he was busy with When You Wish Upon a Lantern, but when he was around, I was so comfortable with him. Now I can't even talk to him about the store, how he's wrong about Kai, how much I miss Nǎinai. When did that happen?

I decide to start small. I will ask my parents about the Qīxì Festival and how much revenue it brought in. If they deflect, I will insist, at least on that one small thing. It's what I deserve, isn't it, after working my (and Kai's) buns off? Then, from there, I will ease into talking about the debt and figuring out how we can save the store. Together.

But it doesn't go as planned. In any way, shape, or form.

I do it at home and not at the store so we won't be interrupted. It's Sunday evening and my parents are sitting on the couch in the living room, teacups full of decaf green tea in front of them, a novel in my father's hand and the Chinese newspaper in my mother's.

I sit between them, my hands clasped around my own cup of tea, which I put down on the coffee (tea?) table. I stare at it as I clear my throat.

"How did we do at Qīxì? I think it was a huge hit within the community and even those outside of it. I'm thinking for our next festival, we can try to branch out to the rest of Chicago too" are all the things I prepare to say, none of which comes out.

Instead, I blurt, "Why do we never talk about Nǎinai?" And before my parents can say anything, it's coming out of me like vomit (but only word vomit this time, thank god). "By avoiding bringing her up, it feels like she never existed! Nǎinai would have known exactly how to help me through a tough time like this, but you did the exact opposite."

I look up and my head turns from one to the other just in time to catch my mother's open-mouthed gasp and my father's gaze dropping to the floor. I didn't mean to attack them, but like that fateful day at Mr. Tang's Bubbly Tea, I can't control what's coming up.

I'm about to apologize, but I don't get the words out before my father says, "You're right, Liya." He lifts his eyes to meet mine. "We're sorry."

I don't know what to say. I didn't prepare for this conversation, and now it feels like I've ripped open my chest cavity and I'm showing my parents my exposed, bleeding heart.

Slowly, my mother says, "We thought it would help you most to not bring her up, so you could move on."

"Moving on doesn't mean wiping her from our lives," I say quietly.

"We know how much she meant to you," my father says, his voice heavy with emotion. "She meant everything to us too, of course, but you had a special relationship with her."

My mother scoots closer to me on the couch. "We don't know how to replace that."

My gaze falls back down to my mug. "You don't need to replace her"—they can't—"but . . . I need you. To be, you know, you. My parents."

My dad scoots closer to me too. They don't hug me because we're not a hugging type of family, but I know the closer proximity is a show of support.

"Yes, of course," my father says.

"Whatever you need," my mother adds.

But despite their words, my father is slowly, painstakingly wringing his hands while my mother sits on hers. They still don't know what to do, how to help (and I still don't know what I need), but at least we've opened this channel. It's a step in the right direction.

And that forward motion gives me the courage to keep going.

"I know the store is struggling," I say. And this time, instead of word vomit, I choose to tell them everything. How I'm worried about our financial situation, how I've been working so hard to try to generate more revenue, how Once Upon a Mooncake is selling wishing lanterns. I originally didn't plan on revealing that last one, worried about fueling the feud, but I'm tired of the secrets.

"I already know what you're going to say, Bǎbá," I

continue, referring to his upcoming rant about the Jiangs, but I'm completely wrong.

The feud seems to be the last thing on his mind as he says, "Liya, aiyah, we had no idea you were going through all this."

At the same time, my mother says, "We didn't know you knew about the overdue rent. That shouldn't be your concern."

"But it *is* my concern," I argue. "I'm part of this family and I'm going to take over the store one day—"

"You're not," my father interrupts.

I swear, my blood goes cold.

"Liya . . ." My mom puts her hand over mine. "We're going to close the store down. Next month. We've worked out a deal with Zhuang Xiānshēng"—our landlord—"who has been very understanding, a benefit of our close community. We're going to continue paying him back with the new jobs we're going to get. Your father and I have both been looking for the past month."

I'm stunned. There's too much to unpack. *The store is closing down. They've known for a month. They're looking for new jobs.*

"How could you not tell me this? What about Nǎinai's legacy? Are the numbers really that bad? Didn't Qīxì help at all?"

My father nods in response to my last question. "Yes, Liya, Qīxì helped us make a large dent into the debt, and that was all accomplished by you."

"We are so proud," my mother says.

There's too much going on in my head. My temples are pounding, all the new information crashing around. "Why didn't you help me? Why were you always in my way?"

My dad sighs. "We were trying to get you to stop being so invested in the store."

Bitterness fills my voice. "Because you knew it was closing."

My mother nods. "We wanted you to move away from it on your own, to expand your interests, and we were trying to nudge you there."

"Well, you nudged wrong. We should have been banding together to *save* the store, not give up on it. What would Nǎinai say?"

My father's eyes grow glassy. "Nǎinai . . . would be so proud of you."

My eyes quickly match his, my vision blurring.

My father's voice is grainy with emotion as he tells me, "Nǎinai never wanted you to take over the store, Liya. She's always wanted bigger and better for you. The store was her American dream, and she achieved it—she came here, eighteen years old, alone, with almost nothing. She worked her way up. As you know, Nǎinai was the eldest of three daughters. Her family spent all their money to send her here, to the United States. The entire family fortune was on her. Can you imagine that kind of pressure? Nǎinai worked hard, of course she did, but it was difficult. She didn't speak English well enough and had a hard time finding a steady job. It was here, in Chinatown, that she found her community. She worked odd jobs for years, ate stale leftover rice and bread that restaurants were going to throw out, and she scrimped and saved until she had enough to invest in the store. It started so small, offering just a few items, in a different location that was tiny and cheap. She grew it from the ground up with the help of the community to the point where she could support herself *and* send money home."

Some of this I know, but I'm enraptured by the memories and the new details I haven't heard before. I soak up every word, especially basking in the fact that my father is talking about Nǎinai again.

My dad continues, "By the time I was in high school, business was good. Nǎinai even saved enough for me to go to college—that is, if I could also earn some scholarships, which I did. I was going to go to UIC—the deposit was paid and I'd selected my first semester courses—but then Nǎinai fell ill for the first time. She didn't want me to, but I stayed home to take care of her and I spent the tuition money on her treatment. After years of fighting, her cancer went into remission and I felt it was all worth it. But she carried the guilt for the rest of her life, I know it, even though she never said anything to me.

She thought I sacrificed too much. But I didn't. We had more time together. And you grew up with her. That's priceless."

He takes his glasses off and wipes his eyes. "When Nǎinai's cancer came back last year, the store was already struggling. Our plan was to let it close and move on. We didn't predict it would fall into this much debt—and perhaps we held on longer than we should have for sentimental reasons—but this is what Nǎinai wanted."

"Because, Liya, the store has served its purpose," my mother says. "Over the years, we've saved enough money for your college tuition. This was Nǎinai's goal all along."

Their words surprise me. I can't talk. I can't breathe.

Wait. We have money.

"We can pour that money back into the store," I say.

Both of my parents shake their heads adamantly.

Sternly, my father says, "We are not going to touch that money until it's to write a check to a college of your choice. That was Nǎinai's wish. And ours."

My mother adds, "Liya, we would rather work multiple jobs than dip into your college fund."

A tear escapes the pool in the corner of my eye and streams down my face. Several more follow. "I don't know what to say."

"This is what parents do, Liya," my father says matter-of-factly.

I shake my head. "Not all of them."

"Well, it's what *we* do," my mother says.

I'm so emotional I can barely talk. "Thank you." I hope they know that these two little words go beyond the money to our whole conversation, to everything they've done over the years.

And in case they don't know, I try to show them with a seldom used gesture in the Huang family: I give my father, then my mother, a hug, holding each of them for several seconds. My father is stiff at first but relaxes into it, and my mother clutches me back.

I wish I had known all of this sooner, but now was better than later. Or never. And I was half of the problem. I should have just asked them when I found the letter instead of trying to shoulder it all myself.

My parents and I still have a long road ahead, but now I have hope. And hope is powerful enough to change winds and move mountains, which many When You Wish Upon a Lantern customers already know.

We're going to be okay.

I'm going to be okay.

30

Dominoes

LIYA

I had been carrying around the weight of my grief for so long by myself that I didn't realize how heavy it had grown. Opening up the channel with my parents lightened the load enough for me to start taking steps forward. The morning after our conversation, I drank my cup of Dragon Well tea at Nǎinai's desk, no snooping, just feeling her presence. Then, a few days later, after waking in a cold sweat from dreaming about Nǎinai's spirit not being able to find me because the store was gone and the wishing lanterns had stopped, I figure out something that I need. And finally, now, I'm ready to do it.

My parents are already at the store and I text them that

I'll be coming in late today. I dress, brush my teeth (and feel better looking at myself in the mirror), then gather the items I'll need: incense, cleaning supplies, and whatever offerings I can find around the house, which turn out to be a couple of oranges and a small stack of joss paper.

Right before I'm out the door, I see an unopened lantern by the shoe rack. It feels like fate. I slip it into my backpack along with Năinai's calligraphy set and make sure I have a lighter. It's not a Chinese tradition to set off a lantern when paying respects to a deceased loved one, but it's going to be my tradition.

The cemetery is a fifteen-minute walk away. It takes me a moment to locate Năinai's grave because I've only been here twice, the day of the burial and on Qīngmíng (the day the Chinese honor their ancestors). My heart sinks when I see that her gravestone is dirty, and I quickly grab the cleaning supplies to scrub off every speck of dirt. We cleaned it in April, on Qīngmíng, but that was months ago.

Once the oblong rectangular light-gray stone is gleaming, I light the incense and bow—once, twice, three times. The oranges are placed on the side, and I find the nearest fire-resistant pot so I can burn the joss paper (a.k.a. paper bills that look like real money but are meant to be burned as offerings to the deceased in the afterlife).

I don't talk to her (it feels weird) but I think to her. I

think-tell her about the store closing and ask whether that is truly what she wanted, not because I don't believe my parents but because I still can't wrap my head around it. All the additional good we would have done, all the wishes Kai and I could have granted . . . how can I wrap my head around that loss? And what now? Who am I going to be without the store? Without the wish grantings?

As I'm watching the last of the joss paper burn, a peach rolls into my line of vision and bumps against my shoe. Curious, I look around.

Uphill, I see a mother and daughter bringing offerings to a loved one. I can't quite make out their faces but it looks like the daughter is searching the ground. I pick up the peach and hurry over. When I'm closer, I see that it's seven-year-old Vivian Law (who wished during Qīxì to see the place her grandpa calls home) and her mother Candice.

I hand Vivian the peach. "Looking for this?"

She shoots me a gap-toothed grin. "Yes! It's Āpó's favorite!" So she's visiting her grandmother today too, just like me.

"Oh, thank you, Liya!" Candice says with relief. "Vivian always insists we bring a peach, and she would've been so sad if we couldn't leave it for Āpó today!"

Candice, her wife, Julie, and Vivian moved here just a year ago so I don't know them well, but they come to the festivals and stop in the store every now and then.

"You're the wish lady!" Vivian says, pointing at me.

I laugh. "That's a pretty cool nickname, thanks."

Candice beams at her daughter. "Yes, the magical wish lady. Remember what I told you about Āgōng and the time he made a wish on a lantern?"

Vivian throws her hands in the air. "It's why we moved here!"

Sometimes the magic happens on its own, I think to myself since I can't figure out what wish they're referring to.

But then I glance at the grave they're in front of and see that it's Lam Āpó, wife of Lam Āgōng. He was the first person Nǎinai and I ever granted a wish for.

"Wait, what did Lam Āgōng wish for?" I ask, my eyes still glued to Lam Āpó's name on the grave. It can't be the one we granted for him; those don't connect.

"Well, it's roundabout, but he was missing home—Macau—and was so desperate he sent off a lantern wishing for a taste of home. Even now when he tells the story he emphasizes how he didn't believe anything would happen!" She laughs. "Then, miraculously, the menu of a new Macanese restaurant appears under his door! With his favorite food, minchi! Isn't that just amazing?"

"Almost too good to be true," I deadpan (I hope). "How did that lead to you moving here?"

"He was so nostalgic eating the food of his home that he

reached out to me." She hesitates before saying, "My parents and I weren't on the best terms then. We hadn't talked in a while. But that one phone call gradually turned into several, then an apology, then a visit. And after a few years of our relationship improving, Julie and I decided to move here, for several reasons, but also so Vivian could get to know her Āpó and Āgōng. We didn't know Āpó only had a little time left, but I'm so grateful now that Vivian had the chance to know her."

My eyes are welling and no matter how many times I blink I can't stave off the tears.

"Sorry," Candice apologizes, believing that I'm thinking about my own grandmother. "I'm sorry for your loss too."

She's only half right. Because yes, I'm thinking about Nǎinai, but I'm also thinking about how we had no idea how far our one act of kindness would go. It was such a small thing giving Lam Āgōng that tiny bit of happiness, and it had taken so little time and energy on our part. And it dominoed to this? I always knew Nǎinai and I created magic together, but I never knew just how much.

Candice smiles. "Anyway, thank you, Liya, for that wishing lantern! Like I said, it's roundabout how it all happened, but our family thanks you and your store."

I nod. Then I wipe my eyes. "I brought a lantern here today to set off for Nǎinai. Would you like to join me?"

"Oh we couldn't—" Candice starts but Vivian screams, "Yes!"

"No, sweetie, we shouldn't impose—" Candice starts again, but I interrupt, "It would be my pleasure to do this one together."

I retrieve my bag and we meet in the middle between the two graves. I write both of our wishes on it (for our grandmothers to be happy and at peace) while saying another one in my head to Nǎinai: that she sees how much good she put in the world while she was here.

Vivian and I set off the lantern together, each of us holding a side. As the breeze catches it and carries it up, up, and away, Vivian sings and dances underneath it.

"Thanks, Nǎinai," I whisper into the wind, referring to the sign she possibly sent me today in the form of Candice and Vivian.

I stand there for a long time after the lantern and Candice and Vivian are gone. I feel the magic. I feel the hope. I feel Nǎinai all around me.

How can I possibly let go of all the good our store could do if it stayed open?

31

Mama Knows Best

KAI

I've been staying away from the bakery. No surprise there. I can't bear it with the lanterns in the window and knowing that Jiao will be taking over. It started as a protest—until you stop selling the lanterns, you lose your baker—but that only made Dad stick to his guns more. He dusted off his apron and got back in the kitchen, which, yeah, okay, I admit it, was the perfect way to strike me in the heart. Because now I'm haunted by all the misshapen buns with questionable flavors sitting in our bakery display. I mean, I wouldn't be surprised if my dad skimped on flour just to save money, hoping no one would notice. Bet Jiao doesn't call my dad a sissy for baking. Maybe that was even enough to make Jiao put on an apron too—nah, never mind. It didn't happen before and it will *never* happen, even if his life—or sadly, the bakery's life—depends on it.

My inability to make them stop selling the lanterns only made Liya's words ring truer. But what am I supposed to do? I tried—really, I did—and no matter how ashamed I feel, it doesn't change the fact that I have no clue how to talk to my dad and brother.

I'm lying in bed awake but pretending to still be asleep, which I've done every morning the past week.

There's a knock at my door. I doubt it's my father or Jiao, who've been spending every minute at Once Upon a Mooncake, destroying the bakery and my dreams. Or something a little less dramatic. Or maybe not.

The door squeaks open just enough for my mother's lightly permed hair and bright eyes to pop through.

My mother took time off when we were young to take care of us, but she's been back in the air as a flight attendant for the past eleven years. I have a hard time keeping track of her schedule, but this must be the start of one of her breaks.

I sit up and motion for her to enter. She's dressed for the day, makeup on.

She takes a seat at the foot of my bed. "I missed you, as always."

"I'm glad you're home," I tell her sincerely. I'd hug her if our positions allowed, but since it's difficult, I just move my hand in her direction.

She tackles me with a bear hug so tight it takes my breath away. My mother is as affectionate as my father is surly. I sometimes wonder if she *has* to be the complete opposite of him to make their marriage work, because otherwise the two of them would just sit and grunt at each other with zero communication. My mother pours so much love onto my father that he has no choice but to respond a little because even his heart isn't made of stone. He's actually kinda cute with her—well, as cute as someone like him can be, that is. He'll buy her balloons and chocolates, and he frequently makes jokes about how she's too good for him—which she kinda is.

When we come apart, her hand caresses my head. "What's wrong, my sweet Kai?"

I try to brush off her question. "What do you mean?"

"You're not at the bakery."

With a huge sigh, I spill all. About how they're ruining Once Upon a Mooncake—I hope as the original designer, she'll be as livid as me but, unlike me, be able to *do* something about it—and about how Dad is leaving the bakery to Jiao.

"Did you know that?" I ask, now realizing that I have no idea how she fits into all this.

She takes a moment to organize her words, and I brace myself because it seems as if I'm not going to like her answer.

"Kai, what do you want in life?" she asks me.

That's not what I expected. "I want to take over the bakery," I answer immediately.

She tilts her head at me, examining. "Are you sure?"

Am I sure? Of course I am. "Why else would I have poured everything I had into baking for so many years?"

My mother gives me a loving smile. "Because you're you. You're passionate and talented and can do whatever you want. Do you know what your name means?"

I nod.

She tells me again anyway. "I chose it because *Kai* means *open*. I originally picked it to mean that your forward road would be open, smooth sailing, no troubles. When you were young, I liked that it matched how open you were with everyone. And now I love that it represents how open your options are because I believe the world is completely open to you, my boy with the big heart. You were meant for more than staying here in this small bakery."

"You want me to leave?"

She shakes her head. "I want you to see the world, *then* decide what you want to do."

"Why don't you want that for Jiao?"

Again, she takes her time, choosing her words carefully. "He can explore if he wants to, but I don't think he will. You two are different, and you don't need as much handed to you."

So I don't get what I want because I'm more competent and I work harder?

She puts a hand on mine. "I'm sorry you feel hurt. If you really want the bakery to be your future, that's an option. But you don't have to decide right now."

"It's already been decided for me," I argue.

She raises an eyebrow. "Not necessarily."

Have you ever felt so awkward you would do anything, even crap yourself, just to get out of there?

This is one of those moments.

My mother shakes my father's forearm. "Go ahead."

My father mashes his lips together, back and forth, stalling.

"*Honey*," she says, a hint of warning in her voice.

He stops mashing. "Jiao . . . has a knack for business."

Why did my mother do this to me? I didn't know *this* was what she'd had in mind—I thought she was going to talk to Dad *without* me present.

"You . . . have other strengths," he finishes. "Which does include baking, of course. And . . . maybe you have shown me recently just how needed you are there. I should have acknowledged that sooner. I am open to discussing things— how you and Jiao can work together."

F. What had I been expecting? For him to suddenly say, "Ah, Kai, how wrong I've been! You're actually the best and you alone will inherit the bakery!" Really, this is the best I could hope for—a joint offering. Which, no thank you.

Maybe my mother was right. I've never considered any future other than Once Upon a Mooncake, and I'm only seventeen—why am I limiting my path so early?

"It's okay," I tell my dad.

My mother starts to object, but I cut her off. "Really. It is." Then, just to her, I say, "Maybe you were right."

She smiles. My father grunts.

I repeat my mother's words back to both of them. "We don't have to decide anything right now." And with that sentence, I feel a little freer.

Then it's awkward again. Are we done now? Can I get up and leave?

My mother clears her throat. "One more thing . . ."

Now my father looks like the one who wants to crap himself to get away. I don't know what's coming, so I don't know how to feel.

With no hint of embarrassment, my mother says, "We need to talk about cute little Liya."

Okay, time to strain on three. How is this worse than before?

She turns to my dad. "*You* need to stop fighting with the

Huangs. I heard what happened at Qixi. It's affecting Kai's relationship with Liya."

My father stands suddenly, hands banging on the table. "That shagua's the one who forbid them from being friends, not me! Take it up with him! But, Kai, he said I have no honor! Who's your loyalty to, that girl or your family?"

My mother opens her mouth to respond but my father is already storming off. She hurries to get up, ready to follow, but I motion for her not to.

"It's fine," I tell her, and again it's the truth. I for sure don't care what he thinks. That's not the obstacle in my way. It's that Liya's father hates me. And now he has more reason than ever—we're selling lanterns.

My mother sits back down. "I'm sorry. That didn't go how I hoped. I just wanted to help."

If that's true . . . "Do you think you can convince Ba to stop selling wishing lanterns in the bakery?"

She gasps. "He's doing that?"

I nod.

She shakes her head in disappointment. "Too focused on the business. He often forgets to take a step back and look at the big picture. But he's been successful because he gets so passionate, and no amount of work scares him. He's just always going, going, forward, upward, downward, wherever he needs to go, pushing harder."

I never looked at my father with that perspective before.

My mother nudges me. "You're more like him than you know."

"Jesus, I hope not," I blurt out.

We both laugh.

32

Continued Magic

LIYA

At the store, I've been watching the window, looking for Kai, but he hasn't been in the bakery lately. Which hasn't happened for as long as I can remember.

Worried, I stop caring about my father's threats. I decide to stop by his house, but only if he's open to seeing me. So I text first. Luckily, he responds fairly quickly and invites me over.

When I arrive, before I can even knock, the door flies open.

"Liya!" Mrs. Jiang greets me. "Don't you just look darling today?" She wraps me in a hug and pulls me inside.

I often wonder where Kai comes from, and then when I

get to see the elusive Mrs. Jiang, I always go, *Oh, of course*.

"Kai's just getting out of the shower. Would you like to join me for some tea?" she asks.

At that moment, Kai appears, his hair still damp. He must have just toweled it off because it's sticking out in all directions. Somehow it's both adorable and sexy.

Mrs. Jiang smiles. "Oh, never mind, I'll leave you two kids to it. Have some pineapple cake! It's fresh—I just brought it back from Taipei!" She gives me another hug. "So good to see you. You're always welcome here."

I wonder if she's just being herself or if she's trying to make up for her husband.

Kai and I settle onto the couch in the living room, where a steeping teapot and snacks are already laid out on the coffee table.

I wait silently as Kai pours us what looks to be green tea. When he reaches for his pineapple cake, I nibble on a corner to be polite. Normally I immediately devour the melt-in-your-mouth, rectangular, buttery shortbread pastry filled with sweet jammy pineapple, but my stomach is roiling right now and I have to force myself to swallow the tiny bite I took.

Kai sips his tea, then puts down his cup so he can give me his full attention. "How are you?"

"I'm sorry," I say, pressing my fingers into my pineapple cake so hard it crumbles. Flustered, I return it to the plate and try to pick up the crumbs. "I'm really sorry about what I said the other day. I didn't mean it."

His eyes don't meet mine as he says, "You were right though." He pauses. "Well, about how I'm a coward with my dad and brother. Not about . . ."

"I wasn't right about any of it." He opens his mouth to argue, but I push on. "You're not a coward. You're *kind*." I pause so the word can sink in. "Kai, I love that about you. I think it's endearing that even when you tell your brother to shut up, you say please."

He laughs. "You didn't find it endearing at the time."

I allow myself a chuckle too. "That was other stuff bubbling up. I was just really scared about the lanterns."

"I know, I get it, and I'm trying. My mom is also on my side—I think we'll be able to get them to stop."

I shake my head. And I'm proud that I mean the next sentence I say: "I don't want them to stop."

His mouth was opening to reply, but upon hearing that, it hangs open in surprise.

I repeat the words, and this time he responds, "Wait, what?"

I tell him everything. How his words sank in and pushed me to open up to my parents, how I found out that they're closing the store and it's what Năinai wanted, and, finally, about my conversation with Candice at the cemetery and how it made me realize just how much magic Nǎinai and I created.

"It's magic that has to continue, regardless of who's behind it," I say. "I want Once Upon a Mooncake to keep this tradition alive."

Kai has been slowly processing the information, holding completely still while his eyes stare at me. Then a slow grin spreads across his face. "You and me?" he says. "Still partners in wish granting?"

How fitting: that's exactly what Nǎinai and I used to call ourselves. "As long as you'll have me," I say with a smile.

He holds a hand up. I move to high-five him, but when my palm meets his, he wraps his fingers around mine. We linger for a moment, his hand squeezing lightly, and then he lets go (unfortunately).

He picks up his teacup for a toast to seal the deal and I carefully clink mine against his so as not to spill. When I sip the tea, I realize it's my favorite. "Dragon Well?" I ask, even though I already know that it is.

He smiles.

I wrap my hands around my cup. "Thank you."

"Thank *you* for moving some of my things back in the kitchen," Kai responds shyly.

"You noticed that?" It was only a couple of items and I should have done more.

He nods. "Of course I did. But I only went back one time

after. I can't bear to be in there. My father's selling fish vests now. They're right beside the display case."

I hold back my laugh because it feels too insensitive, but Kai lets out a guffaw first.

Between chuckles, he says, "Jesus, it's just so him, isn't it?"

I join in and we laugh more than the joke deserves, but our history with his father and the vests has exponentially made it funnier. And perhaps we were also releasing some of the tension from before.

When there's a lull in our laughs, Kai says sincerely, "I'm sorry about the store."

"It's okay." And I really mean it. I'm so grateful for the path my family has laid out for me. I'm sad, of course, but like I said, it's okay. It also helps to know that the tradition Năinai and I began will continue.

For the rest of the time I'm there, Kai and I put our heads together and make plans for the wish grantings in the notebook, starting with fixing my blunder with Sam Tong and Bagel.

33

Genies

KAI

For the next ten days, Liya and I pour ourselves into wish granting. We spend a lot of time planning at Mr. Tang's, the Noodle Emperorium, and Hebian Park. I worry Liya's father will be upset if he sees us together or hears about it through the grapevine, but when I bring it up, she just shrugs.

"I can't stop him from being a baby, but I also don't think it should stop me from seeing you when I don't agree with him," she says.

I'm all for Liya's new perspective, but I also wish he didn't still hate me so much.

Teaming up again with Liya reinvigorates me. But at the

same time, to my chagrin, the more I dedicate myself to wish granting, the more I hear my mother's voice in my head telling me my father and I are more alike than I think. Maybe the hurricane the day I was born was just a strong wind—like my dad, no amount of work scares me, especially when it comes to something I'm passionate about.

Liya and I fill the notebook pages brainstorming different ways we can grant each wish. Because of what happened with Operation Bagel, she's more hesitant than before. I do my best to reassure her, but I also make suggestions for further precautions we can take and ways to get more information before our operations are a go.

Everything comes together when we realize that we can combine some of them—feed two birds with one scone. After that, we're off to the races, right alongside Leads the Way.

Soon, after a couple strike-throughs in the notebook and, phew, several checkmarks, we are on the precipice. We've done everything we outlined and then some, and today is the day we are going to see—from a distance, without any contact—whether our efforts thus far have paid off.

"I'm so nervous I could vomit," Liya says as we walk to Hebian Park, hiding underneath baseball caps. A full picnic basket is on my arm. "I mean, just figuratively, don't worry," she adds quickly.

Weird. Her words aren't as painful as I thought they

would be. I will always love her, with my whole heart as a friend, and maybe kinda as more than friends, in secret. But I've also recently come to realize that when you care about someone as much as I care about Liya, all you want is the best for them. As long as Liya is happy, I'll be okay, even if it's not with me.

"I might vomit for real," I joke. She playfully takes a step away from me.

At the park, we spread out our purple magic carpet. We take a quick moment to be totally silly and pretend we're swooshing through the air. How is it just as fun—if not more fun—than when we were kids?

When we see one of the wishers arrive, we both fall silent. It's Mr. Kwok, who wished for more outdoor time, and hopefully not alone. He's standing in one spot, periodically checking his watch. At the very least, he's outside, so that's one part of his wish, but we haven't checked off the "not alone" part yet.

I open the basket, grab some plates, and hand them to Liya—all while we both watch for the people we came here to see. We pass food, utensils, hand sanitizer back and forth, almost dropping things half the time since our eyes are scanning the park. I take a bite of a curry bun even though I'm not hungry. Liya hasn't even bothered to put anything on her plate except a fork and knife. Ironic—we brought all this food and neither of us has an appetite.

Mrs. Bing arrives and I'm so excited I choke on the food in my mouth. I should've been squealing with Liya but instead I'm coughing. She pounds my back until the fit passes. Jesus.

Then we finally do a rapid succession of high fives because Mrs. Bing has arrived with Bagel—who we believe she has recently adopted—and she is meeting Mr. Kwok for a walk.

We targeted Mrs. Bing for Bagel's new mother for two reasons—one, she was wishing for a companion, and two, she lives in the same apartment complex as Sam Tong. We figured, what better companion than a devoted puppy—especially a rescue with lots of love to give—and what better help for her to have than to ask her neighbor little Sam to come dog-sit when needed. And maybe when it's not needed too.

A few days ago, we volunteered to run the senior center's Bingo night—which Mrs. Bing attends like clockwork—and we brought Bagel along, hoping to introduce them. This time, Liya didn't do any direct pushing and instead announced to the entire group that Bagel was looking for a home. She figured any home, even not next door to Sam Tong, would be a success.

Well, maybe we did a *little* pushing. We found out from the shelter that sausage is Bagel's favorite, so, I mean, how could I not give Mrs. Bing a sausage bao before the game started? When Liya arrived with Bagel, he ran straight for Mrs. Bing and licked her face over and over.

Love at first sight, with some sausage nudging.

Once Mrs. Bing asked us for Bagel's shelter information, we turned our attention to Sam Tong. When Liya and I "ran" into him at the park, we may have planted the idea of a dog-sitting and dog-walking business. Not just for Bagel and Mrs. Bing, but for the other community members too, like Serena Lum, who is worried about her poor dog, Jilly, at home while she works long hours at her new position. We were slightly more involved with this one, giving Sam a few potential client names to get started with, just so he could hit the ground running before he possibly lost interest. Mrs. Tong was especially pleased with the idea of feeding her son's dog passion with something that will also teach him the valuable lesson of running a small business, all while earning a little pocket change.

But we weren't sure until this moment in the park whether Mrs. Bing had followed through with the adoption or not. Or whether our sitting her next to Mr. Kwok at Bingo had led them to talk about going for walks.

Mrs. Bing is currently introducing Mr. Kwok to Bagel, who sniffs his shoes, then rubs his body against Mr. Kwok's legs.

"Abracadabra," I whisper to Liya. Then I pretend our magic carpet has just taken off.

"Look." She points.

I turn to catch Mr. Kwok sticking his arm out and Mrs. Bing looping her hand in.

"Maybe . . ." Liya gives me a suggestive eyebrow waggle.

"Holy crap, yeah, maybe!" I exclaim. "That would be like five birds with one scone!"

"Poor birds, having to share one scone," Liya jokes.

"Don't worry, I'll make them a really big one."

Liya takes out her notebook and puts a checkmark beside Mrs. Bing and Mr. Kwok. It matches the ones already next to Sam Tong's and Serena Lum's names. The rest of the ones on there—Mrs. Ma missing her family in Asia, Mrs. Suen missing her family on the East Coast, and Mrs. Zhao wanting to communicate with her grandchildren who speak English—we're tackling next week. We've set up several classes at the senior center, including How to Use WeChat, How to Video Chat, and English as a Second Language. Liya and I will be teaching the first two, and someone else with proper certification will be teaching ESL.

When Liya looks back up at me, she's glowing—her smile, her eyes, her whole expression. For some reason, I can't read what's churning beneath. Maybe it's the aftermath of what it feels like to create magic. She certainly looks like magic.

"I couldn't have done this without you," she says, still glowing.

I shake my head. "That's not true."

She laughs. "Yes it is! I bungled the one wish I tried to grant on my own!"

Okay, she's got me there. I don't have a comeback for that. She gives me a playful *I win* nudge, which, yeah, that ends it. She does win, always.

We dance around in celebration, then devour the food I brought because there's no better way to work up an appetite than with some successful wish granting.

34

Don't Be Afraid

LIYA

When Năinai told me "Don't be afraid" before she passed, I thought she meant I shouldn't be afraid of losing her because a part of her would always be with me. But now I realize she meant something totally different.

Don't be afraid.

She was always the one pushing me. *Don't be afraid of falling, just get on the monkey bars, I'll be here right below you. Don't be scared of the fire inside the lantern, just be careful when you hold it.* She even insisted that Stephanie Lee wasn't mad at me about the spelling bee incident, but I hadn't believed her because she hadn't been there.

And she was right. I had built up the Lee-bee fiasco so much in my head it changed how I acted socially and it turns out it was for no reason. All of which makes me feel like I'm suddenly untethered and up is down and down is up and it doesn't matter when you mistake spelling bees for bee stings.

It's true that Năinai always thought I was special because I put other people first, but she also constantly worried that I would disappear.

You are the night sky that other people shine against. But you have to remember to put yourself first too, Lili, because no one else will.

Năinai put me first. As does Kai. But she's right, no one else does, including myself.

Don't be afraid.

Not of my parents, not of the world, not of the doubts in my head.

Don't be afraid to put yourself first.

Then the biggest epiphany of all hits me. I make wishes come true for everyone else but I don't work on my own, not in the way that I work on other people's.

Why am I so scared to go after my own wishes?

35

6:45 p.m.

KAI

Liya
Can you meet me at Hebian
Park in an hour?

> **Kai**
> Of course
> Everything okay?

It's a surprise

> Yay!
> . . .
> Okay
> I want to know

What happened to you being
so much better about surprises
than me?

> You were right
> Tell me
> I want to anticipate it
> I said you were right!
> Liya?
> Are you still there?
> How about a clue?
> Please???

I like these turned tables

> Hardy har

One hour

> Liya?
> Are you still there?
> Okay fine
> One hour
> The medicine is bitter

36

Aligned

LIYA

I'm sweating. I don't check my pits because it's only going to upset me (what am I going to do about it now, in the park, with no extra shirts?). But I do awkwardly raise my arms like chicken wings, hoping to air things out a bit.

Is this what Lana Condor or Sandra Bullock would do? No, they wouldn't get sweaty in the first place.

I wait on a bench, my leg jiggling so much there's a chance it might just fly off. My eyes continually scan the park, especially in the direction Kai would be coming from if he was leaving from home.

When I spot his familiar gait (I can't quite make out his

face yet), I reach into my backpack and grab the lantern I brought. I fold it so that the words are hidden (for now) and hold it behind my back as I stand.

Kai's face lights up when he spots me. *He looks at you like you are the sun and moon and stars*, I hear Shue Nǎinai say in my head.

I can do this.

I can definitely do this.

I can't do this.

Kai jogs the rest of the way to me.

"Hey," he says when we're face-to-face.

"Hey."

It's a little awkward as he leans down to hug me without realizing I'm holding something behind my back. I reciprocate weakly with one arm before we break apart.

"So there's a surprise?" His voice and face are so hopeful but all I feel is fear.

Don't be afraid.

This is the moment. It's time. Just rip the Band-Aid off, right now, do it, Liya, just get it over with.

A silence descends, more a pause than an ending. My heart beats faster. Of course, my traitorous mind fills with thoughts of Janie and Jesse.

The sun is setting and it's my favorite time of day, when the sky is streaked with red, orange, pink, blue. I've picked such a perfect setting but I don't feel like the hero of a rom-com or even a reality show.

Do it.

Do it.

My god, *just do it.*

And now I'm suddenly thinking about how I have a new-found understanding for the T-shirt phrase *It Just Do* because it feels like this situation is controlling me.

Kai is watching me, waiting patiently. He knows something's going on, that I want to say something and I'm working up to it. He seems nervous; his eyebrows are slightly furrowed.

You and me both, buddy! I can't help thinking.

I'm still frozen like a weirdo and it's felt like an hour since Kai said *hey.*

He breaks the silence. "Are you okay?"

I manage a nod.

Possibly in an attempt to disperse the awkward air, Kai points to the lantern in my hands that is now only half behind my back. "Are we making a wish tonight?"

"Uh, here." I thrust the lantern at him. But then I pull it back. "No, wait, er . . ."

Kai is staring at me and *not* like I am the sun and moon and stars. More like I am a black hole where all social norms go to die (fair).

I take a deep breath. Then . . .

"Kai, you are my person. The one I go to with the biggest and smallest of worries, and I feel most myself when I'm with you. I don't know what I'd do without you."

Just kidding. Those are the words I practiced in my head. But this—*this*—is what decides to come out: "Kai, you are . . . a person."

My god, Liya. I want to dive into the river. A rom-com this is not.

Kai laughs. "That's good to hear. Thanks for the reminder."

I shake my head. "I meant . . . you're . . ."

He's Kai. *Kai.* How can I translate that into something as simple as words? It can't compute. It's not just about how he knows my history, me, and my deepest, darkest secrets (like how I hate scallions—that's blasphemous in a community like ours!). It's about him. How he takes said scallions off my plate without my having to say a word. How the oranges notebook was the most perfect gift I've ever received. How he can find a way to forgive me when I say things I don't mean. And how he always puts me first, even when he's covered in my vomit or going through something himself.

It blurts out of me, all at once, just like how I fell for him: "Kai, I'm so into you." I'm still holding the lantern. I thrust it at him. I don't pull back this time and he takes it. "I want to be with you, like *with* with you."

Kai's face is blank. Almost as if he didn't hear me. Or maybe he didn't understand.

I reach over and gingerly unfold the lantern in his hands. I watch as he reads the three letters I've painted on it, large and in capitals because I only have two extremes, way too subtle or not subtle at all: *KAI.*

It's silent for five . . . six . . . a million seconds.

My doubt takes over and I start babbling, "But if you're not interested, I don't want it to affect our friendship—"

"Of course I'm interested, Liya. This is all I've wanted. I'm just . . . in shock. This has been my wish for the past I-don't-know-how-many lanterns, up until I thought you didn't want to be with me."

Now it's my turn to be shocked. "Why did you think that?"

"Because you didn't say anything when I asked you out."

My mind blanks. "What?!"

"Liya, I asked you out and *you threw up on me.*"

I'm shaking my head. Over and over and over. That cannot be. It just—it cannot. "I threw up because you made me laugh really hard and I snorted boba up my nose."

Now he's shaking his head too. "No, that can't be . . . I thought maybe . . . But then that means . . ."

I start laughing. I can't help it. Everything got royally messed up *for no reason at all.*

"I didn't hear you ask me out," I say when my laughs

subside. How did I miss something as monumental as that?

"Jesus Christ." Kai lowers his eyes to the ground, then raises them again to meet mine. "Are you serious right now?"

We've already waited way too long, so I quickly reach over, turning the lantern around to show him the other side. Before, I was too scared to say the words aloud, but now I'm not, so I say them as he reads them.

"Will you go out with me?"

"Jesus, Liya, yes, of course!" Kai wraps his arms around me, swoops me up, and turns me in a circle. The lantern's rice paper crinkles against my back.

I'm both swept off my feet and also disappointed that my head is now on his shoulder and I can't see his veins bulging out of his arms.

He puts me down, and his tilted mischievous grin overtakes his face. "So that time you said bakers were sexy?"

I laugh. "I can't believe you remember that."

There's a charged moment between us.

Then he leans down, retrieves the lighter that's peeking out of my backpack, and flips it on. "We have to send this lantern off."

How does he always know the perfect thing to say or do next? I'm embarrassed by the extent to which I'm the opposite. But this time, a past faux pas becomes the perfect thing to say.

"That sounds gruper."

He laughs so hard his exhales extinguish the flame.

Together, we light the lantern. We've done this so many times before but it's never felt like this. Instead of the magic being all around me in the universe, it's right here beside me, breath mingling with mine, smile warming me from the inside out.

We each grasp one side of the lantern's base, holding it at eye level. The fire dancing inside feels like an embodiment of my feelings for him, and I almost want to dance alongside it.

Without saying a word (we don't need to), we inhale together, then exhale as we lift our arms in sync. We guide our lantern into the air and the wind scoops it up, lifting it gently and elegantly. We watch in reverent silence as it whirls and twirls in the sky, celebrating.

When I look into Kai's eyes, I see home. The snuggle-under-a-blanket, fire-crackling-beside-you, snacks-in-your-lap kind of home.

I hold up three fingers. One, I point to myself. Two, I flap my arms like a bird, then pretend to scroll on a phone and click something. Three, I point to him.

It takes him a second, but I see when he puts together that the bird represented Twitter, and that I was pretending to like a post.

"I like you too," he responds with a grin. "A lot."

We share a smile, and it electrifies the air between us. I can't wait anymore. It feels like I've been waiting forever. I start leaning in, just a smidgen, because even though I want it, I've never done this before and I'm feeling self-conscious.

But when Kai starts leaning toward me too, the doubt evaporates and I confidently close the rest of the distance between us.

Our lips meet. The kiss is chaste but as sweet as I imagined it would be (and oh, how many times did I imagine it!). One thing I couldn't have predicted? I feel it in my heart, my stomach, even the tips of my fingers.

When we come apart, my lips are tingling. My toes are tingling. I want to float right off the earth and into the sky.

We smile, maybe a little shyly, and then Kai slips his hand into mine. His palm is warm and cozy. Curling my fingers around his feels like taking a sip of hot cocoa after a long day out in the cold.

Kai gestures toward the sky with his free hand. The sun has set but it's not dark enough to see stars yet.

"I look for Niúláng and Zhīnǚ whenever I'm outside at night now," he tells me.

"Me too," I admit. And sometimes, in my head, I go back to us lying on the magic carpet staring up at the sky before our parents showed up. Now I don't have to go back, I realize. Now those moments are my present. Better even.

Niúláng and Zhīnǚ may not be aligned tonight, but Kai and I are. Finally. Because I wasn't afraid to go after my own wish. Because I fought for myself.

He walks me home, his hand holding mine the entire way.

The next morning, a mooncake special shows up at my door-step. The red-and-gold box is tied shut with a golden bow, and it's so beautiful I don't want to open it at first. I do so carefully, planning on keeping everything for a long, long time.

Inside there's a mooncake that I already know is filled with lotus seed and a note. I'm about to break the mooncake open so I can see the note immediately, but then my eye catches on an unexpected object underneath. I lift the mooncake to retrieve a red paper rectangle. Upon further inspection, I realize it's a sealed envelope. On it, in Kai's blocky handwriting, it reads **THE AMAZING DATE**. Oh my god, if the envelope were yellow and black, it would look exactly like a clue from *The Amazing Race*.

I tear it open with the kind of impatience and excitement I imagine real racers feel on the show. I just can't wait.

Liya,

Would you please accompany me on our first and long-overdue date? It will coincidentally also be the very first episode ever of <u>The Amazing Date</u>! You are the only contestant eligible for the show—congratulations!

If you read this first—which I predict you did—the mooncake holds the time and place where <u>The Amazing Date</u> will start.

Here's a list of things you will need:

- SPF and sunglasses
- Comfy clothes and shoes okay to walk a lot in
- Not to have eaten lunch yet
- The best smile (✓)
- A sense of humor (✓)

I absolutely can't wait.

Yours,
Kai

My heart swells that he already knew I would stress over what to wear and bring. It's like I'm on a reality show catered to my personal well-being and fun, and nothing else.

I already know the time will be when I'm free (he texted late last night and asked about my availability) but I have to know exactly when. I'm so excited I'm tempted to tear into the mooncake with my bare hands, but I don't, instead hurrying to the kitchen to grab a knife. Carefully, I cut the beautiful, perfectly crafted mooncake in half and retrieve the note.

The Amazing Date is not for several days. Days! How can I wait that long?

"What's that?" my father asks suspiciously. He and my mother are at the kitchen table eating breakfast.

"Kai and I are dating," I tell my parents. Confidently. Without regret.

My father drops his chopsticks. "What?!"

I wanted to figure out the best way to tell them, but the most important thing is no more secrets.

I look him in the eyes as I say, "If you'd like to give him a chance—actually get to know him, who is a separate being from his family—we can invite him over for dinner."

"Liya." My father's tone is ominous.

I take it down a notch. "Please, Bǎbá. For me."

He holds back whatever he was going to say next. But he doesn't say okay.

My mother reaches over and places a hand over his. "We can do dinner. Can't we?"

"Just Kai," I clarify. "Not his family."

My father still doesn't say yes. He's glaring into his rice porridge. Before, I would have never dared make this joke, but now I square my shoulders. "Do you have to live up to your zodiac animal *this* much?"

My father the ox doesn't say anything. My mother giggles at my joke, then nudges his forearm.

"Nǎinai loved him," I say, my final attempt.

Still, he doesn't respond, but his face does soften. My mother shoots me an *okay, enough* look so I retreat, hoping I've given him plenty to chew on.

At the very least, I told them and they didn't freak out (that much).

I told them the truth.

The Amazing Date

KAI

Today is my first date with Liya. *My first date with Liya.*
What is even happening?

Is this my life?

Thank you, Yu Huang Dadi or the universe or whoever, for finding my sent lanterns, seeing how royally messed up our misunderstanding was, and stepping in. I'm frustrated by how many months we lost but I'm simultaneously relieved it wasn't more.

I've spent the last few days planning. It gives me a new appreciation of just how much work Liya does for her festivals. It feels like a mix of that and wish granting, but easier because I know Liya really well and there's a wealth of shared history to draw from.

I feel like a bit of a dweeb standing in Hebian Park in a blue checked dress shirt holding a single white-and-pink lily behind my back. But, phew, when Liya shows up and her face glows like a lantern, all hints of dweeb-worry evaporate on the spot.

She runs to me and I hand her the flower. "For you, Lili," I say. It's not an exact match for pronunciation, but I hoped it might remind her of Nainai.

Somehow she glows even brighter. "Thank you."

She's dressed in comfy cute sneakers, formfitting capris, and a loose flowing top. Perfect for today.

"You look beautiful," I tell her, taking a second to marvel that I *actually get to tell her that for once*.

"Right back at you," she says, turning a little red. This is still pretty new for us. "Thanks for the instructions. You know me well."

"Are you hungry right now or would you rather eat lunch in an hour or two?" I ask.

"Right now," she answers immediately. "I took your instructions too strictly and didn't eat breakfast either."

"Oh no!" I should've specified further. I reach into the backpack beside me on the ground and retrieve the clue I'm looking for.

"What would've happened if I said an hour or two?" she asks.

"You would've gotten a different clue."

She frowns. "Well, I want to know both of them."

I laugh. "You will, eventually. This day is going to be hard for you with all the surprises, huh?"

"I'm not entirely convinced you didn't plan it this way just to torture me."

I give her a mischievous smile as I hand her the clue, which she grabs and tears open with a ferocity I didn't know she had.

Her eyes scan rapidly, full of excitement.

DETOUR—Since you're hungry, both of these options involve food. Make your way to our favorite lunch spot and choose STOMACH or SWEAT.

"Noodle Emperorium!" she yells. "And, um, I choose stomach."

And we're off.

"This is so cute," Liya gushes to me as we reach the restaurant. "All of the places are *our* places!"

"We've only been to two so far."

She grins. "Humble Kai, as always."

Mr. Chen greets us with a happy yell and two hugs. I called him a couple days ago to fill him in on the details and he had also yelled on the phone when he heard we were together.

"I have to say," he says to Liya as he leads us to our cozy two-person table in the back corner, "and I think I speak for the entire community when I say, *finally*."

She gives him an embarrassed laugh.

"So happy for you two, really, so happy," he continues, oblivious to her flushed cheeks. "Blessings, blessings."

He leaves and I apologize, "Sorry, I told people when I was planning."

"Don't apologize," she says sincerely. "I'm happy for people to know." She looks around. No one else is here. "I hope he's doing okay," she whispers to me.

I nod. "I'll leave a big tip."

"*We* will."

Of course she's going to make us fight over the check later even though it's *The Amazing Date*.

She gestures to our empty table lacking menus. "So I'm guessing I don't get to order since this is a detour?"

I nod again.

"Do I get to find out what sweat would have been?" she asks.

"Spicy challenge."

She scoffs. "Easy."

Just then, Mr. Chen brings over a large steaming bowl. I texted him earlier when Liya picked stomach.

"Enjoy, enjoy!" He waves his hands at us.

I dish out the noodle soup into small bowls for each of us. "All right, Liya, are you ready to stomach this?"

She examines the bowl. "What's the catch? Isn't this one of our usual orders?"

It's Taiwanese sweet-and-sour soup. Mr. Chen's version is unique because he, of course, adds made-from-scratch noodles to it, whereas traditionally there are no noodles.

I lean toward her. "Here's the catch . . ." I pause for suspense. "It's exactly our usual order, but if we were truly on *The Amazing Race*, they would make this into a challenge because it contains an ingredient they would consider weird."

A confused Liya wracks her brain and even takes a slow sip, trying to figure out what I mean. I use my chopsticks to pick up a small dark cube from my bowl. Congealed pig blood.

She starts laughing. "I totally forgot that was in here! And that white people find it weird! I also forgot that it's blood since it doesn't look like blood, you know?"

"Do you remember the first time we had this?"

She thinks for a moment, then snaps her fingers. "We came here to cheer you up after your dad went to see Leads run instead of going to that local baking competition. Which you *won*," she says with emphasis, and it warms me how much she's on my side.

We dive into our soups happily. Everything feels exactly the same and completely different, in the best way. We're as comfortable as always but now I can reach over and hold her hand, or tell her how happy she makes me—both of which I do.

After we finish the soup, we order some dumplings because we're still hungry. I've always loved that Liya doesn't need to eat appetizers, entrées, and dessert in the prescribed order.

While we wait, I hand her the next clue.

"Is this the one I would have gotten if I said an hour or two?" she asks.

I laugh. How adorable is it that she needs to know? I shrug. "Maybe. Maybe not."

"Stop torturing me."

"It is, it is."

She rips it open. "Roadblock," she reads off the top. "I assume it's one I have to do?"

I smile. "You got it." Normally on the show, you choose one of the partners to tackle a roadblock, but today is all about her.

When she reads the challenge written on the paper, she starts laughing.

"No! I don't want to do this!" she exclaims, half serious.

"Did you pick this just to make me laugh over the memory of it?"

I hold up two hands in pretend surrender. "Guilty."

Her challenge is to memorize the first few lines of a Chinese poem that she then has to recite correctly to Yang Po Po. This poem—oh man, this poem. Where to begin? It's about a lion-eating poet in the stone den, and it's famous because it contains ninety-two words, all of which are "shi" but pronounced with different tones. When they taught this to us in Mandarin class, Liya could *not* hold it together. She was trying—really, so frickin' hard—but every time the teacher said *shi shi shi*, the laughs would explode out of her.

She was so embarrassed, I could tell, and it was so cute I couldn't help laughing either. Of course, then *that* caught on and led to a lot of students laughing uncontrollably. The teacher was pretty pissed. Liya thanked me later for joining in so she alone didn't get in trouble.

"How am I going to get through this without laughing?" she laments.

"*That* is exactly the point." I would do anything to hear my favorite sound in the world.

She starts reading aloud and only gets through three *shi*s before the giggles hit. "Oh no."

Soon we're laughing so hard my stomach hurts and I worry about keeping my sweet-and-sour pig's blood down.

She tries again and only gets one line out.

"Did you memorize this?" she asks.

"Are you trying to see if you can just say *shi shi shi* over and over again in random tones without actually memorizing the poem?"

"Definitely not," she answers with a *definitely yes* smirk.

My lips curl in a devilish grin. "I figured you would, so that's why you're reciting it to Yang Po Po." She's a huge poetry fan.

"Right. Ouch. Well played." We share a smile. Then, suddenly, she says, "Hey, you know what? Not that I'm superstitious or anything, but—"

"Of course not," I manage to say with a straight face.

She pushes my arm lightly. "Anyway, the first time we learned this poem made me think a lot about *shi* homophones, and I think that was when my thing with the number four started."

I'm surprised. "You didn't know that's when that happened?"

"You did?"

I smile. "I've always noticed everything with you, Liya."

She looks at me like she doesn't deserve me, which couldn't be further from the truth.

Then she studies the poem in silence—smart move—while we nibble on the dumplings that have just arrived.

When we step into the senior center, everyone in the common room begins freaking out. Massively. Like we're their favorite celebrities who they've been shipping for years, and we've just gotten together.

"Finally finally finally!" Yang Po Po screeches as she scuttles over to us. "Liya, I have to tell you, when Kai called me, I fainted. Well, not really, but if I were in a cartoon or movie or soap opera, I would have."

Mrs. Hong yells out, "If you were in a soap opera, everything would make you faint!"

"Stop being so crabby—we know you love them even though you're always making fun of them!" Mrs. Suen says with a laugh.

Mrs. Zhao adds, "Yeah, you're always the first one in front of the TV when there's a new episode of any Chinese drama!"

"That's because I like to make fun of all of you for loving them so much!" Mrs. Hong retorts.

Mr. Quay ignores the drama from his spot on the couch and says to Liya and me, "We are all so happy for you."

"Why are we happy for them?" Mrs. Chew asks.

"They finally got together!" Mrs. Goh yells from the other side of the room.

Mrs. Chew is still confused. "Weren't they already?"

Liya and I share a look and then we have to bite our lips to keep from laughing.

Liya correctly recites the first few lines of the poem for Yang Po Po. Or Yang Po Po just felt bad and let any mistakes go since this is a date, not an academic event. God knows I don't care which it is. Yang Po Po hands Liya a second lily, and I hand her another clue. The last clue.

"Long leg," Liya jokes as she tears it open, referring to how most *Amazing Race* legs include just one detour and one roadblock.

"I saved the best for last," I tell her.

DETOUR—Dessert is next. Go to the place where it all started and choose MOON or STARS.

Liya points out, "Well, technically, our friendship started in the alley by the dumpster."

I laugh. "Okay, fine, go to the place next to where it all started."

She smiles. "To Once Upon a Mooncake we go! Um, is it going to be . . . I mean, we don't have to worry about . . ."

"Jiao and my dad won't be there," I reassure her. It hadn't been easy, but in exchange for using the space and closing slightly earlier than normal, I told them I would come back to the bakery. It would be hard being there while they messed it up, but I missed baking, and better for there to be someone present other than Dave & Buster's number one and two fans, right?

"I choose . . ." She hesitates, nibbling on her bottom lip.

I think about kissing it, but it's not the right moment. "Whatever you choose, I'll tell you the other choice when we get there and you can switch or choose both."

Her smile is so wide her cheeks push into her glasses. "Moon," she chooses immediately, able to now that she knows it's not final.

As we leave, she slips her hand into mine. The hooting and hollering from the senior citizens make Liya's cheeks flush, but she holds on to me tighter.

I unlock Once Upon a Mooncake and breathe a sigh of relief that it's empty. Even though we had an agreement, I wasn't 100 percent sure they'd abide.

I turn on the lights and drag an extra chair into the kitchen in case we need it.

Liya's bouncing off the walls. "Okay, so what are my two options? You promised."

To make it even more fun, I decide to charade them to her.

I point to the **MOON** on the clue, then hold up two fingers. Then I repeat her genius charade from all those days ago. One, I pretend to moon her, and two, I bring out an imaginary birthday cake and mime blowing out the candles.

She laughs. "Are we going to make one?"

I smile. "Yeah, together."

She emits a squeal-adjacent noise. "Okay, what's the stars option?"

Shoot. This one is a *lot* harder to charade. Especially when I can't copy one of hers from the past. I come up with my game plan for the charade by asking myself how she would do it.

Three fingers for three words. Third word. I pretend to pick up something squeezable. Unscrew the cap on top. Then I squeeze something all over my free hand. I make a disgusted face and struggle to move my fingers, trying to show it's sticky. After a few seconds, I pretend to peel it off.

When she doesn't get it, I try another route. I pretend to take out a small tube, uncap it, and smear it on something. Then I pick up the something and put it on the wall.

"Glue!" she realizes. Then she laughs. "Were you putting Elmer's glue on your hand, letting it dry, and peeling it off?"

I smile and nod. We used to do that in her store as kids and her parents would get mad at us for wasting glue. Nainai thought it was hilarious, laughing her resounding *ha-ha-ha* as she helped us grab that elusive first corner piece that would lead to the glorious one-shot glue skin peeling.

"Okay, third word, glue."

I shake my head. Then I make the universal *keep going* signal with my hands, telling her it's another word for *glue*.

"Um . . . glue stick? Elmer's? Paste?"

I clap my hands.

"Paste!" she says confidently.

Okay. One finger. First word. I pretend to crack an egg into a pan.

"Egg. Cooking an egg."

I nod. I pretend to flip it with a spatula.

"You're frying an egg."

I nod and wave my hands at her, telling her she's on the right track. I point to the egg in the pan.

"A fried egg?"

I nod frantically, pointing at her to tell her she just said it.

"Fried?"

"Yes!"

She pauses. "Fried something paste? Ew, let's not make fried paste."

I laugh. Then I quickly charade the second word by holding my hands really close together. But she doesn't need it because she's already put it together.

"Oh my gosh, fried thin pastes! Qiao guo!" She laughs long and hearty. "I never thought about that name! Why is it so bad?"

"It's not the only one. What about scallion pancakes? That is not a pancake, nor do those two things go together."

"Scallions don't go with anything," she jokes. "Okay. I'll stick with my original choice of moon even though I'm guessing it's the harder one to make. But I want to see you make what you're best known for."

I've made too many mooncakes to count, but I'm suddenly nervous.

"How in-depth do you want this to be?" I ask.

She looks confused. "What do you mean?"

"We can start from scratch or a later step. Or we could just eat them. I have mooncakes in all stages depending on how much work you want to do."

She chuckles. "This is very different from *The Amazing Race*." I try to keep my face neutral, but she reads my disappointment anyway and quickly clarifies, "This is better. Way, way better."

I smile.

She thinks for a second, then decides. "I want to make them from scratch, to get the best idea of what it's like. What your day is like."

Adorbs.

Together, we start mixing the dough. Since she seemed to want the full experience, I don't tell her I have premeasured ingredients and instead let her scoop from the flour bag, measure the vegetable oil, et cetera. I hand her a whisk and let her do the honors, though I worry because the first few stirs can be a bit tough. The whisk sticks and she lets out a soft *oof*.

Instead of handing the bowl back, she shyly asks, "Can you maybe help me a little?"

From behind, I wrap my arms around her so I can apply pressure to the whisk, helping her push it through the mixture. Her eyes travel from my hands up to my forearms, then to my arms. I'm so aware of how close we are that I can't focus on anything else. Her hair is under my nose and I'm overwhelmed by her scent, which is so uniquely her it makes me feel weak in my knees.

She stops whisking. I follow her lead. She places one hand on my forearm, caressing my skin, and then she turns within my arms so we're face-to-face.

I push the mixing bowl away from us across the counter. Her arms circle around my neck and mine instinctively wind around her waist.

She leans in first, her nose approaching mine, then brushing against it. Then I lean in too.

It happens so slow I can taste the anticipation. Then I'm tasting her.

Her lips are soft, warm. They part and glide until my bottom lip is between hers. Her teeth lightly graze the surface, just enough that all my nerve endings are firing.

She tastes like everything good in this world. Like sugar and spice and everything nice. Like magic.

38

Finally

LIYA

Oh my god. Kai's strong gorgeous arms wrapped around me, his lips covering mine . . . I am now speaking from beyond the grave.

For the first thirty seconds of the kiss, I floated out of my body and asked the heavens, *Is this really happening?* Now, back in my body, I weave my fingers into the soft hair at the base of Kai's head. I deepen the kiss by gently pressing his face closer to mine.

As much as I enjoyed our first kiss, this one is a completely different breed. It has all the sweetness as the one that came before, but now there's a wild abandon to it. A hunger.

My stomach feels like it's in free fall in a good way, the best part of a roller coaster.

I never want this to end. I never want this feeling to go away.

This day has been perfect, just perfect. The time and thought that went into each detail blew me away. *The Amazing Date* combined everything I love into a day full of laughter and smiles, and every part of it showed how well Kai knows me.

How can Kai feel like home and also so exciting and new at the same time? It's the feeling of wearing pajamas but also getting glammed up, or enjoying a cozy cup of hot cocoa while at an energetic dance party. He's somehow the best of everything.

We kiss until our lips feel raw. Until we're so thirsty we have to stop so we can guzzle down water like we've been hiking in the desert.

Suddenly I don't need to bake the mooncakes from complete scratch like I wanted earlier. Now I just want to eat them.

Luckily Kai indeed has mooncakes at all stages ready to go, so we split a finished one.

We've barely swallowed the last bite when we come together again. Kissing kissing kissing until it's almost my curfew. Maybe we're making up for lost time, or maybe we're just this drawn to each other. My guess is that since we've been best friends for so long and we've been building our foundation (while pining), this is like starting a relationship at lightning speed. Because there's no way any other first-date kiss would feel like this. It can't. This has to be the most butterfly-inducing, passionate, overwhelmingly wonderful first-date kiss of all time.

I feel like the hero, not of a rom-com or a reality show, but of my own story. A story I'm starting to appreciate for what it is without wanting it to be something else.

Finally.

39

Ghost Festival

LIYA

Kai and I have been inseparable since *The Amazing Date* less than a week ago. Which isn't that different from before except it's also completely different. I still haven't gotten used to the hooting and hollering that breaks out when community members see us holding hands or canoodling. It's both the best and worst being a part of a small community—embarrassing as hell but also nice to know they've been shipping us.

Unfortunately, my parents still haven't invited Kai over. As expected, the culprit is my father, who hasn't even acknowledged that Kai and I are together now. Though I haven't witnessed anyone asking him about my new boyfriend, I'm

100 percent sure people have and I'm 95 percent sure he just doesn't say anything.

But I haven't given up. I've been telling him story after story after story. About Kai's kindness, his giant heart, his humble spirit. And I have plenty more. Today at Ghost Festival will be the first time he will have to see me with Kai. And I am not going to hold back just because of him . . . Well, I will to some extent. If I'm being honest, I don't think I can kiss Kai in front of him regardless of the feud because I might combust on the spot from embarrassment. But he better be ready to see some PG hand holding!

Not yet though.

I'm meeting Kai early, before the evening festivities, and I have a surprise of my own planned. I can't top *The Amazing Date*, but I have something for him in celebration of Ghost Day.

Zhōngyuán Jié is the day when the gates between the realms open and the deceased visit our world. A lot of the traditions revolve around placating ghosts with offerings and preventing them from visiting homes or bringing bad luck, but Nǎinai turned our version of it into time to visit with lost loved ones and to visit with each other. And my surprise for Kai is a fun interpretation of our version.

I can't wait to see his face when I give it to him. Maybe I'm starting to understand why he doesn't like to spoil the surprise beforehand, though I'll never admit that to him.

Thank god I texted him that I was coming over. Not just because I tortured him about having to wait for the surprise (which was delicious) but also because I didn't think this through enough. Currently, as I'm standing on his doorstep, I have no free hands to knock or ring the doorbell.

"Kai?" I yell. I twist my torso and try to use my elbow. I'm too short for it to reach the doorbell so I bang it against the door. Ouch. Some liquid spills over the side of the bowl I'm holding.

"Whoops, sorry, buddy," I whisper.

Finally, I hear footsteps. I wish I could put the present behind my back, but that's definitely not possible.

"Surprise!" I yell as the door flings open.

It's Jiao. Literally the worst person who could have opened the door. Because at least Mr. Jiang would have said nothing and let me inside in peace.

He starts laughing. "What the hell is that?"

I mimic him in a snotty tone, but only in my head. It's all I've got and even I know that comeback is sad.

"Kai?" I yell inside.

"Coming!" I hear from much too far away, because anywhere not here is one more second I have to spend with Jiao.

"At least you two weirdos found each other," Jiao says. "No one can argue that you aren't perfect together. Took you long enough though, jeez."

He walks away without leaving any space for me to

respond, and weirdly (so freaking weirdly), his words mean a lot because they came from a jerk like him.

Kai appears a second later, a towel around his shoulders and his hair damp, and I'm so distracted I forget about the surprise.

"No way!" he exclaims.

"Ah, surprise!" I say too late. It's all Jiao's fault.

I hand him the plastic fishbowl with Crabby Hermy the Second inside.

"Liya . . ." He's looking at me like I'm the sun and moon and stars, and even though it's been a week, I still don't know what to do with it. At first I felt undeserving, but now I'm trying to just enjoy it.

"It felt fitting for Ghost Day," I explain. "Crabby Hermy the First—I mean, his spirit—can come meet Crabby Hermy the Second." I don't really believe in all that, but I like taking part in the traditions. "And we can get him a friend after we do more research about who gets along with who."

He smiles. "I love it. Want to help me get him settled in my room?" he asks as he takes the bowl from me.

I return his grin, then bite my top lip in anticipation. I'm hoping it'll also lead to some kissing on his bed.

"Sorry about Jiao," Kai says as he leads me down the hall.

"You heard?"

He shakes his head. "I just assumed."

I laugh. "Well, it wasn't as bad as I thought it would be."

In fact, it was kind of nice, but I don't want to say that. It feels blasphemous, somehow, like I'm not fully on Kai's side, and besides, why should Jiao get points just because he's so awful that anything slightly positive is an improvement?

Kai is adorable trying Crabby Hermy in several spots, wanting to find the best place for him (with sunlight but not too much sunlight, and does he have a nice view from this vantage point?). He takes so long that when he finally settles on a place (near the window beside his award-winning sculpture but to the side for some shade), I practically throw myself at him. He's ready. He scoops me into his arms.

Even though we come together quickly, our kiss is still sweet. I always make myself slow down because I'm scared of bumping his teeth or nose or chin. His lips caress mine and I inch him toward the bed. When he's sandwiched between the bed and me, I press forward, tipping him backward onto the mattress. He uses an outstretched leg to close the bedroom door.

Our kiss grows hungry. We're all moving limbs and heavy breathing. I place my knees on either side of his torso. He's running his hands up and down my back. I'm clutching his shirt over his chest.

A knock sends me scrambling off Kai and off the bed, which I realize after the fact probably sounded more suspicious through the door than if I hadn't moved.

"Stop dry-humping each other," Jiao yells from the other side. "I'm leaving in five minutes!"

Kai remains sprawled on the bed, his face toward the ceiling, his lips and cheeks tinged red. "When does the fall semester start again?" he jokes. Since Jiao's been home, they've been sharing a car, and of course they tend to play more by Jiao's schedule than Kai's.

As if reading my mind, Kai says as he sits up, "It's getting better though."

"Did you talk to him?" I ask, perching back onto the edge of the bed.

Kai nods.

At that exact moment, Jiao yells, "I mean it—five minutes, Poop Son!"

Kai rolls his eyes. "Okay, it's only a little better." He checks his watch. "One piece of that being, today's carpool revolves around our schedule. But we still have to leave soon to have enough time to stop by the bakery and pick up the snacks I made for the festival."

When I see the time on his watch, I stand quickly and smooth out my dress. "When did it get so late?"

Kai's hand reaches out and circles my wrist gently. When I stop and look at him, then his lips, he pulls me closer. He's sitting on the bed, his legs slightly apart, and I slip right between his knees. He kisses me slowly, passionately, but only for a second.

Then he pulls away and his face softens. "Are you okay today? It's the last When You Wish Upon a Lantern festival."

I sigh. "I'm more okay than I would've guessed a few weeks ago. I'm glad I at least have this. A chance to say goodbye. And I'm really glad the bakery is going to keep up the traditions, and you and I are going to keep granting wishes." It hurts a little less each time I say it.

Kai squeezes my hand. "You amaze me."

I blush, not knowing how to accept the compliment. He gives them out so freely and so often.

"Really, Liya. You're so strong. You've inspired me."

"In what way?"

He reaches up and tucks a piece of my hair behind my ear, gazing at me with such admiration I almost want to look away. "You've been so resilient yet flexible," he says, eyes still on me. "You're grieving the store but also making plans for the future."

I've been spending some time at the library researching colleges and have been updating Kai on my dream schools. He's been supportive, so supportive, but this is the first time he's admitted that it's affected him at all.

He draws in a breath. "It took a little time, but thanks to you, I'm starting to get excited about some of my options. Before, it felt like a punishment that I wasn't going to get the bakery after everything I put into it, but now I'm slowly seeing it more as a gift. It's freedom. I can do whatever I want. For the first time last night, I asked myself what that is, what do I really want." He looks at me. "You, of course"—I smile— "and I want to grow. I think culinary school could be cool. Very cool. I can broaden my skills, and from there?" He shrugs. "I feel like I can do anything."

"That's so exciting, Kai," I tell him honestly. "I'm still sorry about the bakery, but wow. This new dream is so awesome and so you."

"I'm finally starting to realize that I'm not responsible for what my family does. Just what I do."

I nod in wholehearted agreement. If only my dad could see that.

Still in between his legs, I lean forward and give him another kiss.

Jiao bangs on the door again, and I jump. Again.

"Five minutes are up!" he calls.

Kai gives me a peck on the tip of my nose, then we reluctantly say goodbye to Crabby Hermy the Second.

The car ride is awkward, mostly silent, and best of all, short.

After Jiao drops us off at Promontory Point, Kai turns to me and says, "Thank you for Crabby Hermy." And then his lips take on that telltale mischievous tilt. "I have a surprise for you too."

I'm about to beg him to tell me, but even that has to wait. My parents are already here, and they've spotted me and Kai. Holding hands.

Kai starts to pull away, but I clamp down, remaining steadfast. His eyes meet mine with a question in them, and I answer with a smile.

We make a beeline for my parents. But when we get close, I let go of his hand, though I'm not entirely sure why.

"Ǎyí, shǔshú hǎo," Kai greets them, bowing his head slightly, the epitome of guāi háizi, just like Nǎinai used to call him.

"Hi, Kai," my mother says, a warm smile on her face.

My father says nothing but does stop setting up the table to stare (glare?) at us.

My mother gestures to the giant bag of pastries Kai is carrying. "Thank you for contributing."

"*Selling*," my father clarifies. "Just like they're selling lanterns."

"I'm sorry—" Kai starts to say, but my dad cuts him off.

"Your father sent over a box of fish vests. As a gift."

"I'm sorry," Kai says again, dead serious.

My dad laughs. "I'm sure that attempted peace offering was more from you than from him. And, well, like my wife said, thank you. For that, and"—he gestures to the bag of pastries in Kai's hands—"for the egg tarts and pork sung buns and beef curry buns . . ." He trails off. Then he clears his throat as his gaze drops to the ground.

"I didn't like . . . beef curry buns at first. Because I didn't like chicken curry buns, and they seemed closely related. But now that I've tried them," he says slowly, "they, uh, grew on me."

I'm disappointed he had to use a metaphor, but I'm also relieved he's finally coming around.

"Thanks, Shǔshú," Kai says kindly. Too kindly. "And I get it. I'm still figuring out how to swallow those chicken curry buns myself."

My father places a hand on Kai's shoulder and pats once. It's just a start, but . . . it's a start.

Kai and I only make it fifty feet before we bump into Stephanie and Eric.

"Well, *hello*, Lili, Kai," Stephanie greets us. She can't stop grinning.

I texted Stephanie pretty shortly after Kai and I got together, and she sent me more emojis than I have ever sent in my whole life.

Eric claps Kai on the back. "I'd say 'finally,' but I'm pretty sure you've heard that enough lately."

We laugh and catch up before making plans to grab dim sum together soon, and then they break off to celebrate their twenty-month anniversary. (Just like the first fart, I didn't know that was a thing.)

I take Kai's hand again and lead him away from the tables closer to the water, for some privacy. And, selfishly, for my surprise.

Kai already knows what I'm up to. "Not yet," he says with a laugh.

The surprise comes later when the festival begins.

I should have known because the community is gathering in an organized, collective, quiet way they are not known for. But I'm distracted, having spent an hour setting up, then the last twenty minutes playing charades with Kai. Instead of communicating sentences through the windows, now we just come up with fun words to charade to each other. Bonus points if it involves an inside joke.

I'm currently miming driving a car (to be followed by shooting a bow and arrow, then gulping down a glass of water: car-bow-hydrate), but I stop when Shue Năinai clears her throat and takes a spot at the center of the group.

Then I'm frozen in place as Kai joins her.

"Happy Zhōngyuán Jié, everyone!" Shue Năinai starts. "We are happy and sad to be gathering here today to welcome our loved ones who have passed on, and also to say goodbye to our beloved When You Wish Upon a Lantern. This store, and more so the wonderful people behind it, have been such an important, supportive part of this community, bringing us together time and time again and making our wishes come true."

She looks directly at me, then sneaks a glance at Mr. Tang, who is nearby and looking at her like she is the sun and moon and stars. She bows her head slightly to me, as if to say thank you. I waffle between giving her my best confused look and just admitting it with a nod, but she's already turning away back to the others.

"We are so happy to welcome Huang Ying Yue's spirit today," Shue Năinai says, and hearing the name of my năinai springs tears to my face. I sometimes forget her name because she's always just been Năinai to me. I'm reminded in this moment just how beautiful it is, meaning "reflection of the moon." We both have names revolving around the dark night, and Năinai once pointed out how close that made us.

She also, I'm now remembering, once joked about how unfortunate it was that her last name was Huang and not Jiang, since the name Jiang Ying Yue would be especially poetic, meaning "a reflection of the moon in the river." She used to joke about how Huangs and Jiangs should go together somehow, and I didn't understand it at the time. But now . . . was she referring to Kai and me? Did she know and was trying to push me in the right direction?

I guess I'll never know.

Kai steps forward. "In honor of Huang Ying Yue, the

Once Upon a Mooncake bakery is going to continue as many festivals as they can. Our first inaugural one will happen in two weeks at Hébiān Park, only . . ." He pauses.

I tilt my head at him in confusion. There isn't a holiday in two weeks, not that I know of.

A smile of pure joy stretches across Kai's face as he says, "The celebration is going to be to rename the park. To Huang Ying Yue Community Park. To honor her for all that she did to build this community. This family."

Everyone is staring at me. And my parents. I'm in disbelief.

My father moves first, walking over to Kai and hugging him.

"It was a group effort," I hear humble Kai saying.

"It was your idea," Shue Nǎinai says (loudly, to make sure my father hears).

With the news and seeing my father hug Kai, the tears spill over. I rush up and as soon as my father lets go, I'm on top of Kai.

"Thank you," I whisper in his ear.

The solemnness breaks and everyone returns to the cheering, chattering, rowdy bunch I've known my whole life. They take turns hugging me and my parents.

Then, finally, my parents come up to me. And they hug me, together, in a big, fierce three-person hug.

We don't say anything. We don't need to, for once.

My heart feels as if it's going to burst out of my chest. This bittersweet day has somehow become more sweet than bitter, and everything makes me want to cry.

Mrs. Bing and Bagel are here, with Sam Tong not too far away at all times. She and Mr. Kwok are attached at the hip, splitting pastries and burning joss paper together in the designated areas we've set up.

Everywhere I turn, people are sharing their favorite stories about Năinai, many of them revolving around past wishes. And so many are sharing their current wishes, which Kai and I jot down in the notebook to work on in the future.

I light incense with Yang Pó Pó and place oranges on the offering table with my parents. Shue Năinai gives me the biggest hug, then Kai, and gives us blessings. She invites us to double-date with her and Mr. Tang over free tea at Mr. Tang's Bubbly.

"Maybe no boba for you," she jokes. Kai looks at me, surprised that I told her about the boba incident. Then he breaks into laughter, going and going until he clutches his stomach.

It's the first time we laugh about the incident and it feels amazing.

The When You Wish Upon a Lantern table is covered in more items than normal, a part of our everything-must-go sale. Things are flying off the table, making me hopeful that our debt will be smaller and my parents will have less pressure soon. My dad is finalizing a job at the bank thanks to a good word put in by Stephanie's dad, and my mother is interviewing for a position at the senior center next week.

When Kai and I break away to write on our sky lantern, together, like we always have, I don't know what to write for the first time in my life.

I'm happy.

Kai is writing his wish first, in secret, making a big show of not letting me see.

I decide to wish for things to keep progressing, for both of us, in all dimensions, because there's still so much room for everyone to grow, us included.

When he finishes and hands the lantern to me, I see that he's wished something similar. I write my version on it anyway, showing him when I'm done, and he kisses the top of my head. Somehow that feels just as intimate as our other kisses. This one makes me feel cared for and seen in a different way.

The sun begins setting. Kai retrieves our magic carpet and we post ourselves facing the lake in preparation for the lanterns to come. Snuggled up with his arm around my shoulder and me leaning against his side, we watch the sky change colors in comfortable silence.

In the dark, the water lanterns are lit first. They're dropped into the lake in succession, the current pushing them to form a wavy line, giving directions to lost spirits.

Kai holds the top of our lantern as I light the fuel cell. Once it catches, I grab one side of the lantern and Kai the other. Together, in one breath, we lift it into the air.

"May our wishes find the light," I whisper.

Our eyes follow the lantern as it floats gracefully, bobbing as it soars higher. It joins the other lanterns already in the sky. All of them swirl and whirl and twirl, dozens of individual dances coming together to form one massive celebration.

Just like our community.

It feels just as magical as before. Maybe more so. Because after seeing both the joys and pain that life can offer, the good has even more magic to it.

We watch the sky lanterns drift off. The water lanterns continue to hover, the line now broken but the flames still dancing.

Then, suddenly, dark clouds roll in and the skies open up. A classic Chicago summer thunderstorm.

I let out an embarrassing yelp as Kai tries to cover me. I try to cover him back. It does not feel romantic (I'm soaked through and cold) but we're laughing as we scramble to help my parents pack up the last of the items.

When Kai and I are in the back seat of my parents' car, shivering and snuggling together for warmth, I can finally appreciate the rain.

"It's Ghost Day," Kai whispers to me.

I nod, confused why he's stating that fact. Then I catch on to the meaning behind his words. I turn to the window and place my fingers against the glass, following some raindrops down the side.

Nǎinai.

I don't really believe, but maybe there's a chance the lanterns led her spirit back to us. And maybe, like on Qīxì when the Chinese believe that Niúláng and Zhīnǚ's tears are felt as rain on Earth, these tears are from Nǎinai. Tears of joy. From the park renaming, her legacy continuing, and seeing all the good she put out into the world. And, I hope, from seeing Kai and me together and how far we've each grown. I'm still awkward and shy and socially inept, but that's okay.

There is magic on this sometimes wretched, unremarkable Earth. But often, you have to make your own wishes find the light.

Author's Note

Dearest Reader,

This is a contemporary book about the magic that can be found in the real world because even though it's rare, it does exist. Our most magical moments aren't necessarily the ones we would have imagined. Mine are simple, but they took decades to find: laughing with my husband over an inside joke until I can't breathe, feeling comfortable in my own skin, getting to write stories for readers like you.

Sometimes in this world you have to make your own magic. Switching careers and going after my dream job was one of the hardest decisions I've had to make. But four books in, I cannot imagine another path for my life. Being an author was the wish I wrote on my metaphorical lantern and sent into the air years ago. Thank you for helping my dreams come true.

This book is also my love letter to Chinese culture. It contains my favorite holidays, traditions, folktales, food, and more. Thank you for allowing me to share them with you.

May your wishes find the light,

Gloria Chao

Glossary

The meaning of the majority of Mandarin words in the novel can be inferred from context. However, for those who need a reference or would like to know more about the terms that are more vaguely defined, here is a glossary.

Āgōng: Grandfather. Also a term of familiarity and respect for a man who is a couple generations older than you.

Aiyah: An expression of dismay, exasperation, or surprise. Can be positive or negative. No accent marks are used since this word is common enough that it has found its way into some English dictionaries.

Āpó: Grandmother. Also a term of familiarity and respect for a woman who is a couple generations older than you.

Ǎyí: Auntie or madam. A polite way to address a woman who is a generation older than you.

Ǎyí, Shūshú hǎo: A polite way to greet a man and woman who are one generation older than you. Similar to "Greetings, madam and sir" or "Greetings, Auntie and Uncle."

Bà: Shorthand for "father," akin to "dad."

Bǎbá: Father.

Bǐng: Thin flour wraps similar to a tortilla.

Cìxiù: Embroidery.

Dāoxiāomiàn: Knife-shaved noodles.

Dēng mí: Lantern riddles. An activity often accompanying many Chinese holiday celebrations.

Èr: Two

Guāi háizi: "Good kid." As Liya says, this term "can be condescending in other languages, but it's the golden compliment in Mandarin when it comes from an elder."

Hébiān: Riverside. Name of the fictional park in the story.

Jiě: Older sister. Also a term of familiarity and respect for a woman who is slightly older than you.

Lái: Come.

Lāmiàn: Pulled noodles.

Lǎo (as in Lǎo Kao): A word sometimes added to a surname to add familiarity. Would only be done with a very close friend.

Lǎo dà: Eldest child.

Lǎo èr: Second child, number two child.

Lǎo sān: Third child, number three child.

Lí: The first part of Liya's name has a few meanings, including "dark." When combined with "yǎ" it means "will be graceful."

Mā: Shorthand for "mother," akin to "mom."

Mǎmá: Mother.

Nǎinai: Paternal grandmother

Niúláng Zhīnǚ: The Cowherd and Weaver Girl. One of China's four great folktales, dating back more than 2,000 years.

Pó Pó: Grandmother. Also a term of familiarity and respect for a woman who is a couple generations older than you.

Qiǎo guǒ: A Qīxì Festival food made from flour, sesame, sugar, and honey. Also known as "fried thin paste."

Qīngmíng: The holiday where the Chinese honor their ancestors, often by cleaning graves and making offerings. Also known as "Tomb-Sweeping Day."

Qīxì: Means "Evening of Sevens" and is sometimes called Chinese Valentine's Day. The holiday is inspired by the Niúláng Zhīnǚ folktale.

Ròu jiā mó: A street food originating in Shaanxi Province sometimes known as a Chinese hamburger. It consists of crispy flatbread called baijimo filled with pork (Shaanxi), lamb (Gansu Province), or beef (Xi'an) seasoned with cumin and pepper.

Róu yī róu: Knead (the dough) a little.

Shǎguā: Fool.

Shŭshú: Mister or sir. A term of respect used for a man who is a generation older than you and younger than your father.

Tiāndēng: The Mandarin phrase for wishing lanterns. "Sky light," translated literally.

Wáng (王)*:* Surname Wang. Also means "king."

Wŭxiá: A genre of Chinese fiction that usually follows a martial-artist protagonist.

Xiānshēng: Mister or sir. A term of respect for a man close in age to yourself.

Xīwàng nĭ de yuànwàng zhăodào guāngmíng: May your wishes find the light.

Yă: Elegant, graceful.

Yéyé: Paternal grandfather.

Yī jiā yī: One plus one.

Yŏu qí fù bì yŏu qí zi: Like father, like son.

Yuèliàng Dàibiăo Wŏ de Xīn: "The Moon Represents My Heart," a Chinese love song most famous for the version sung by Taiwanese singer Teresa Teng in 1977.

Zhōngyuán Jié: Ghost Festival, which takes place on Ghost Day, the fifteenth day of the seventh month of the lunar calendar, the day when the gates between the realms open and spirits visit the living.

Acknowledgments

Thank you to my readers. Thank you for taking the time to walk through these pages. Your support means the world. I hope you felt a little of the magic that I felt while writing this book.

Thank you to Kathleen Rushall for your guidance, wisdom, and tireless efforts. Having you as my agent is a dream and a comfort. Thank you to everyone at Andrea Brown Literary Agency for your support and encouragement on this project.

Thank you, Jenny Bak, for your enthusiasm for this story from day one. You answered the metaphorical lantern that was this book. What an honor and dream come true it is to work with you. Thank you for bringing out the best in these characters and this story and for being such a champion for it.

It's also an honor to be a part of the Penguin Viking list. I now share a publishing home with many authors I SparkNoted in high school. Teenage Gloria would have never predicted this and most days I still can't believe that my life has taken this path.

Kaitlin Yang and Kat Tsai: Thank you for creating magic. The cover is somehow even better than my dreams.

Thank you to every single person at Viking Children's and Penguin Teen. Putting a book out in the world is no small feat, and I'm grateful to each and every one of you for your time and expertise. Special thanks to Sola Akinlana, Gaby Corzo, Christine Ma, Peter Kranitz, Abigail Powers, Lily Qian, Vanessa Robles, and Marinda Valenti.

Thank you to Kim Yau for all your support throughout my career, including this project.

Thank you to the friends who brainstormed with me, provided advice, cheered me on, and supported my books. Special thanks to: Susan Blumberg-Kason, Rachel Lynn Solomon, David Arnold, Kerri Maniscalco, Laura Taylor Namey, Emiko Jean, Axie Oh, Kelly Yang, Dahlia Adler, Sarah Kuhn, Nina Moreno, Suzanne Park, Marisa Kanter, Rena Barron, Traci Chee, Emily Wibberley, Stephanie Kate Strohm, Samira Ahmed, Jessie Ann Foley, Kat Cho, Lizzie Cooke, Ronni Davis, Anna Waggener, Eric Smith, Amber Smith, Amy Spalding, Rebecca Podos, Ashley Herring Blake, Farrah Penn, and Lexi Klimchak.

Thank you to the librarians, teachers, booksellers, book bloggers, and indie bookstores for the important work that you do. Rachel Strolle, Kathleen March, Andrew King, Stephanie Heinz, Teresa Steele, Renee Becher, Audrey Huang, Lauren Nopenz Fairley—thank you for your support.

Thank you to my family. Thank you, Mom and Dad,

for helping me research traditions and holidays and talking through so many things for this book. I love that these stories give us a chance to discuss and learn more about Chinese culture. Thank you to Diana Fowler, Dan, and Matt.

Thank you, Anthony, for being the best partner. What a silver lining it was to have worked on this book with you figuratively and literally beside me. Thank you for reading everything I write many, many times and for endless brainstorming. I hope other readers can find a way to appreciate all the inside jokes and Easter eggs I write for you in my books. (For any readers who made it here, I charaded *carbohydrate* to my husband in the MIT Bio Café a few months into our relationship. Other people saw; I was pretty embarrassed.) There is too much to say here and since I could fill a book with that—and I do, all of the romances I write are inspired by our love—I will simply say that I love you infinitely and am grateful to you for everything. Thank you for guiding my wishes into the light.